Undercover Hero - *Book Four*
By Melody Anne

Printed and published in the United States of America.
Published by Melody Anne
Editing by Karen Lawson and Janet Hitchcock

Table of Contents

Dedication

This is dedicated to Larry Jones. You are loved and missed. I'm so glad I got to know you, spend time with you, and was welcomed into your family. Your memory will live on in your wife, children, grandchildren, and all those lucky enough to have known you.

Melody Anne's Titles

Click on any title to go directly to the books Amazon page

Romance

BILLIONAIRE BACHELORS

*The Billionaire Wins the Game

*The Billionaire's Dance

*The Billionaire Falls

*The Billionaire's Marriage Proposal

*Blackmailing the Billionaire

*Runaway Heiress

*The Billionaire's Final Stand

*Unexpected Treasure

*Hidden Treasure

*Holiday Treasure

*Priceless Treasure

*The Ultimate Treasure

BABY FOR THE BILLIONAIRE

*The Tycoon's Revenge

*The Tycoon's Vacation

*The Tycoon's Proposal

*The Tycoon's Secret

#6 Virgin to Conquer – Melody Anne

SURRENDER SERIES

*Surrender – Book One

*Submit – Book Two

*Seduced – Book Three

*Scorched – Book Four

UNDERCOVER BILLIONAIRES

*Kian – Book One

*Arden – Book Two

*Owen – Book Three

*Declan – Book Four

FORBIDDEN SERIES

*Bound – Book One

*Broken – Book Two

*Betrayed – Book Three

*Burned – Book Four

HEROES SERIES

*Safe in his arms – Novella

*Baby it's Cold Outside

*Her Unexpected Hero – Book One

*Who I am with you – Book Two – Novella

*Her Hometown Hero – Book Three

*Following Her – Book Four – Novella

*Her Forever Hero – Book Five

BILLIONAIRE AVIATORS

*Turbulent Intentions – Book One (Cooper)

*Turbulent Desires – Book Two (Maverick)

*Turbulent Waters – Book Three (Nick)

*Turbulent Intrigue – Book Four (Ace)

TORN SERIES

*Torn – Book One

*Tattered – Book Two

7 BRIDES FOR 7 BROTHERS

#1 Luke – Barbara Freethy

#2 Gabe – Ruth Cardello

#3 Hunter – Melody Anne

#4 Knox – Christie Ridgway

#5 Max – Lynn Raye Harris

#6 James – Roxanne St. Clair

#7 Finn – JoAnn Ross

Thrillers

CONFESSIONS

*Dance in the Dark – Book One

*TBA – Next Book in the Series

Young Adult / Fantasy

PHOENIX SERIES

*Phoenix Falling – Book One

*Phoenix Burning – Book Two

*Phoenix Ashes – Book Three

*Phoenix Rising – Book Four

**All links are part of Amazon Affiliate program

Note from the Author

It's always difficult for me to write the final book in a series. For one, I don't want to let the characters go. And for two, I want to make sure I wrap up the loose ends I've left open and not disappoint my fans. There's nothing I hate more than to get invested in characters in a book and then not see them get their happily ever after. Sometimes I have to wait because of other projects, and sometimes because I'm not sure what I want to do. This book took a while because life got in the way. But I'm glad it did because I've enjoyed Declan and Angela's story a lot. I love when a tough guy breaks. I think I do because my dad was such a tough guy, but when it came to the women he loved, he was a big marshmallow. I still miss him every single day and it's been nearly two years since I lost him. I don't think that pain will ever go away. But just like my hero and heroines say in the books, I can smile when I think of all the good times I did get with him.

I love writing so much because I get to control my worlds. Life isn't always that easy. But I'm also discovering that again, just like my characters say, the imperfections are what makes life so amazing. It's not the perfect moments we think about, it's the ones that don't go anything like how we planned. We don't talk about the fish we've caught. We talk about the ones that got away.

While working on this book, we lost my fiancé's father. It was utterly heartbreaking for the entire family, and he'll be missed. There was a time I wanted to stop loving people because the loss of them hurts so much. But

I've learned that even if we lose these people too soon, it's never a tragedy to love. And that's why I truly believe we will get to be with them again someday. It hurts beyond reason to lose a loved one, but it would hurt so much more to never have them at all.

I ran a contest for this book to submit a scene for Declan. The winner was chosen who wrote an incredible chapter. Let's see if you can find it in the book. The winner was author Sophie Wyld. Thank you for your time, and for being a part of this universe I love so much. You did amazing!

Thank you again for all of your messages, for your love, and for all you do to give me this life I live. I get to write and express my love, joy, and grief through my books. It's gotten me through the best and worst times in my life. Thank you for all you do to help me.

Prologue

A chill rushed down Angela Lincoln's spine. Unfortunately, it was something that happened far too often. Some people might truly heed the warning, but she was beginning to think she was simply paranoid, jumping too easily at shadows. There was enough horror in the world to fear, so she didn't need to be afraid of the make-believe.

It had been three years since she'd fled California with her son. It felt like only yesterday and she still didn't feel safe. There was so much danger and pain in the world; it was hard to let it go. She was trying though, and if she didn't feel safe in the community of Edmonds, Washington, she wasn't going to feel at ease anywhere.

There were times in life that stayed with you no matter how much you hoped they'd go away. Why was it that people forgot a lot of the good, but *always* remembered the tragic? Maybe because the bad left a scar that never fully healed.

Goosebumps popped up on her arms and a tremor ran through her. "Stop it," she muttered. She was being foolish. The only reason she was freaked out was because she was obsessing. She kept walking, placing one foot in front of the other. She was through with letting fear hold her back.

It was an amazing spring day in Edmonds, and she knew any season in the Pacific Northwest could produce a myriad of weather patterns, so she wasn't going to waste this beautiful, sunny afternoon. She wasn't going to tuck tail and run inside just because she had a bad feeling.

Her eight-year-old son, Timothy, was in school, and she only had a couple of hours before she needed to pick him up. She had just enough time to grab an iced coffee and pastry from the local bakery, then enjoy people watching at the park.

Because Angela had had her son at the tender age of eighteen, she had a bond with him some parents might not have a chance to form. He was her entire world. It had been the two of them through thick and thin, and there was nothing she wouldn't do for her child.

She ran her fingers across her stomach with a sigh. She'd always hoped to have a large family with at least four kids to run down a giant decorated staircase on Christmas morning with giggles in their voices and magic in their eyes. But life didn't always work out the way you planned. Sometimes that was a good thing. She wouldn't be having more children, but that only meant her bond with her son would be that much stronger.

With the unusually warm weather there were quite a few people moving about her small town. She'd been there for three years and they'd embraced her. She truly felt it was home now; she knew the storeowners' names, and the bank teller greeted her with a smile. She made it through the coffee shop in minimal time thanks to missing the lunch rush.

She'd only taken a couple of sips of coffee before a man ran into her so hard it nearly knocked her to the ground. Her cup flew out of her hand, and she watched in horror as the drink painted the sidewalk. Then, to her surprise, he kept on going, not even bothering to say *excuse me* or *sorry*.

She waited a moment before she called out to him, "Did your mother not teach you any manners?"

She wasn't expecting much, but she wished she wouldn't have said anything when the man turned. The feeling of eeriness that had been with her the last couple of hours washed over her again as his dark brown eyes met hers. She froze in place.

He looked familiar, and he certainly looked like a person she never wanted to see again. He was short and stocky, and there was something so evil about his expression she couldn't move. If he headed toward her she'd turn and run . . . *if* she could unlock her legs. This wasn't the type of man she'd expect to pass on the sidewalks in Edmonds. Maybe in her old location—but definitely not in this quaint little town.

Something tugged at her memory, and she pushed it back. She didn't want anything to do with this man. He stared at her another moment and started to step toward her, before a group of children rushed out of the ice-cream parlor.

Thankfully, he changed his mind and didn't come after her. The glance couldn't have lasted for more than a few seconds at most, but it was one of the uneasiest moments of her life.

What a horrible human being. She shook her head and tried to push him from her mind. She'd lost her joy in the beauty of the day. Maybe it was a good thing she'd dropped her coffee because her stomach was now churning.

She turned toward the park and decided to take a walk before she headed to pick up her son. She wanted to ease her tenseness and have a smile on her face when she met him. She loved when school was out, loved her time with her favorite little man.

When a person had a feeling though, they should listen; some said it was intuition and some said it was a higher power. Angela was beginning to think it was a higher power, because as soon as she turned a corner in the park, she knew she should've gone straight to the school and waited for her son.

Now, she might not have the chance.

Standing in a small clearing was a group of men holding guns with several large duffel bags at their feet. A man lay on the ground by them, but she didn't have time to survey the situation, to see if that person was okay. She stepped backward and her foot landed on a twig, making several heads turn in her direction. There was no graceful way of backing away.

The eyes she connected with were more evil than they'd been on the sidewalk a few minutes earlier. His lips had turned down as he glared at her. She would never forget what he looked like or the blackness of his gaze. There was nothing good about that man.

"We meet again," he said.

His voice was so familiar. How did she know this man? She'd swear she'd never seen him before this day, but everything inside her screamed that she had. Maybe he was just talking about their meeting on the sidewalk. She sure as hell wasn't going to stick around and find out.

Angela realized the power of fight or flight, because without hesitating a second more, she turned and ran. The first gunshot rang out, a sound no one should understand as it came toward your back.

She didn't feel pain, but with her heart thundering and the amount of adrenaline rushing through her, she wasn't sure she'd feel anything other than the need to escape. She had a son to get to who needed her alive. She had to escape, and she had to do it now.

A branch shattered next to her head as she turned the corner. She didn't slow. She moved faster than she ever had in her life. Her ears were buzzing so she had no idea if anyone was on her heels. She didn't hear the men speaking, didn't hear shouts, and thankfully, didn't hear any further gunshots. She broke out onto the street where people were milling about.

She continued to run, looking straight ahead. She needed somewhere safe, but her mind was so foggy she couldn't think of where that might be. So she mindlessly went as far as she could.

When she saw a cop car ahead she nearly wept she was so dang happy. She waved her arms in the air and probably looked like a mental patient. She didn't care. She'd prefer getting arrested to being shot in the back. She hadn't turned around once to see if they were on her heels. In every horror movie she'd ever watched, the victim always got caught because they kept turning and then tripped or did something else foolish like run into a dark alley. She was determined not to be an easy victim.

The cops stepped from their car, looking at her warily. "Angela?" the younger one asked. Right now she was appreciating again those advantages at living in a small town. *Everyone* seemed to know their neighbors. That's why terrible things weren't supposed to happen in a place like Edmonds.

"Drug deal," she gasped. The men looked behind her before glancing at her again. The unknown older one surveyed the area and the younger one she vaguely remembered as Officer Miller looked directly at her.

"Take a breath and tell us what's happening."

She took a few breaths, still too afraid to turn. Then she stiffened her shoulders and looked the officer in the eyes.

"I was walking, and there was a huge drug deal going on off the path at the park. I was so stupid to stumble onto it. I'd run into one of the guys a little earlier and somehow walked straight into the middle of his operation. I know him. But I don't know how. There were guns, and it looked like someone was lying on the ground. I couldn't tell if he was alive or dead." She was still breathing heavy, but her voice was coming back.

"Did you get a good look at them?" Miller asked.

"Yes and no. I could describe the one guy to a T, but I'm not sure about the others. It was so stupid to walk there," she exclaimed.

"You should be able to walk wherever you want, especially in this town. But this will end soon," Miller promised.

"You don't know that. The bad guys are everywhere," she said. She panicked, bile rising in her throat. It didn't seem to be safe anywhere she went. What kind of world was she bringing her son up in?

"Let's get you in the car and somewhere safe, then we can talk more about this and maybe look at some pictures," Miller said.

She heard his partner on the radio as he called in the report. She didn't hear the reply. She stood there unmoving for a moment.

"Come on, Angela, let's get you to the station," Miller said again, remaining calm.

"I have to pick up my son," she told him.

"We'll pick him up and make sure he's safe," Miller told her.

At those words some of the tension released from her body. She climbed in the car. It was better than standing in the open, waiting to be shot.

"We're bringing Angela Lincoln in," Miller said. "We need her son picked up from the grade school. Copy. Be there in five minutes."

The next couple of hours went by in a blur. Angela was taken into a room in the station she'd hoped to never see again. Lieutenant Bonthu entered and picked her brain, but the longer she sat there the fewer details she was able to give.

"I know this is a lot, Angela, but we believe you ran into the ringleader of this entire syndicate. He's a very wanted man," Bonthu said.

Terror filled her at those words. She'd been spotted by the ringleader of the drug organization that had been terrorizing this town for years. He had to feel the noose tightening around him with Declan Forbes on his tail. And now he was aware she'd spotted him. Everything within her needed to run, needed to keep her son safe.

Declan was the lead FBI agent on the case that had been plaguing Edmonds for three years now. They were in the schools, had people in power in this place and others, and were growing bigger. Declan was there to stop him, and he was getting closer and closer.

"Can you look at these pictures?" Bonthu asked.

She was afraid to. What if they came after her? But she nodded. He pulled out a folder with a couple dozen pictures in it. On the fifth page, she froze. A shudder ran through her as she had a flashback. Something was tugging on her memory that she didn't want to know—didn't want to remember.

"That's him," she said, her voice barely above a whisper. "That's the man on the sidewalk. That's the same man in the park, with the gun."

The Lieutenant was quiet for a while. "That's what I thought. We've been looking for him for a while. He's a ghost. This is a lucky break."

"How in the world can you say this is lucky? He will hunt me down," she gasped. Fear filled her.

"We'll keep you safe," Bonthu promised her. She didn't believe him, didn't trust him. "But if you saw him, that means he's coming out of hiding. We *will* get him."

"I need a break," she said. "Please, let me take my son home."

Bonthu looked as if he wanted to argue, but then he let out a sigh and nodded. "A break might be good. It might clear the cobwebs."

"Thank you," she told him.

They walked her from the room to where Timothy sat at an officer's desk playing a game of Uno. He smiled at her.

"I'm beating Officer Jayden," Timothy said.

"Yep, he's whooping me," Jayden said with a chuckle.

"How about we go home?" she asked.

Timothy threw down his cards and raced to her, throwing his arms around her waist. She'd truly miss these days once he decided he was too big to do that. She wanted to stop time.

"I'm having fun, but I'm hungry, so home sounds good," Timothy told her. She loved the adoring way he looked at her.

Officer Miller gave her and Timothy a ride home, asked if there was anything she needed, then left them alone. It was what she wanted, but it felt eerier than she thought it would. She sat down on the couch and let Timothy tell her about his day, but the longer they sat, the more worried she became. She realized she was waiting for her door to get smashed in.

She couldn't stay.

Yes, she knew she had friends in this town. But they didn't know of her past, and they didn't know what they were signing up for by helping her. The best option for everyone involved was for her to leave.

"We're going to take a trip," she told Timothy.

"Really? Where?"

"It's a surprise," she said with a forced smile. She couldn't let Timothy know anything was wrong.

"Yea!" he exclaimed before jumping up and running to his room.

Angela went to her room, grabbed a bag, threw some clothes in, and then went to help Timothy. Within an hour they were ready to leave. She threw what she had to have into her vehicle, and they left the town of Edmonds as quietly as they'd arrived.

She was doing what she had to do, though her heart was breaking into a million pieces. She had friends in this town who'd become family to her and her son. She didn't want to leave, but she was scared and didn't see another choice. She was doing what she had to do.

She didn't know what would come next. She wasn't sure she wanted to know.

Chapter One

Declan Forbes wasn't a do-it-by-the-book kind of man. No one would say he was an easy guy to work with or a pleasure to be around. That didn't mean he wasn't the absolute best of the best. It meant he was a royal pain in the ass—especially to criminals.

He was good—and he knew it. But there was a price that came with being the best. He always wanted more. And he didn't stop until he got it. When he was stumped on something, he took it far more personally than he should.

And right now, Declan was stumped. His case was unsolved, and no matter how many hours he put into it, he wasn't getting closer. Just when he thought he was getting a break, getting one of the bad guys, ten more sprang up. They needed the ringleaders, and they were harder to find than Osama Bin Laden.

There was a crime syndicate that reached far wider than the town he'd been assigned to. He was fed up with the bad guys getting victories. It was enough to make him want to find another line of work. But that would be tragic because one: he didn't give up, and two: he wasn't letting one more piece of scum have the upper hand.

He walked toward his office where his boss waited to find out what was going on. Declan hated having nothing new to report. He felt like a failure. It was an unfamiliar feeling.

In a bad mood, he moved through the hallways of the local FBI office and into the back room he'd made his own. He wasn't pleased to see his boss sitting at *his* desk looking as if he planned on making himself comfortable.

"You're late." Declan smirked at his boss's words. He wasn't late, never was, but anything less than ten minutes early was late in the director's eyes.

"Director," Declan said as he moved forward. He didn't feel like taking a seat. Declan had learned long ago there was power in stillness. He'd gotten more than one perp to speak without having to say much at all, just stare him down. He'd been told many times he had a terrifying look.

Director Dorsey stared back. He knew this game well. They were an even match if Declan would admit it . . . which he wouldn't.

Finally, Director Dorsey chuckled as he leaned back. The power game was officially over. Declan cracked his own smile that couldn't be described as pleasant. He might like working alone, but he did respect this man and hadn't been steered wrong by him so far.

"How are you enjoying your time in this sleepy little town?" the director asked.

"Sleepy?" Declan said, raising his brow. "I hardly think that's an apt description with all the crap that's been going on."

"I prefer the city. This is far too quiet for me," Dorsey said. "Even with drugs, fires, and murder."

"I'm glad to see you have your sense of humor," Declan deadpanned.

"I learned long ago that if I didn't find humor in this horrific world, I couldn't stay in this job. Some might take it wrong, but I do what I have to in order to not bring it home to my family."

Declan nodded. "I can respect that."

There were times Declan became so disgusted with how people treated one another the only thing that kept him grounded was his family. He had a tough-as-nails hide on him, but there was only so much bad a man could handle before it was too much. He had to get away from it all. He knew for certain he couldn't do this job if it wasn't for his family. They might not realize it, and he certainly didn't tell them, but it was the truth.

His job was the main reason he didn't do relationships. He was too hardened to be the kind of man who could be called *husband*. He'd watched his three younger brothers marry in the last couple of years and was very aware of the changes in them. There was a small part of him that felt jealous, an entirely new emotion for him, but the larger part knew he would never marry.

Angela Lincoln.

He couldn't say *or think* her name without a growl emphasizing the five syllables. She'd been in Edmonds, which wasn't too far outside of Seattle, for a couple of years now. He'd been trying to find out the connection and he was getting closer.

Danger surrounded her, and if he didn't crack this case soon, she just might become another name the FBI couldn't help. They'd already failed her once. He wasn't willing to let it happen again.

He was there to learn her side of her story and keep her safe. She was off limits otherwise. So why in the hell was he thinking her name and marriage at the same time? Something had to be seriously wrong with him, and he hoped like hell he figured it out sooner rather than later.

He couldn't dismiss that vulnerability in her eyes, the secrets she tried to keep masked, and the longing he felt in her to break free. It was more than clear the woman didn't trust anyone, but she worked for his brother part-time, and she'd forged friendships with his sisters-in-law, giving him the in he needed.

He was sure she was beginning to trust the Forbes family. It was time to get her to open up to him. He could do it; he'd just need to brush off some of the harshness his brothers were so fond of telling him he wore.

When Declan had decided to become an FBI agent, he knew his life would be isolated. He'd served as a Marine for eight years and had seen things he'd never tell anyone about. But when he left the Corps, he'd needed a career that motivated him, challenged him, and more importantly, gave him the opportunity to do something right in a broken world.

For the most part he felt his job gave him that and more. But sometimes it was frustrating. It was hard at times to tell the bad guys from the good. Criminals had grown smarter over time and he wasn't sure which side of the law most people were on anymore.

He did have faith in Angela. He knew part of her story, though he'd tried to find out more. He *would* get to the bottom of it, and then maybe he'd retire and start the next chapter of his life.

The possibilities were endless for Declan just as they were for his siblings. Though they'd grown up with proverbial silver spoons in their mouths, they hadn't taken that as a right to do nothing with their lives. They'd wanted to carve their own paths without the power of their name behind them.

Declan was different from his brothers, more hardened, but over time his tough exterior had started to crack. Maybe it was being with his family so much, and maybe it was due to a particular woman he couldn't keep off his mind. But whatever it was, he was changing. He wasn't sure he liked that.

"Did you go somewhere?" Director Dorsey asked.

Declan gazed at his boss. "I'm right here," he said. He had drifted a bit. He didn't normally do that, but he was in a safe environment, allowing him to let down his guard.

Dorsey nodded. "You've always done exceptional work, Declan. The way you think makes you an ace agent. We've allowed you liberties because of that. This case is stumping us all. Even the men at the top haven't a clue how to crack it. What are your thoughts? What's being done?"

Declan decided the time had come to sit. He moved to one of the uncomfortable office chairs and took a seat. He didn't like not having all the answers, and Dorsey was aware of that. He was also patient for the most part. Dorsey knew Declan didn't spout words to hear himself talk. When he spoke, there was meaning behind what he was saying.

"We've made breaks in the case," Declan finally said. "We just can't seem to find the men at the top, though we have a good idea of who they are."

"Or the women," Dorsey pointed out.

Declan smirked. "Are you being politically correct?"

"I've been in this business for what seems like forever, and I learned long ago not to underestimate the power of a determined woman. Power is an aphrodisiac to us all, and women can get into places and do things men can't. They make damn fine criminals, and they're harder to catch."

Declan almost chuckled. "I came to that same conclusion. I don't know in this case, though. We have too many leads pointing to one man."

"We know this ring stretches far and wide. We need to tighten the circle," Dorsey said.

"I think there are more insiders than we originally thought. The group has too much power to not have help from higher levels than we were originally aware of."

Dorsey didn't blink. "Why do you think we're having this meeting one on one?"

Declan didn't trust most people in general. That was why he worked so well with Dorsey. His boss was less trusting than he was, and that was saying a lot.

"I'm not sure why we're having this meeting at all," Declan told him. "I don't have any updates. Don't think that doesn't piss me off."

Dorsey stood up. Declan did too. "I wanted to talk in person. I'm not sure who's doing what right now, but I don't trust our secure phone lines. I want this case solved yesterday, and I want more answers. We have a few leads and I'm expecting some calls, but again, I'm not trusting that the information we're getting through the phone is for our ears only. I want you to report to me in person when you can. I want as little information over the phone as possible."

The director stood and Declan joined him. "I can do that."

"I'm heading out for now. I have another meeting, but walk with me to my car."

Declan didn't argue. He followed the man he'd worked with for several years.

They left the office, continuing to talk as they moved through the small building and stepped out back where a large black SUV waited. As they approached the vehicle, Declan's mind was busy calculating everything he'd learned in the past few years. It was hard to have a decent conversation with anyone, even his boss.

The back door opened, and a man stepped out, calling inside as a sleek silver lab jumped down and immediately sat at the man's feet.

"Nice dog," Declan told Dorsey.

"Yeah, I wanted her to be your partner, but I don't think now's the right time. But soon."

Declan glared at his boss. "I don't work with partners, not even canine ones."

"You don't always get what you want," Dorsey told him as he signaled and the lab moved to his side, waiting for a command. If they did place the dog with him, at least he was pretty sure it would obey.

"I don't get what I want most of the time," Declan said. He glared at the dog who didn't seem offended or interested.

"That's all for now. Give me good news, Declan . . ." He paused for a long moment. "And do it soon."

Declan had no doubt this was an order. He didn't do well with orders any more than he did with rules. He never should've joined the FBI.

"What's the mutt's name?" Declan asked.

"Cynder." Dorsey was smiling big now. He was truly enjoying himself. Declan wasn't going to show him how irritated he was. He was also done with this conversation.

"She makes a great partner for you. Enjoy her," Declan said. He was glad he wasn't taking her. Dorsey didn't respond.

"Cynder, come," Dorsey said. Just like that, the dog stood and followed him.

Declan began walking away. He wanted out of there before the director changed his mind and sent him home with the dog. He had enough to deal with without taking on the responsibility of a pet.

"Sir," someone yelled. Declan stopped his exit. He moved back to the director as an officer approached, out of breath.

"Calm down and talk," Dorsey said, his feathers not easily ruffled.

"A big deal just went down. We didn't catch them, but we have a witness," the officer said before hanging his head. "Or we *did* have a witness. We've lost her."

Declan watched as the director's head nearly came off his neck.

"What are you talking about?" Dorsey asked. "And you better explain in as few words as possible."

"That means talk fast," Declan added.

"Angela Lincoln spotted who we think is the head of the whole syndicate. She came to the station . . . and now she's nowhere to be found."

Declan desperately wanted to punch someone—hard.

"Was she abducted?" Declan asked, trying not to freak out.

"No, she fled. The officers went back to her place and she'd left a note. She apologized and said she had to keep her son safe."

Declan let out a relieved breath when she didn't appear to be in immediate danger. He was well aware that could change if she really had spotted the head of the organization.

"Do you know where she went?" he asked.

"No," the officer said.

"Why wasn't I called right away? Why wasn't I brought to the station?" Declan demanded. The officer shifted on his feet.

"I don't know. I'm just the messenger," he said. Declan had the urge to smash his fist into something again. He had to clench his fingers together and try desperately to calm himself. "We didn't think she'd run, though."

"She's terrified. She shouldn't have been left alone," Declan told him.

"There's no way any of us could've known what would happen," the officer replied.

"Are you new to the force?" Declan asked in a deceptively quiet voice.

"No, I've been on for about five years," Miller replied.

"Then you should've known a scared witness is a dangerous witness. There's no excuse for this."

"I'm not in charge," Miller said. Declan growled a bit, causing Cynder to tense next to Dorsey. Miller sighed. "But yes, we screwed up."

"I'll find her," Declan said. "And *I'll* be the one keeping her safe until we catch these guys." The authority in his voice was so final, not even the director tried to argue with him. He needed to get on her trail immediately if he had any chance of keeping her and Timothy out of danger.

"You'll do it," Dorsey said. "Let's not let these guys get away with anything else. They've terrorized this town long enough."

Declan didn't say anything else. He walked away this time, more determined than ever before. He'd go to her apartment first then make some phone calls. He'd find her no matter how long it took. He just hoped it was sooner rather than later.

Chapter Two

Angela tossed and turned in her bed, sweat beading all over her body as she cried out in her sleep. "Please, please, stop. Please don't do it. Please stop," she whimpered. The blankets twisted around her legs, trapping her, causing her to panic as she tried getting away, caught up in the darkness of a nightmare.

"Are you scared, little girl? There's nowhere to run, nowhere to hide. I have you right where you I want you. Aren't you having fun?" The voice was all around her, in her head, above her, in a dark tunnel. There was no escaping it. Tears streamed down her face as she continued to twist in her bed.

"Yes, I'm scared. Please, you've done enough," Angela said. Somewhere she knew it was a nightmare. She wanted to wake up. It had been so long since she'd had one this bad. It always changed, but the fear was the same. Someone wanted to get her, and they weren't going to stop until they did.

"I like you scared," the voice said. She tried to twist away again, but it was too late. Searing pain ripped through her stomach. It was odd how accurately she remembered that pain. It wasn't just a slice, it was a ripping that came from the inside out, though that was impossible.

"Mmm, I love the smell of copper," the voice said with an evil laugh.

"Why would you do this? How can you be this cruel?" Angela cried. She was clutching her stomach as she twisted again, another searing pain in her side. She grew weaker. She couldn't stop this.

"Because I can. Because I want to. *Because* you're wanted dead. Because once you have a taste of this power, there's no going back," the voice said. It was closer to her, looming and shadowy. It would blanket her. She knew what came next—total darkness.

She was losing the will to fight. She wanted to give up. It hurt too much.

"Mom, Mom, please . . ." That voice came from farther away, through a tunnel, through the woods, and over the oceans. It was so still, so quiet. But it was much more powerful than the evil voice surrounding her.

"Mom, wake up. Please, Mom, I'm scared," the voice said, growing stronger, getting closer.

She could fight this. She knew she could. A scream ripped from her as she twisted hard . . . and then she was falling. The impact of hitting her bedroom floor finally pulled her from the nightmare she'd been stuck in.

It took a moment of confusion before Angela realized her son knelt beside her, tears streaming down his cheeks.

"It's okay, Mom, it's okay," he said as he grabbed her hand with his small fingers and comforted her.

"I'm so sorry, Timmy. I'm so sorry." She stopped her own tears and pulled her eight-year-old son into her arms and clung on tight. "It was only a bad dream. I didn't mean to scare you."

"You were crying, Mom," he said as his little body shook against hers.

"I know, baby. I'm sorry. Sometimes dreams seem real, and this was a really bad one. But I'm awake now and everything will be okay," she assured her son.

She'd worked so hard to protect him, to keep the horrors of reality away from her precious son. But she couldn't protect him in her sleep. Maybe it was time to talk to someone. She'd thought she was okay, but with all of the things happening in Edmonds, she realized she might not be. Maybe there was no place she could go where she'd be truly safe, ever feel that she could keep the evils of the world away from her son and what they'd already gone through.

"I'll take care of you, Mom. I'm a young man, as Mr. Joseph says, and it's my job to protect you."

"Oh, baby, you do take care of me, and I appreciate it. But you're still a little boy, and it's my job to keep *you* safe. I think the roles will change as you get older, but don't grow up too quickly."

"I like growing," he said.

She smiled as she rubbed her cheek against his soft black hair. He was growing so quickly, but he was still small and sweet. She didn't want to lose this time with him and didn't want to see that guarded look in his eyes she saw on so many teens.

"I know you do, Timmy, but I promise time will fly by so fast you won't know what's happening. Trust your mom and enjoy being a kid. I promise not to watch any more scary movies so I don't have bad dreams that frighten you," she assured him.

"I don't like scary movies," he said with a shudder. But then he leaned back and smiled the sweet smile that turned her heart to butter. She leaned down and kissed his forehead. She was sad to think there'd be a time he wouldn't sit in her lap any longer. She'd successfully distracted him, though.

She looked at her alarm clock and saw it was only two in the morning. She knew she was going to have a hard time getting back to sleep, but she could at least tuck her son back into bed.

"Let's lay you down," she said.

"I'm scared," he told her.

"Then I'll read you a story." She stood up and cradled him in her arms as she walked the short distance to his room. He was almost too big for her to carry anymore. Time was going too fast. Life always did when you least wanted it to.

She picked out his favorite story, *Brown Bear Brown Bear What Do You See*, and he was back asleep before she was halfway through the story. She sat with him a bit longer, so grateful she had him. She couldn't imagine her life without her son.

They'd made it to San Diego. She should've chosen a different location, but she'd wanted some familiarity.

Timothy had been sad when he'd realized they weren't going back to Edmonds, but he'd adjust. He'd done just fine three years earlier. At least she hoped he would.

She finally rose and walked into her kitchen to heat water for a cup of tea to soothe her nerves. It had been a long time since she'd had a nightmare like that one. It had been a long time since she'd been so brutally attacked. Maybe the stuff that had happened in the past couple years in Edmonds had triggered her. Was it related? She wasn't sure. She'd been badly hurt, but she couldn't remember many details. It was a terrifying feeling.

She sat on the couch and drank her tea, calming herself. Then she hopped in the shower. She'd worked up quite a sweat during her nightmare. She wasn't sure if it was her memories of the assault trying to break through, or if she was only scared.

She was grateful she couldn't remember what had happened to her four years earlier. That way she only really had to deal with it in her nightmares, which had become few and far between. She was making a new life for herself and she was thankful for it.

She did remember the pain. That was never going away. She'd woken up in pain and until that moment she'd thought she was a strong woman. She'd never felt so weak. She wouldn't wish that feeling of helplessness on her worst enemy.

Her gut clenched and she ran her fingers over her abdomen. The knife had done more damage than she ever spoke about. Enough that she'd never be the woman she was before the accident.

She couldn't think about that now. If she did, she'd fall apart all over again, and there was no way she'd wake her son up again with screams or tears. She'd done her best to protect him his entire life, and she'd continue doing that. As long as he was healthy and happy, she was as well.

It was after three when she was finally calm enough to lie back down. She moved into her room and frowned as she looked at her torn up bedding. It was damp from her sweat. Too tired to do much more than rip the bedding away, she pulled it off and stuffed it in the corner, then threw a sheet over her mattress and fell on top of it.

Even though morning was only a few hours away, it would be a brand-new day and give her a new start on life once again. She'd discovered sleep truly could heal the soul as much as it healed the body.

She was asleep in seconds. And she was right. The fear faded away.

Chapter Three

Angela tried to get comfortable in the cafeteria she was sitting at in the southern tip of California. She felt she was far enough away from Washington to be safe from danger, and since she'd lived there before she felt secure in the familiar surroundings.

She'd found a tiny two-bedroom apartment and was thankful for the savings she had in her bank due to the generous pay from the Forbes family and her income from the café she'd worked at in Edmonds. Those jobs were both long gone since she'd left without a word. She hadn't even taken her cell phone; too afraid it could be traced.

She had to assure herself the drug cartel didn't know her name, just her face. But the man *had* recognized her. She didn't know how. He'd seemed familiar to her as well, but she couldn't quite make the pieces fall together. But she'd never sleep again if she let herself worry too much.

Angela loved to people watch, and she enjoyed the crowds surrounding her. This place wasn't quite like Edmonds, and the warmer weather and the different personalities made her feel as if she was a nobody. It was perfect. She didn't want to stand out, didn't want anyone noticing her. She wanted nothing more than to blend into the sea of faceless, nameless individuals.

Timothy was in school under a different last name. That hadn't been too difficult, but she knew it wouldn't last long. If the case in Edmonds wasn't solved soon, she wasn't sure what she was going to do. It wasn't easy to give yourself a new alias in this age of paranoia.

Her coffee and biscuit were set before her, and Angela thanked the waitress. She really shouldn't be spending any extra money, but she hadn't been out in weeks and needed to be around people in a place she felt somewhat safe.

Nightmares had plagued her for a long time when she'd first arrived in Edmonds, and now they were back again. At only twenty-six, she'd seen a lot of bad in her lifetime. She hoped she'd seen the last. She didn't want to worry about life, didn't want to live at half-mast. She wanted to soar, and she was determined to get to that point.

She sat quietly reading a book, munching on her biscuit smothered in strawberry jelly, and sipping on her mocha. If she could forget about why she was in this location at this time, she could almost smile at the nearly perfect day.

The last time she'd lived in San Diego had been nine years ago. It had been a happy time in her life. She'd been in love with her high school sweetheart, had good grades, and was excited for her future. She hadn't known the things her boyfriend or her father had been into, and she hadn't had a clue how much darkness was out there in the world.

She was more than aware of all of that now.

She refused to think of how it had all ended, and instead thought of the romance of that summer: fishing in the ocean, tanning on the beach, and laughing with friends she'd thought she'd have for life. It had only been nine years, but it felt like a lifetime ago. It was so strange how everything could change so quickly.

It had always been her philosophy to not live with regrets. It was hard to stick to that when she knew taking a right instead of a left could change your entire life. She remembered that movie *Sliding Doors*. How different would her life have been had she never met Robert? She wasn't sure. But she wouldn't have regrets. Because everything happened for a reason.

And Timothy was a very, *very* good reason for her to have met Robert. Though she truly wished Timothy didn't have to go his entire life without a father. She just hoped she was enough to make up for it.

Robert had promised her the moon and stars. But those promises had been nothing but words. The second she'd found out she was pregnant he'd changed. And then she'd learned more about him than she'd ever wanted to know. She'd walked away, but it had been too late to keep her from the horrors that real life could be. Robert had died soon after. She'd been heartbroken, but almost relieved too since he'd turned into such a terrible person.

Angela finished her coffee and snack, put down a couple bills, and walked from the café. She easily moved down the familiar street, trying to convince herself this was like any normal day. She'd pull herself together, and she'd figure out where she and Timothy were going to make a permanent life together. She didn't want to keep moving him all over the country. Maybe they should go to Mexico or even farther, somewhere like Italy. But those places required passports, and that was very traceable.

She couldn't imagine some criminal in Washington would want to chase her around the world, but she'd learned not long ago to never underestimate evil. They didn't like loose ends. And Angela had no doubt whatsoever that she was indeed a loose end. If she only had to worry about herself, she might want to just face it. But the moment she'd become a mother her life had changed, and she had more than herself to be concerned about.

She hoped she'd be able to return to Edmonds someday. But she might've burned those bridges with her abrupt exit from the town. She'd made friends there, and she had no doubt they'd be hurt by her departure.

Angela tried pushing these thoughts from her mind as she moved to the Saturday market and browsed the selections. She wasn't used to not having a job, and she was wondering if she should try to find temporary work. She'd have to give her social security number, though, and that scared her. She wasn't sure how deep the crime syndicate ran, and she didn't want to find out.

She purchased some food, then looked at the time. Timothy would be out of school soon, so she needed to get back to their temporary home. He hadn't been thrilled when he'd had to go to a new school. That had broken her heart. He'd made friends in Edmonds and she hated to uproot him from that. But Timothy was such a good kid. He'd accepted her explanation that she'd do all she could to take him back there, but sometimes situations were out of a parent's control. She hated that he had to accept her explanation and that she might be making him grow up too quickly. It wasn't easy making decisions for her child.

When she was close to home, she felt that chill down her spine again. And this time she was worried about it. She'd ignored it the last time and she'd had to uproot her entire life because. She stopped and looked around. She didn't see anyone. But she picked up her pace. Maybe they'd be moving sooner than she wanted. She just didn't know where she was going to go next.

Chapter Four
One Week Later

One day continued to turn into the next. Wasn't that how time was? Her loneliness was all in her head. But each day she took Timothy to school, then fretted about what to do next. Then it was time to pick him up again. Something had to change soon, or she was bound to go crazy.

She was once again alone when a voice she hadn't been sure she'd ever hear again spoke from behind.

"Angela."

Her insides turned to instant mush and she wanted to kick herself right where she was standing. But if there was one thing Angela had learned over the years, it was how to keep a straight face and not show fear. Well, it wasn't exactly fear she was feeling at the moment.

It was lust, pure and simple.

Declan Forbes was too good-looking for his own good. Seriously! He was intimidating as hell with a stare that made her want to admit to everything she'd ever done wrong, including the time she'd snagged a five-cent sucker at the store because her mother had told her she couldn't have it.

The guilt of taking that sucker had haunted her for years. By the time she'd turned twenty-one she'd paid for that dang thing a thousand times over, leaving a nickel in the change dish on the counter every time she'd gone back into that store. A life of thievery wasn't meant for everyone.

But back to Declan. The man had shoulders suited for a linebacker and arms that could either hold a criminal in place . . . or a woman against a wall. His eyes were nearly black, and his hair was always in place. He looked completely comfortable in a suit, and his jaw had a slight tick when he was thinking.

She'd avoided him while in Edmonds because he terrified her. She wasn't afraid he'd hurt her physically; she was afraid of the spell he cast on her without even trying. If the man put real effort into interacting with her, she'd be putty in his hands. Working part-time for his brother, she'd seen him more often than she'd wanted to, but other than that she'd always run in the opposite direction of Declan.

Somehow, he was now in California, far away from Edmonds, and standing in front of her at the small mom-and-pop café where she was trying to enjoy a cup of coffee. What were the chances of that happening?

"Are we going to have a staring contest?" Declan asked, and she realized she'd been standing with a blank look on her face. Maybe if she continued to do so he'd give up and walk away. Maybe she'd wake up and this would be nothing more than a dream.

His lip turned up the slightest bit in his trademark smirk, and she seriously wondered if the man could read her mind. She let out a sigh.

"Possibly." She kept it short and sweet . . . but not too sweet.

Before Declan said anything more, the bell on the door rang and in walked Owen Forbes. The resemblance between the brothers was obvious, but where Declan had a hard edge, Owen had a lightness that automatically drew people to him.

"Sorry I'm late. It took forever to park the car and then Eden called, and you know how that goes," Owen said with a smile that could've lit up the entire city.

"Newlyweds," Declan muttered. She was sure he wasn't saying it for anyone but himself, but that one word released her tension. She turned and faced Owen, missing her friend. She didn't normally go more than a few days without seeing Eden.

"The honeymoon phase must still be in full affect," she said with a genuine smile, forgetting for a moment that the two of them shouldn't be there.

"I plan on it staying that way for the rest of our lives," Owen said. "When you have a woman as amazing as Eden you don't ever lose sight of how lucky you are."

"Well, you did almost blow it," Declan rudely pointed out.

"Biggest mistake of my life. Luckily, she forgave me, and now I have a lifetime to show her how thankful I am."

"Yeah, you don't deserve her," Declan said with a clap on his brother's shoulder. The words were followed by a real smile, erasing the sting.

"I know I don't, but she sure as hell loves me so I'm not going to tell her that," Owen said.

They both turned back to Angela. She had to admit she enjoyed being around whenever the brothers were together. It was fun watching them talk and seeing how much they cared about each other. She also didn't like their focus on her. It was intense, to say the least.

She finally sighed. "Why are you here, Declan?"

"I think we're beyond asking questions as if we don't know what's going on. You witnessed a drug deal, saw who we believe is the head of the entire organization, and the more I dig, the more I see a connection from your incident four years ago. I asked Owen to come because he's been working the case with me and can fill in any blanks. Can we go somewhere and talk?" Declan asked.

"I left for a reason. I don't want to talk anymore. I pointed out the man I saw, gave my statement, then left," she said, feeling her heart pick up its pace. He raised a brow as if to tell her she wasn't going to hide. She knew better than that, but she could sure as hell try.

"We need to ask you more questions."

She looked from Declan to Owen and back again— and her shoulders slumped. She hadn't been able to run from her past. And the present was even scarier. There didn't seem to be anywhere far enough away to hide.

As good as Angela was about keeping her composure, she felt tears building behind her eyes. This was something she didn't want to face. But with everything that had happened it appeared that was no longer a luxury she could afford.

"What do you want to know?" she asked. The bell rang and two people walked inside.

"I think we should do this in private," Declan said. He reached for her and she tried to pull back, but he took her hand. She wanted to run, but she'd already done that, and it obviously hadn't been far enough. There was nowhere she could hide from this man. It had been so easy for him to find her. She wondered if the cartel could as well. Maybe her feelings of being watched were genuine.

"I don't understand why you'd chase me all the way here," she said.

Owen got a phone call and apologized as he took it and walked away, leaving her alone with Declan. She wanted to call him a traitor. She *absolutely* didn't want to be alone with Declan.

"You saw something I wish you wouldn't have seen, but you did, and we need you as a witness," he said. She flinched. Of course, it wasn't personal. As if he could read her thoughts again, he squeezed her fingers. "I also want to make sure you and Timothy are safe. That's my *top* priority."

"I'm afraid, Declan. I don't want something to happen to my son. They go after family members to keep a witness silent."

"I won't let anything happen to you or Timothy," Declan said with a glint in his eyes that told her he meant what he said. But even if he were Superman, he couldn't guarantee that. There was no way for him to be with her twenty-four/seven. The thought of that was almost scarier than the criminals getting their hands on her.

"I'm fine here. Just ask your questions, get it out of the way, and leave," she said. He flinched. "I'm not trying to be mean. I'm sorry. I just don't want to go back."

"You aren't safe here, Angela." He didn't add more, and her eyes narrowed.

"What are you talking about, Declan?" He didn't answer fast enough. "Please just spit it out." She was growing more and more agitated.

"You shouldn't have run away. I can protect you."

"You can't be with me all the time, Declan."

"If for some reason I couldn't be there, then my brothers can," he pointed out. "At home. This is about Timothy too."

She flinched. "That's a low blow, Declan. You know how much I love my son."

"Yes, I do. But people don't think straight when they're scared. You can't do this on your own. And more importantly, there's no reason to when you have friends willing to lay down their lives for you."

She was shocked at those words. "Why would any of you do that for me? I've only been there a few years."

"And it only took a day for us to care."

The look in his eyes told her he wasn't just spouting words. She didn't know what to think or feel about what he was telling her. It was hard to stay defensive when she knew Declan didn't lie. He also didn't say something just to hear himself speak. He was a man who said little but meant everything that did come out.

"I'm so grateful for everything your family has done. Arden took a chance on me and gave me a job, letting me in his house. You've embraced Timothy and invited us to family events. You've gone above and beyond. But you have nieces and nephews to consider now. If someone truly is after me, I should be far away from you. I can't repay your kindness by putting everyone you love in jeopardy."

She hated that she was trying to talk him out of helping her. She could tell herself all day long he was just doing his job, but she knew this went beyond his badge. He cared about his family. He'd do anything for them, and since she was friends with them that made him feel more responsible. That's just how honorable he was.

She watched his eyes narrow. She was making him mad but didn't understand how. She was speaking from the heart and didn't feel she was doing anything wrong. She could easily give him her statement from here and then go back and testify when the man she'd spotted was safely behind bars. Though she knew even if he was in jail she wasn't necessarily safe. There was no way a man like that had gotten where he was without having people in his pockets. She knew of witnesses who ended up dead even when the main villain was in jail. It happened more often than people realized.

There was nowhere far enough away to hide when someone really wanted to get to them. Hell, people were even slain in jail.

"Your pride will get you killed," he said. She stepped back from him. She knew it wasn't a threat, but he didn't have to be so blunt.

"They have to find me first," she replied. "Or they'll move on to someone else."

"You can't bury your head in the sand and hope this goes away. Help me get this guy and take down this organization, and I'll take care of you."

"Whether I can bury my head or not, I'm going to continue to do just that. You can't physically remove me from this place." She was finally finding her backbone.

He shook his head. "I'm trying not to scare you more, Angela," he told her. He didn't break eye contact as he waited for her reply.

"What aren't you telling me?" she asked. There was something he didn't want to say, and she wished he'd just spit it out.

"You *are* in serious danger, even down here."

She waited.

He didn't say more.

"Why do you keep saying that?"

They stood there for at least a full minute with a thousand questions running through her mind. She wasn't going to ask more. She'd wait to see if he'd just lay it all out. They could dance all day long, but she wasn't going to change her mind unless he gave her a good enough reason to do just that.

Finally, he shrugged. "How do you think I found you?"

"You're some super-secret ninja spy," she said only somewhat kidding.

That got the smallest of smiles to show on his firm lips. He shook his head.

"That's true, but that's not it. You aren't as stealthy as you believe."

"Why do you say that? I didn't even take my cell phone with me."

"Your house was broken into the day after you left, and you had notes jotted down. It didn't take me long to figure out you went to California. It just took me a while to find out where. And I have a lot of resources at my fingertips. But I guarantee you they aren't far behind me."

"Was it them?" she asked, her voice quiet, fear truly seeping in. It was always there in the back of her mind, but it was in full force right now. She wanted to get to Timothy, assure herself he was safe and where he was supposed to be.

"It's them, Angela. You might be the only witness to see this man at work. He won't stop until he finds you. The only way to keep him from accomplishing his goal is for me to be at your side. I can do that so much better at home."

"Closer to him?" she gasped.

"There is no place far enough. My house is a fortress."

"They know who I am?" she asked, tears filling her eyes. She assumed they did, but to hear it confirmed scared her. They'd know she had a son, know that would be her biggest weakness. They'd be correct. If testifying put Timothy in danger, there was no way she'd do it.

"Let's get Timothy and get out of here. I don't like it. There is nothing at all safe here."

"I don't want to go back," she whispered.

"I know. But let me do my job. Trust me to do what's best for you."

She looked at him, not knowing what she wanted to do next. Making rash decisions didn't seem to be getting her anywhere so she needed to slow down and think. She couldn't do that with him standing in front of her.

Chapter Five

Declan's phone rang and he cursed. He was making progress with Angela, and he didn't need the interruption. He let it go to voicemail, but it rang again, and he glanced down. Dammit!

"I have to take this," he told her.

"It's okay. I need a minute to think. I'm just going to step out front."

Declan didn't like that one bit, but he wasn't too worried since Owen was out there. What in the world was taking his brother so long anyway? They needed to get out of this place. Declan didn't like being in unfamiliar surroundings. He'd rather be in a territory he knew.

He answered.

"Make this quick. I've got limited time," Declan said.

"Is that any way to speak to your boss?" Director Dorsey asked, sounding tense.

"You're eating up your time," Declan replied.

He normally liked chatting with the director. The man was good at his job and Declan respected him and the work he did. But right now he was anxious and in unfamiliar territory, and the last thing he wanted was to lose sight of Angela.

"There's trouble here, Declan," Dorsey said, getting to the point. They might be able to quip with one another but now wasn't the time for it.

"What's happening?" Declan asked. His entire body was tense. He wanted this job over and done with. He wanted the bad guys in jail where they belonged.

"There was another bust."

"Did we get him?" Declan asked, not holding out a lot of hope.

"No, but we got someone who's giving us info," Dorsey told him.

"Who?" Declan wanted to know.

"The kid's name is Don Klien, but he doesn't matter. The info he's giving us is what counts. We know this all comes down to Mario Vasquez, but it's bigger than we initially thought."

"Explain," Declan said. He didn't want this drawn out.

"We know Mario is heading this operation in Edmonds. We also know it stretches farther than this town. What we didn't know was Mario has a brother," Dorsey said.

The line went silent at those words for several tense seconds.

"How did we not have this information?" Declan growled. He was pacing in the small café grateful the place had emptied.

"They have different fathers, and they've been very smart in keeping it hidden."

"How reliable is this Don kid?" Declan asked.

"We've looked into it already and Mario does have a brother. Emilio Coronado. He belongs to a cartel, the Coronados, that's been rising on our radar."

"Of course, I know who they are. I can't believe we didn't know the connection to Mario," Declan exclaimed. "They are wanted here and in Mexico."

"The amount of crime they're responsible for is shocking. We've never been able to corner Emilio. He's a ghost. No one has ever seen his face. And now Angela is one of the few who have seen Mario."

"*If* it was Mario she saw," Declan pointed out.

Dorsey let out a groan. "We need her home, and we need her protected. With this new info she's in more danger than she could possibly realize. They know who she is, and she stands in the way of a lot of money for them."

"I know that," Declan said, his voice going dangerously quiet.

"If Mario sends Emilio after her, she could pass him on the street and have no clue who he is. But they don't need to go after her on their own and risk being exposed. They have a lot of minions willing to do their dirty work for them," Dorsey pointed out.

To the outside world, Declan would've looked calm and in charge. No one would know his blood had run cold or his heart was thundering. He knew he could protect Angela, but he also knew how evil these cartels could be. He was afraid for her, and he wasn't sure how he was going to get her to listen.

"Why is this kid giving up info?" Declan asked. He had to focus on the case. The sooner he solved it, the sooner he could assure Angela's safety.

"He wants out. He's afraid," Dorsey said. "He promised us all the information he has if we place him in witness protection."

"Then the cartel shouldn't be as focused on Angela," Declan said.

"They'll want them both," Dorsey said, popping that bubble.

"I know. I'm just grasping at straws," Declan told him.

Declan was feeling confined. He moved to the front of the café and stepped outside. He didn't see Owen or Angela. He moved down the sidewalk while he continued speaking to Dorsey. Where in the world were they?

He was on high alert as it was, but something inside him was screaming that all wasn't right. He never ignored his gut instincts, and right now they told him he needed to have his eyes on Angela, and he didn't think it was just because of this call. These men wanted her, and he'd found her far too easily. They could too.

He moved about a block down the street and turned a corner to find a crowd of people. What in the hell was going on? He couldn't keep talking.

"I've got to go. I can't see Angela," he said.

The director didn't argue. "Call me back as soon as the situation is resolved," Dorsey said, and the line went dead.

There were vendors in the streets and crowds of people, women, children, dogs, strollers—lots of targets. And too many in the way of finding the woman he needed to take care of.

He wanted to keep her safe for the case, but he wasn't going to lie to himself and say it was only that. He cared about this woman. He didn't know why or how it had happened, but sometime in the past couple of years he'd begun looking at her in a different light. And he wasn't sure what in the hell that meant. He never would know if some criminal got to her. He'd never forgive himself if that were to happen.

He was more scared now, knowing Mario was associated with Emilio Coronado. This operation stretched so much wider than he'd imagined. Mario had almost taken down their entire town with his fires. This man wasn't afraid to run over anyone who stepped in his path. And unfortunately, Angela had done just that.

Declan picked up his pace as he pulled out his phone and dialed Owen. There wasn't an answer. His gut continued screaming. Something was wrong. He just didn't know what in the hell it was.

He put his phone away and moved. He had no idea if he was going in the right direction, but he couldn't stand still. He wouldn't feel better until he laid eyes on the woman he needed to care for.

He skirted around pedestrians, most people instinctively moving away from him, like the sea parting. His eyes had to look wild, and the firm set of his lips was enough to make anyone pause. He wasn't a small man. Many people had pointed out that he looked as if he should be a linebacker on the football field. Right now he didn't mind, because he was willing to plow through anyone to get to Angela.

Where in the hell was she? Apparently, she hadn't taken his warnings seriously or she never would've wandered off.

The longer it took to find her, the more his gut clenched. His instincts had saved him more than once in his years in the military and the FBI. He wasn't going to stop listening now. He moved forward.

The crowd grew thicker as he continued through the busy vendors. Kids laughed and cried, dogs barked, and strangers brushed against him. His eyes continued scanning, looking for dark hair and a red sweater. Thank goodness she had a penchant for bright colors. But in a sea of people that wasn't as helpful right now.

The call from Dorsey hadn't helped ease his sense of foreboding. His need to keep her safe was pushing him on. He had no choice but to make her listen. And if he needed to tie her up and drag her home, that's exactly what he was going to do. This wasn't a game, and they didn't have the luxury of taking their time, not when they were dealing with a gang as powerful as the Coronados.

She might think she was safe a couple of states away from Washington, but she was in their playground in California. She was in far more danger there than back home with Declan and his family.

This gang was smart. She'd run back to a place she was familiar with. It wouldn't take much guessing on their part to hunt her down in this city. While it might not be small, it wasn't impossible to find her. It had been far easier for him than he'd liked. He'd been grateful for that when he'd located her, but he knew that meant they could too.

The only proof that Angela was in danger right now was his gut. But that was all the evidence he needed. He pushed through another large group of people . . . and prayed he wasn't going to be too late.

Chapter Six

Angela knew she shouldn't have wandered off. She was very aware Declan was going to be furious with her. But she was scared, frustrated, and needed to think. She hadn't seen Owen outside, so she'd decided to take a walk. She was sure if Declan had found her once, he'd certainly find her again. But that didn't give her a lot of time to figure out what she was going to do next.

She wasn't a fool. She knew there were men out to get her. She just hadn't thought of the possibility they'd come looking for her in San Diego. This was a safe and secure place. It was familiar and the only spot she'd thought to come. She was just a small fish in a very large pond. Her philosophy had always been out of sight, out of mind. If she wasn't around, she'd hoped they'd feel she wasn't a threat. Declan was making her think she'd been wrong to assume that.

As she wandered through the festival she'd stumbled upon, she hated how her heart pounded and her adrenaline spiked. She hadn't been afraid . . . much . . . since she'd arrived in California. Sure, she'd been spooked a bit easier than she had been before, but she'd felt a sense of peace.

Declan had shattered that false sense of security. She was angry with him for that. She couldn't be a good mother if she was constantly looking over her shoulder. Right now, she wanted a cup of coffee and another muffin to calm her stomach. Then she'd gaze out at the water, take some calming breaths, and wait for Timothy to get out of school. She was sure Declan would track her down before too long.

She might not want to admit it to herself, but she felt a bit safer knowing he was looking out for her. Yes, she also felt smothered, and yes, it scared her. But there was a sense of security in knowing a man as capable and strong as Declan Forbes wanted to keep her alive. She wanted to tell herself it was only because of the case, but she wasn't sure of that. Of course, she wasn't sure of much of anything anymore.

This city was comforting with people coming and going all the time. Of course, there were the locals, but there were also a lot of people visiting for fishing and recreation. This long weekend looked to be a festival event.

That meant there were extra people in the city, and normally she loved every minute of that. She loved to people-watch and try to figure out what they were doing or thinking by their expressions. She could paint a story in her mind of young lovers on their honeymoon or a couple celebrating fifty years together. She watched mothers pushing strollers and teens flirting while eating ice cream. She loved the different stages of life people went through. Some of those times were good and some bad, but all told a unique story that gave a beautiful picture to anyone who took the time to see it.

But right now, instead of imagining wonderful stories, she was searching for danger. Was that man leaning against the tree near the alley looking at her? Did he have an agenda? Was the woman sitting on the steps sending furtive glances around calling in her location? Was there really someone after her? Or was it all in Declan's head? She didn't know. She hated the fear and uncertainty, and she hated even more the distrust in her fellow human beings. She'd never been that woman and didn't want to start being her now.

Declan wanted her to go back home. But wasn't that exactly like going straight into the lion's den? It seemed so much safer to be right where she was. She wanted to go home eventually, if it would still be home after the way she'd left. But she was hopeful. It was a place that, for the first time in her life, she'd felt safe and cared about.

Angela shook off those thoughts. This wasn't the time or place for them. She needed to pay attention to the here and now and what was happening around her. For the most part she'd felt safe until today. She'd thought she was comfortable and secure, and more importantly, that Timothy was.

She made it to the water and felt her stress practically dissipate. Water had always been a safe haven for her. She could fish, swim, or simply dip her toes in. But sometimes all it took was watching the way the waves splashed on the shore. No ripple was ever the same. Most people didn't know there wasn't a single ripple that looked like another; they were as unique as people were.

The sound, sight, and smell of a lake, ocean, stream, or river was soothing. She'd be more than content to own a home in the backwoods with a river running right past her front door. That was her idea of heaven. Maybe after Timothy was grown, she'd find something just like that and live out the rest of her days there.

Again, she had to smile and shake off her thoughts. She wasn't being observant at all. She was living inside her own head. Maybe Declan had a point about her safety. She didn't seem to be worried enough about it.

With the smell of the water before her and the aroma of pastries and coffee behind her, she was hungry. She'd been too busy and then too stressed to put anything in her stomach. But now seemed like a good time for a delicious mocha.

She turned around and looked at all the vendors, sure there was something delicious if the smells were any indication. She'd grab a quick drink and a bite to eat, then head back toward the café where she'd left her full cup of coffee . . . and Declan. She was sure he wasn't there now and would almost bet her life he was searching for her, but she'd run into him. If not, he'd find her at home. She smiled, having no doubt he knew where that was.

She didn't mind some people finding her. Others she hoped would never spot her again. That thought took the smile right off her face.

As she headed toward a coffee stand, someone ran into her, nearly knocking her to the ground. Instant déjà vu filled her along with a sense of foreboding.

"Excuse me," the woman said with a hurried gait and apologetic smile. Then she was gone. Angela took a deep breath.

"You're being stupid now," she muttered to herself. But how could she help it when Declan had put so many thoughts into her mind? It was easy to get bumped in this crowded place.

She made it to the vendor and waited for several minutes before she was able to order a mocha and blueberry scone. The first sip was heaven. She turned back toward the crowd and wasn't sure which direction to go next.

Still was filled with a sense of unease that she desperately tried to squash down. She was perfectly safe. Nothing could happen to her in the middle of a crowded city center. A person would be foolish to try something with so many witnesses. Even knowing this, she couldn't shake the feeling that something was wrong.

She walked along as she finished her coffee and scone, barely tasting the treat. Declan was to blame for that. Normally she'd get the utmost enjoyment out of a walk on a beautifully sunny day. But instead of people-watching and browsing, she saw danger everywhere she turned. Instead of enjoying the differences in the people she passed, she watched for weapons. She was a hot mess.

Of course, Declan would see danger everywhere he looked. That was part of his job description. He was FBI, and that had to change a person and make them more cynical. The world needed people like him. It also needed people like her who saw petals on the roses instead of thorns on the stems.

She refused to let criminals take away her love of life. She refused to give in and be afraid of everyone and every sound. Yes, she needed to be cautious, but that didn't mean she had to change the very fabric of who she was.

Still, one thought ran through her brain—if Declan had been able to find her, wouldn't the bad guys be able to do the same? That was like a mantra in her brain. It was removing the joy from her life. If she went home she might feel better. Maybe tomorrow would bring her peace.

She had to have her act together before Timothy got home because she wouldn't allow her son to live in a world of fear. She'd lived her life well, making very few mistakes. And the ones she had made had shaped her into the woman she was today, so she was glad she'd made them.

Her life was exactly as it had been at this time the day before—before Declan had shown up and reminded her of what she'd fled from. If she could get that through her brain, she'd be fine. The only thing that had changed was the arrival of Declan and Owen.

But even with her pep talk chills traveled down her spine. She looked around again and didn't see anything out of the ordinary, so she tried to shake it off.

She moved down the street and turned. The crowd parted. And that's when her heart lodged in her throat.

Maybe her paranoia had been for a good reason. There was a man standing in the shadows, and no one else seemed to be aware of him. Angela couldn't help but notice the small man. He wasn't just standing there. She knew that glint of the sun on metal. She knew exactly what he was holding. And she knew it was aimed directly at her.

She did the only thing she could do at that point. She turned and ran. She prayed he didn't fire, prayed she didn't get someone killed. Maybe she should've listened to Declan. It might be too late to ever tell him that.

Chapter Seven

There was a reason humans survived the impossible. Declan firmly believed there was something out there greater than himself, greater than any of them. He believed that gut feeling a person had was something on the other side telling you to take a step backward or forward. He cursed the fates and the heavens when a child came up missing or a person was killed. He lost his faith and gained it back.

He believed in a higher power.

And when he heard a gunshot rip through the air, his blood froze. His gut had been telling him to get to Angela; she needed him. And he knew why. She was in danger . . . and he might be too late.

He was running before the smoke cleared. Chaos erupted around him as screams filled the air. There was nothing more terrifying than the sound of a gun going off in the middle of the city. In the country a person wouldn't blink twice, but in the city there were too many bad guys intent on bringing others down.

"Angela!" he cried. He couldn't help himself. He had to find her. He refused to think it was too late, and there was no doubt this wasn't a coincidence. Someone was after her, and he was deathly afraid she'd been found.

Another shot rang in the air, and instead of terrifying him more, it gave him a sense of relief. He prayed no one was hurt, but two shots meant the first hadn't hit its target. He hoped and prayed the second one hadn't as well.

There were too many people around him. He couldn't get through the crowd, still he pushed his way forward.

"Turn around," someone shouted. "A guy is shooting." The words trailed off as the person trying to warn him continued past.

Sobs and screams filled the air as he tried to make his way through the swarm of people. He was used to rushing in while the rest of the world flew past. That was his job. It was his obligation. But never before had he felt such a deep sense of urgency.

Declan carried his own sidearm safely tucked away, and he wasn't going to pull it. There were too many potential victims around. There was too much fear. He didn't need a weapon anyway. His hands were as deadly as a bullet. He'd take this guy down, or he'd die trying. He realized he'd give his life for this woman. But he didn't think he'd have to. There was no way some punk with a gun, willing to shoot it into a crowd of innocent people, would get the upper hand with him.

As he got farther into the crowd, it began thinning. There was still chaos all around with people hiding in doorways, peeking out, and others crying as they ran past. Children were screaming, and parents were holding them close. He hated that they had to witness this horror and feel the sense of powerlessness that came with it. The world had become a less safe place. He'd give about anything to go back to his grandfather's time when there wasn't a thought of shooting inside a school, or a mall, or a movie theatre. What had happened to humanity and loving your neighbor? He might never get that answer.

He was focused as he moved forward. Those thoughts were running through his head, but his main objective was getting to Angela. He had to get there in time, had to protect her. Get her out of this city. Her and Timothy. Thank goodness her son was in school. As soon as he had her secured, they'd pick up Timothy and get the hell out of there. She no longer had a choice.

Another shot rang out and his adrenaline spiked. It had been a long delay from the second shot to the third. Was the man closing in on her? Had he gotten close enough to feel he could fire again? Where in the hell were the local authorities? There was some sort of fair going on; shouldn't they be there for crowd control? He didn't see a single blue in sight.

He was going as fast as he could while he scanned for her in all directions. Finally he broke through a group of people and the mass diminished. Most were now behind him. The faces he saw looked confused as if they had no idea what was going on. There were abandoned vendor booths and spilled drinks on the ground. Sweaters had been abandoned, and a purse was overturned in the center of the street. Safety was all anyone was thinking about.

Something caught his eye, just a glint, but it was enough. He spotted the gunman moving ahead, his eyes locked on something. He was trying to conceal the handgun in his coat but the barrel stuck out. He moved with purpose.

The man's arm lifted, and he shot again. Declan's head whipped around and he spotted Angela. His heart stopped. The moment froze. She turned and looked right at her potential killer . . . but she wasn't hit.

She ran and the rest of the people around did as well, all of them going in different directions. No one knew where the shots were coming from. Declan couldn't unsheathe his weapon. It would only terrify the crowd more. He was in a suit, not a uniform, and they wouldn't know who the bad guy was. He did the only thing he could. He shouted.

"Hey!" he yelled at the top of his lungs. The gunman stopped his aim and turned. Their eyes locked. Declan started running straight for him.

Chapter Eight

Angela's blood had grown cold. There was no way to deny the shots were being fired at her. What made it even worse were all the people around. They were in imminent danger because of her. Four shots had been fired, and not one had hit her. She wasn't sure if they'd landed in someone else instead. She wasn't sure she'd forgive herself if that had happened.

She should've listened to Declan. He'd tried to get her to leave. If she hadn't wandered off, none of these people would be in danger. There was elderly who couldn't run, children who didn't know what was happening, and strangers who were confused.

She didn't know where to go. She wanted to lead the gunman away. She didn't have a death wish, but she also didn't want to live at the expense of others. She didn't have time to think, to make a plan. Who was this? It wasn't Mario Vasquez. She didn't know who in the hell it was. All she knew was there was someone willing to take her life, and he truly didn't care how many witnesses there were. He would shoot her and disappear again.

Angela ran toward the water. It might not be the safest move on her part, but it was away from the other people. Maybe she could lead him there and jump in. She could hold her breath for a really long time. That might be her best chance to save the people around and her own life.

It was so hard to think.

She was in shock and terrified. She'd been chased down by these guys, and that told her she wasn't safe no matter where she went. Which meant her son wasn't safe— and that was unacceptable.

She didn't have time for those thoughts, though. She didn't have time to panic or think about what she'd done wrong. A bullet could travel far faster than she could run, so she had to be smarter than the person shooting.

She moved ahead when she heard the shout. She didn't turn, but it sounded like Declan. Hope filled her. If it was, she might have a chance. She kept moving as fast as she could. Every little sound made her blood turn to ice. She could barely breathe.

Her heart was pounding so hard she could feel it pushing out her chest. She most likely looked like one of those cartoons where the heart was about to pop out of the skin. She didn't care how she looked. She only cared about survival.

She tried to focus on what people were shouting as she passed them. Which direction were they going? Was the gunman right on her heels? It felt as if she could feel his hot breath on the back of her neck. That thought brought tears to her eyes. She wouldn't turn around; she knew if she did it might cost her life. So, she kept on moving, and hoping, and praying.

This all felt as if it were taking hours, but she'd be surprised if less than five minutes had passed since the first shot rang out. Items were being dropped as the chaos increased. The word gun was shouted over and over again.

With the sheer number of mass shootings over the past decade, she wasn't surprised. This was something that should never occur. And this time it was all because of her.

Panic surrounded her. No one knew where to turn, where to go. She continued to move, but the crowd was unorganized. Everywhere she turned she ran into someone, and she was growing tired.

She shouldn't have left Declan's side. That was her one consistent thought. But maybe it still would've happened, and maybe he would've been killed. She couldn't live with that either.

She moved forward and tripped over a dropped bag. As she fell to the ground, she almost hoped to get knocked out. At least she wouldn't see her death coming.

Chapter Nine

As soon as Declan moved toward the shooter, the man turned and ran. Declan chased him for a minute then stopped. He was torn. He wanted this man, wanted him desperately, but he didn't know if there was more than one person after Angela.

He looked toward the fleeing shooter then in the direction Angela had run. His gut told him to get to her and ensure she was safe, then try to find the man who'd made a huge mistake in going after her.

He was cursing himself because that man should never have come near her. He shouldn't have taken the call and let her walk out the door. He shouldn't have assumed his brother would trail behind her. He should've done his damn job and not let her out of his sight. And now he was having to live with that. But she'd be okay. He'd make damn sure of it.

He didn't look at anyone as he searched the chaotic crowd, trying to find her. When he did, all the color in his face drained as his heart stopped for at least a full two seconds.

He didn't stall long. She was lying on the ground . . . not moving.

"Angela," he cried as he dropped down next to her. Had she been shot? He flipped her onto her back and did a quick visual, searching for blood. There was none.

Her eyes fluttered open. She looked calm for a second before panic set in and her head whipped past him.

"Shooter," she gasped. "Shooter!" Her voice grew louder as her body began moving.

"It's okay, Angela. He's gone." Declan didn't know that for sure, but he needed her calm so he could assess her injuries and get her to safety. She wasn't going to calm down until she felt safe.

He had to fight the bile rising in his throat at how close she'd come to getting killed. Declan didn't care how long it took, he was going to take down that cartel and he wasn't going to be gentle about it. He was beyond frustrated and needed an outlet for it.

This wasn't the time nor place though. He needed to stay calm for her sake. If he freaked out, she was going to as well, and that wouldn't help either of them.

"Were you hit, Angela? I can't see blood," he asked her. His hands were running down her legs.

"No. I tripped. I think I knocked myself out for a second," she said. "My head hurts a little and my hands, but I don't think I was shot," she told him. "But there were several shots. I don't know if anyone else was hit."

"I don't know either," he told her. "I was worried about finding you, not looking at other people."

"We need to see if everyone is okay," she said as she sat up. She looked a bit disheveled but only had a few minor scrapes.

"The local authorities will be here soon, and they can assess the crowd," he told her.

"You *are* the authorities," she insisted.

"I want to get you out of here, Angela. I only saw one shooter. I don't know if there are more," he demanded.

He looked around them and the scene seemed to be calming. People were wandering around looking lost and scared. The booths were still abandoned, and he watched as a couple teens snatched some purses and took off running. It was sad when people took advantage of situations like these. He wanted to go knock them out, but he wasn't going to leave Angela for some petty thieves.

He looked in her eyes again and watched them fill and spill over as a sob ripped from her. Declan didn't know what to do. He would protect her with his last breath, but consoling someone was far out of his comfort zone.

"It'll be okay. I'll keep you safe. You just have to stay with me," he told her as he took her hand in his and squeezed her fingers.

"It's not okay. Don't you see that? People are scared. There's probably more that are injured. You have to check on them," she said, her shoulders going firm as she wiped away the tears as quickly as they'd come. She was such a strong woman, no doubt about it. He wondered what had happened in her life to give her such thick skin.

"Let's get up," he told her. "I don't like being vulnerable." He didn't like their position on the ground. It was too easy for someone to attack. He wasn't worried he couldn't fend off the enemy, but he didn't want to try to protect her while doing it. If he had to, he'd rather be on his feet.

"Okay, but I want to check on everyone," she said.

They stood, and he looked out at the crowd. There were a few people on the ground just as she'd been, but no one seemed to be severely injured. He could only see a small area though. Some of the people who had fled were coming back to check on their things, return to their booths, or look for lost family members.

"Where's Owen?" she asked.

"Did you see him when you came out?" he asked.

"No. He wasn't there so I decided to go for a walk. I know it was foolish, but I really didn't think there was danger like you'd thought," she admitted.

Declan pulled out his phone and dialed. Owen picked up this time.

"Where are you?" Declan snapped.

"Sorry," Owen said. "Eden had an issue and there was a couple fighting right by the café so I moved down the street where I could hear her. By the time I came back you were both gone. I'm sure I'm almost to you. I heard the shots," Owen replied. "Is Angela okay?"

"Yes. She's shaken up, but she's okay," Declan told Owen. "I want to get her out of here."

"Of course. We need to get Timothy too," Owen said.

"Right away. Get the car and meet me on the corner next to the fish market."

"Done," Owen said before hanging up.

There were sirens in the distance. They were finally on their way to the square. As the initial shock wore off, more people began talking about what had happened. Declan didn't want to get mixed up in it.

If the authorities questioned him, it could take hours. He was a federal agent and trained to be aware of a lot more than civilians were aware of. One part of him wanted to scoop Angela up and walk away.

But that same training that had taught him what to look for had also taught him not to abandon a scene. He just hoped like hell it didn't take all day. They had to pick Timothy up in two hours so whomever he spoke to better make it fast. He was getting Angela and Timothy out of this city before the perps came back for a second shot.

"Thank you for being here, Declan," Angela told him, bringing him out of his thoughts.

"What?" he asked, confused. She hadn't been happy to see him earlier.

"I wasn't too thrilled to see you, but because you were here, I'm alive, and so are all these people. Who knows what would've happened if you hadn't come? I owe you my life. There's no one else I can say that to," she told him before reaching for him.

He was in a bit of shock as she wrapped her arms around his neck and squeezed. She held on tightly as a shudder wracked through her body. Declan took a moment and hugged her back. He wanted to get moving, but he didn't want to let her go.

"I didn't do anything extra, Angela. You made the right decisions, and you probably saved a lot of lives by running toward the water."

"No one would've needed saving if I hadn't been here. I should've listened and gone straight home."

"They probably know where that is. We need to get out of here."

She let him go and the fear in her eyes made him feel guilty, but he was only trying to keep her safe. He had to be honest with her in order to do that.

"I truly thought I was okay here. I didn't think they'd care enough to hunt me down. This is a long way to come. I was hoping they'd see I was gone and just wanted to live my life. I didn't think I'd be a threat to anyone. But they really do want me dead," she said with a little sob.

"They want anyone who stands in their way dead. But they aren't going to get their way," he assured her.

"You can't promise that," she said.

"I promise to keep you safe, and if you listen to me, I can do that."

"I'll try," she said.

Declan gave her the tiniest bit of a smile, which was rare for him. He respected her honesty. "I guess we're both going to try stepping outside our comfort zones here," he said.

"It won't be easy."

"No, we can both agree on that," Declan told her.

He led her away. He wanted her safely in the car. He knew he'd have to talk to the authorities, but he wasn't letting her be alone for even a minute. They'd deal with that or they weren't getting his statement.

Chapter Ten

The first responders were at the scene in droves. Declan didn't want to deal with what had to be done; he wanted to get Angela out of there. But he was a lawman and couldn't just walk away.

"I'm going to take you to the car with Owen while I give my statement. I don't want them to know the gunman was after you. I want to assess the situation first," Declan told her.

"I'm sorry I dragged you away from home and made this mess."

He could never predict what would come from this woman's mouth. She had so much compassion and seemed to be far more worried about everyone else's needs than her own. He didn't understand.

"We'll talk about this later, but I need you to quit apologizing. You're a mother, and you did what you had to do to keep your son safe. I understand that fight or flight feeling, and I get taking flight. But we're going to do this differently now. So, sit tight with Owen and I'll be back quickly."

"Shouldn't I talk to them too?" she asked.

"No. Right now I don't trust anyone," Declan said.

"Even the police?"

He sighed. "I have the utmost respect for the men and women who serve in all aspects of law enforcement. But just because someone dons a uniform doesn't make them the good guy. Just like there are bad apples in every aspect of life, there are people who get into law enforcement for the wrong reasons. I can honestly say I don't often see it. But your protection is all I care about right now, and I'm not taking any chances."

"I'll trust you," she said. She was well aware of someone using their authority to get what they wanted. It was tragic and made the good guys look bad. It made it hard to trust the people you should be able to trust the most. Though she'd had a negative experience, she still trusted them. She wasn't allowing a few people to question her faith.

"Okay, stay put," he said as they reached the car. Owen held open the door for her.

She smiled, and it was like a rainbow after the storm. He had to fight not to lean down and plant a solid kiss on those perfectly pink lips. He waited to leave until she was safely in the car.

"Take care of her," he told Owen.

"Of course," Owen replied.

He knew his brother wanted to go with him, but Owen wouldn't let Angela out of his sight—not again. That's why Declan wanted to get her home so badly. He could keep her safe there. In Edmonds he'd be able to have eyes on her twenty-four/seven. He couldn't do that in San Diego.

He turned and moved toward the emergency responders, the scene filled with cop cars, ambulances, and fire trucks. When a shooter was involved, they didn't hold anything back. Declan wasn't sure if there had been any injuries beyond scrapes and bruises. He hadn't had time to assess the situation.

The sooner he spoke to the cops, though, the faster he could get her out of this city. He wasn't sure how they were going to do it. They needed to pick up Timothy, and they had two vehicles. He'd figure that out next.

She wouldn't fight him on leaving, not after what had happened today. She now knew these men could find her anywhere. Maybe she'd be safe in some Midwest town if she went into witness protection, but that was very difficult to explain to an eight-year-old. All Declan knew for certain was that she wasn't safe alone.

As he stepped closer to the hub of the police, he noticed the people around him. The panic had dissipated, replaced by curiosity. Those who hadn't been in the direct line of fire wanted to know what had happened. Some smiled and chatted. Others picked up lost items. Most people in this world were good, and when tragedy struck, they banded together to help one another.

Sadly, all the negative was broadcast across the country. A crime was tragic, but if the news focused more on the humanity of the community coming together and picking up the pieces, the criminals would lose the glory of their actions, and it would happen less.

When Declan had started school, there'd been no such thing as a school shooting. The first had been

Columbine. Until then, the worst school tragedies were courtyard brawls. Detention had been a big deterrent in his days. No student wanted to be stuck in that dark room while the sun was out, and his peers were running around chasing girls.

But in today's world, all you heard about was another attack and violence across the entire country. What had happened to the days his grandfather and father had spoken about? Maybe someday they'd get them back. Maybe someday the cartels like the one after the woman he cared about would actually be the losers. He'd fight every day of his life to make that happen.

The sirens had stopped now that the emergency vehicles were parked, but lights flashed brightly, drawing attention to the center where orders were shouted, and teams were organizing.

Paramedics walked the streets helping people. He watched as someone was placed on a stretcher, but the woman appeared to be alert. Declan hadn't seen any casualties, one positive in an ugly situation.

He easily spotted the man in charge: a large white-haired man with a captain's badge on his chest. His mouth was grim as he spoke with authority, sending his men in all directions. He wanted witnesses interviewed before they disappeared. Then maybe, just maybe, they had a chance of catching the shooter.

He approached and the man stopped speaking, eying Declan.

"You look like law," the captain said.

Declan's lip turned up a bit as he held out his badge he'd already pulled from his pocket. Better not to reach into a dark jacket in a tense situation.

"Declan Forbes, FBI," he said.

"Not from here," the captain said.

"No, from Washington. I've been on a trail, but I'll be heading back home today," Declan told him.

"Trail go cold?" the captain asked. "Or did you decide to bring your mess here and leave it on my doorstep?"

This wasn't a man to be fooled. And he didn't want a song and dance. Declan had the utmost respect for that.

"There are things I can't say," Declan said.

The captain smirked and Declan had the feeling he wanted to roll his eyes. "Yeah, yeah, I know FBI talk," he said. "Captain Singer." The man held out his hand. "What can you tell me?"

"I saw the shooter but can't give a great description," Declan said. "I'm also not here to step on toes. I just want to give an account of what I saw and be on my way."

"Captain, we have two shooting victims, nothing fatal. There are a lot of witnesses, but the accounts vary," a young cop said as he skidded to a halt in front of the captain, appearing eager to please his boss.

"Keep trying to get information. If enough people collaborate one story, we know we have something," the captain said. The young cop ran off as the captain turned back to Declan.

"I saw the gun, but he was good at keeping it hidden. He had on a dark hoodie, but I could see his olive complexion. Male."

"Mexican?" the captain asked.

"I can't say. I also didn't hear him speak."

Declan assumed the shooter was from the Coronado gang, but he couldn't say for sure and wasn't going to voice assumptions.

"This is a mess down here. I want you to go to the station and sit with my guy. Let's see if we can jog your memory a little more," Captain Singer told him.

That was exactly what Declan hadn't wanted. He needed to get Angela on the road.

"I don't see the point in that," Declan told him.

The man's lips pursed. "Humor me, then. This is chaos, and I don't like cleaning up messes in my city. I like nice easy days. Sometime in the near future I'd like to think my city is secure enough for me to retire and spend my days on a sailboat with a fishing pole instead of on hot pavement smeared with blood."

"I can appreciate that," Declan told him. The man looked worn.

"Head down there now. I'm going to be right behind you. I just have to get this a bit more organized. I should have you in and out fast," Singer assured him.

"Yes, Sir," Declan said, giving the man the respect, he'd obviously earned.

Declan knew he'd been dismissed. He turned and walked away, anxious to get back to Angela. His brother was more than capable of taking care of her, but he didn't like having her out of his sight for too long with all of this going on.

In the chaos, Declan had forgotten to call Dorsey back. Even in the middle of the worst situations Declan didn't normally forget anything. It had to be Angela. She meant more to him than simply being a person needing protection. He just wasn't sure what that was.

He decided to call Dorsey as he walked. He answered immediately.

"Sorry for the delay," Declan said as a greeting. "The gang found her. There was a shooting. She's secure now, and it doesn't appear as if there are any casualties."

"I'm watching it on the news right now. It said there are two gunshot victims, but no fatalities," Dorsey replied.

"News travels fast," Declan murmured, thinking back to his earlier thoughts. He wondered if the news was showing how the community was coming together right now to help each other. He doubted it.

"I saw the gunman but didn't get a good description. I think Angela did. We're going to talk more about it. I need to get her back home. Definitely need to get her and her son out of here," Declan said.

"Agreed. We've been doing a lot of research into this Coronado gang. They've been all over the United States and Mexico. They have a lot of blood on their rap sheet, but there's no telling how many members there are."

"I'll get her home and we'll go from there," Declan told him.

"Just be careful, Declan. I don't know how many higher-ups these guys have in their pockets. I know there's a lot of money involved, though," Dorsey said.

"I never trust anyone, so that's easy," Declan said with his idea of a laugh. The sound was cold enough that a person nearby stepped farther away from him as he moved through the waning crowd back to Angela.

"That's a tough way to live, but I get it," Dorsey said.

They ended the call as Declan reached the vehicle. Angela and Owen were safely inside.

"We need to go to the police station. I want you to wait with Angela while I go inside. This should be quick," Declan said.

"We have to pick up Timothy in just over an hour," Angela reminded them.

"We'll be there," Declan assured her.

"If you take too long, I'll take her to get him," Owen said.

"I won't take too long."

There wasn't much information he could give. He was stopping in as a courtesy, and he'd be in and out of there in thirty minutes max. They were all silent as they moved through the busy city streets of San Diego.

He went into the station, basically repeated what he'd said to the captain, made it official with his signature, then walked out much to their irritation. He didn't have time to wait around.

His director's words were also ringing in his ears. He shouldn't trust anyone, not even the cops. He'd feel a hell of a lot better when they reached Washington. There, he knew exactly who he could trust. He just hoped there wasn't an argument from Angela. For her own good, she needed to listen to him.

If she didn't do it for herself, he was sure she'd do it for her son. He'd use that if he needed to. He'd do whatever it took to keep her safe.

Chapter Eleven

"Is there anything you need from your apartment?" Declan asked as they drove to the school to pick up Timothy.

Angela had been very quiet since he got back in the SUV. He was sure she was in shock and trying to pull herself together before her son was there. If kids only knew how much parents suppressed to keep them warm and bubbly, they'd have more appreciation for the sacrifice's parents made. Then again, he'd been told that really wasn't something most people realized until they were parents themselves. Then half the time, they still didn't look back.

That was another big change from the days of his grandfather. Some changes were amazing and needed. Others he could do without.

"There's not much, just some clothes and maybe Timothy's books. I didn't take a lot with me when I left Washington, and I'm renting the place week by week. I didn't think they'd find me here, but I also wanted to be able to go quickly if somehow they did."

Declan was impressed. She wasn't as foolish as he'd thought; she did want to survive. Some victims gave up because the emotional toll was too much to deal with. Not Angela. She'd never give up.

"Are you ready to go home?" he asked.

She sighed. "I don't want to put my friends in danger." She gave a humorless laugh. "That is *if* I still have friends after the way I left." He tried to say something, but she held up a hand. "I do want to go home. It seems there's nowhere truly safe, so at least there I know Timothy will be taken care of if something happens to me."

Her words broke his heart. She seemed so damn defeated right now. It was easy to feel hopeless after something like this happened. He took her hand and squeezed her fingers.

"You still have friends, plenty of them, who will do anything to protect you and Timothy. Going home is the smartest thing you could do," he assured her.

"Being a single mother isn't easy. There are so many women out there who make it look like a piece of cake, but I second-guess every single thing I do. And the world has changed so I don't know right from wrong half the time. Morality has been flipped upside down, and it scares me. What if I do it all wrong? But at least this mistake is something I can fix," she said, a tear in her eye.

"Would you want to live in a perfect world?" he asked.

That stopped what she'd been about to say. She smiled as she wiped away a tear. Owen was silent, and he was grateful his brother was giving them this moment to talk. He was pretty sure Angela had forgotten his brother was even there.

"Of course, I would. Isn't the dream to live in Utopia?"

"That's not my dream," he said. "I'd love it if innocent people quit getting hurt. But how boring would it be to have a life of perfection? I think part of what's wrong in the world today is we don't have to work so hard." He pulled back his sleeve and showed her a scar. She ran her finger along it, and his gut clenched. He loved her touch. He'd like to have a lot more of it.

"I got this scar when I was twelve. I thought there was nothing in the world I couldn't do. There are times I still think that, though the older I get, the more I realize my body will age. I'm not slowing down yet, but someday I might," he said with a chuckle. "But I decided I was going to ride bulls. My dad didn't tell me no. He believed in letting me do whatever I wanted, so he took me to a rodeo."

"You rode a bull at twelve?" she exclaimed. That drew a chuckle from Owen.

"Not a chance." He chuckled again. "He let me ride a sheep. My dreams of riding ended that day. I got the orneriest one there and that thing threw me into the fence. I was mighty proud of this scar. We watched the bulls that night, and I saw a guy get gouged in the leg. Then my dad took me back to speak to the riders, and I saw how beat up they were. I wasn't afraid of riding. I knew I could do it. But I didn't want to be thirty years old and limping. I decided a less dangerous profession like the Marines was the route I was going to take."

"Less dangerous?" she gasped.

He chuckled, a real heart-felt chuckle. "That was my idea of sarcasm. I wanted to be a hero. I didn't realize then that a hero doesn't want to be one. A hero is the woman who protects her son. A hero is the grandma who teaches her granddaughter how to sew. A hero is an everyday person who does what they do because they want to give. A person who wants to be a hero will never be one."

She was silent for a moment, then she shocked him when she leaned in and gave him a kiss. It wasn't a long kiss; it wasn't a romantic kiss. It was a thank you. He wanted to take the thank you deeper, but his freaking brother was in the front seat. She pulled back and cupped his cheek as she smiled.

"Thank you, Declan. You will forever be my hero. Not only for saving my life, but for making me feel like a better person."

They arrived at the school and Owen parked the car. "Keep your hormones in check. We have a herd of animals exiting the school."

"You're just a riot, Owen," Declan told him.

Angela stepped out of the car and ran up to her son. Timothy threw his arms around his mom, and Declan didn't doubt for one moment how much love the two of them shared. They came back to the car as Timothy talked a hundred miles an hour.

When she opened the door and he saw Owen and Declan, he beamed. "Mr. Owen, Mr. Declan!" he exclaimed. "I've missed you."

Declan saw Angela's flinch, though she covered it quickly. He could see she felt guilty for taking her son from the home he'd loved. But she'd done it to protect him. She was right, no choice was easy for a mother, or father, for that matter.

"We've missed you too, buddy," Declan said.

"How are you?" Owen added.

"Great. We painted today. Summer is almost here, and Mrs. Bowers said she's ready for vacation," Timothy said.

That got a chuckle from all three of them. "I bet she is," Declan said. "A roomful of kids all year round calls for a two-month vacation."

"Why?" Timothy asked in all his innocence.

"Want to explain that one?" Angela asked, a sparkle in her eye. Declan loved seeing that sparkle.

"Because she has to plan the next school year and she wants it to be perfect," Declan said with a waggle of his brows.

"Good save, brother," Owen said with his own laugh.

"What are we doing?" Timothy asked, the conversation going over his head.

"How about we go home?" Angela asked.

That made Timothy's smile stretch so far, Declan thought his cheeks might just split open.

"Really? We get to go back?" he asked. "Yahoo!"

"I guess that solves it," Angela said with a shrug. "How do we do this?"

"It's simple. We have two vehicles, so let's have Timothy ride with Owen so he doesn't get lonely, and you and I will drive back in your car," Declan said.

He wasn't telling her that he'd rather Timothy was away from them in case danger followed, but by the knowing look in her eyes, he could see she perfectly understood that.

"That sounds fun," she said. "Do you want to ride with Owen and keep him company?" Angela asked.

"Can we stop at Taco Bell?" Timothy asked Owen, who laughed.

"Taco Bell is my favorite. I think we must stop at Dutch Bros too. I like my coffee."

"Do they have kid drinks?" Timothy asked seriously as if he had to consider this extra stop.

"The best kid drinks ever," Owen assured him.

"Good. Then I say yes," Timothy said. "When do we leave?"

"Right now," Angela told him. "We're all ready to go."

"It's a looooonnnnngggg drive," Timothy said. "Coming here took forever."

"Yeah, buddy, it is, but we'll make some stops and stay somewhere with a swimming pool," Owen assured him.

"This is the best day ever," Timothy said as he threw his fist in the air.

"I'll talk to you on the phone anytime you want, but it'll be a couple of days until I see you," she told Timothy with a slight sheen in her eyes.

"I'm a big kid now, Mom. You'll be okay," Timothy assured her.

"Yes, you are. I'm so proud of you," she told him.

"We better get going. I want some Taco Bell desperately now," Owen said as she hugged her son. "Buckle up and I'll take you to your car."

They all buckled, and Timothy talked non-stop on the way to her car. They got there too quickly. She hopped out, obviously not wanting to let her son out of her sight, but knowing it was best for him right now.

Declan stood back as she hugged her son extra tight again, and then he placed his arm behind her back and held on as Owen and Timothy walked to the car and drove away. He wanted to leave immediately, but he gave her a minute.

"He's going to be just fine, and I'm going to be able to protect you better if I'm not worrying about him."

"I'll worry about him," she said. "They come after children to get to the parents."

"They won't lay a finger on him. I promise you that," Declan said. And he vowed that was a promise he'd keep forever. No one would harm that child. "We're traveling different routes just to make sure we aren't followed. That won't be easy for you, but it's what's safest for Timothy."

She nodded. He could see how difficult it was for her to keep her tears at bay.

"Then let's hurry inside and grab my clothes then get on the road. I want to get back to him as soon as possible."

"Of course," he answered. They packed in less than ten minutes, then he walked her outside and helped her into the passenger side of her ridiculously small car before he jumped into the driver's seat. He barely fit. This wasn't going to be the most comfortable drive, but he'd manage.

"Thank you again, Declan. Thank you for caring. I know this goes above and beyond your job description."

"You're family now, Angela," he told her. And he realized as he said those words, he wanted them to be true. He wasn't sure when or how, but he wanted this woman to be family. What in the world had happened to him?

He wasn't sure, but he didn't mind. Maybe he'd fallen under the same spell as his brothers. And maybe that wasn't the worst thing in the world.

Chapter Twelve

Angela was exhausted. The day had begun with her life perfectly normal. She'd dropped Timothy off at school, gone to her favorite café, and then Declan had shown up. Twelve hours later she was entering Santa Barbara. It felt like a week had happened in a day.

She'd walked away again without telling anyone. She'd pulled Timothy out of school *again*. She'd uprooted her life, and she'd done it without blinking . . . again.

She wasn't sure what she was going to do next. All she knew for sure was that the roller coaster had to come to a stop soon. No one could live their life on an adrenaline high for long without it wearing them down. She wasn't sure how SEALS did it, or how the firemen kept it up. She'd only done this for a day and could barely keep her eyes open.

"I wanted to get farther tonight, but you look as if a slight breeze could blow you over," Declan said.

"Yeah, this seat is broken so it's impossible to get comfortable," she told him. "But I'm okay. I don't want to keep Timothy waiting and since we're taking the coastal highway and they're on the freeway, it's already going to take us a lot longer."

"You were napping for a few minutes, so I talked to Owen. They're already a hundred miles south of San Francisco. Timothy is full of Taco Bell, and Owen has lots of energy so he's going to drive a few more hours. He's getting a hotel with a pool and letting Timothy swim for one hour in the morning, then they are getting on the road again. We'll stop for the night, then switch over to the freeway to speed us up. No one is following," he assured her.

"That we know of," she said.

He smiled. "If someone was on our tail, I'd definitely know."

"Is there anything you aren't confident about?"

"Nope," he said.

"I believe you."

Her stomach rumbled and he laughed. "Let's get a place and find food. I haven't eaten since the muffin I had early this morning," he told her.

She really was hungry, but she was determined not to complain about anything. She'd already complicated this man's life by leaving and making him chase her down. And she wasn't going to starve if she didn't eat for a day. But she also wasn't going to stop him if he wanted to get food. She felt as if she could eat an entire cow right now. Maybe it was the adrenaline of the day or the stress of the past few weeks, but whatever it was, she'd found the appetite that had been gone for a long time.

"If I have a coffee, I could probably go longer," she said.

"Let's just have an early night and leave first thing in the morning."

She had zero desire to argue with that. They drove through town, and she was more than happy when he found a nice hotel right on the beach. She'd been living in San Diego for a couple weeks, but she hadn't had a lot of time to play. To look out at the ocean tonight sounded like the perfect stress-relief. Her small apartment certainly hadn't had a view. Places in San Diego with a view were way beyond her budget. Nothing was for Declan, she realized.

He'd grown up wealthy. But she respected and liked that he didn't use that as an excuse to live a life of ease. Neither he nor his siblings did. They might have some expensive toys, but they also were assets to society. There weren't a lot of people who could say the same, unfortunately.

She waited in the car while he checked in. Though tired, she was getting a burst of energy from the relief of stopping. She hadn't had time to stop since this had all begun.

"We're all set," he said, startling her when he opened her car door. "Grab your bag and let's put our things away, change, then walk down the beach. The manager said there's a nice place with outdoor seating and a great view."

"Oh, that's just what I want," she said with a sigh.

He helped her from the car and carried her bag. She appreciated that. She wasn't sure she could even carry herself at this point.

The room was spectacular, and when she realized they were sharing it, she felt a bit of a twinge in her gut. It was a suite with two bedrooms and a small kitchen and living room, but still, to be that close to this man was making her think thoughts she hadn't been sure she could think anymore.

"I'm sorry about one room, but I don't want you far from me. I don't trust anyone right now. I have an agency credit card I use for things like this, so we aren't traceable, but with all that's happening I need to know you're okay," he said.

She had to fight tears. It seemed she was doing that a lot on this day. It had to boil down to how tired she was. But at the thought of them sharing a room, her exhaustion seemed to evaporate. It seemed the power of hormones was stronger than a need for sleep or food.

"I understand," she told him. She did, but she was scared too. Not scared of him but scared of her reaction to him.

They left the room and began walking down the dimly lit path along the beach. She was very aware of how Declan kept watch all around him. To someone passing by they might seem like a normal couple taking a romantic evening stroll, but she was very aware that he was one hundred percent the FBI man. He was assessing every person they passed and, no doubt, profiling them. She felt safe with him.

They reached the restaurant and she winced. It was beautiful. She'd been expecting some small beachfront café, but this looked like a five-star resort. There was a patio with heaters, candlelight, cloth tablecloths, and an impeccably dressed staff. This was the kind of place she never could afford. But the smells drifting out were making her stomach rumble embarrassingly loud.

She was way underdressed. "I don't know if we can go in there," she said, feeling slightly shy.

Declan laughed. "We're fine. Lots of people spend the day on the beach then crawl up here, starving, in nothing more than a beach cover-up," he told her. "I'm not at all worried."

"If we get kicked out, I blame you," she said.

"Okay, deal," he replied.

They stepped up to the outside hostess platform where a man greeted them with a genuine smile. He didn't seem at all worried about their attire. She was glad Declan had changed from his suit to jeans and a light jacket. She knew he wore the jacket to cover the gun he carried. That gave her an added sense of security.

"Two this evening?" the man with the tag saying Jefferson asked.

"Yes, outside please," Declan said.

That's when Angela *really* looked at him. Declan carried his wealth on him whether he lived like a rich man or not. She glanced at his watch, which probably cost more than her car, and the shoes on his feet, which she knew cost more than her entire wardrobe. He might not be a snob, but he was used to the finer things in life, and she was sure people on staff at this place could easily spot that. They could also see that he was way out of her league. She was trying not to let that dampen her mood.

Declan took her hand and placed it on his arm as the host led them to a table tucked into the front corner of the patio with a spectacular view of the ocean. The curved table had a bench and Declan sat next to her their thighs almost touching. This was so much like a date it was making her heart thump.

She had to tell herself repeatedly it wasn't a romantic evening. The restaurant happened to be the closest dining location to where they were staying. She didn't want to read more into it than was there. Declan wasn't the settling down kind of man, though his brothers had all done that. And she was in no position to be thinking along those lines.

Still, she tried convincing herself sex was an incredible stress relief. She was sure there'd be nothing wrong with a night or two in this man's huge arms. But then she'd have to face him on a daily basis, and that could be extremely awkward. Angela never had been a casual fling kind of girl. Did she really want to start now? Did she have any choice if she ever wanted to have sex again?

She couldn't believe the thoughts running through her mind. They were crazy.

"You seem pretty intense there," Declan told her. "What are you thinking about?"

Angela felt her cheeks heat as she looked down at the menu for the first time. Their waitress stopped at the table, saving her from answering.

"Have you had time to choose a drink?" she asked.

Angela looked at the woman as if she were a knight in shining armor. "I'll have a Pinot Noir please," Angela told her.

"I'll take a Scotch on the rocks," Declan said.

"Coming right up." The waitress left. Someone else stopped and filled their water glasses and placed bread and butter, along with oil and vinegar, on the table. She thanked them and didn't consider being ladylike and pretending she didn't want any. She grabbed a piece of warm bread, slathered butter on it, and took a big bite.

"Oh my gosh, this is pure heaven," she said after swallowing. Declan wasn't far behind her with his own piece. She didn't hesitate to grab another. "I don't want to ruin my dinner, but I can't stop."

He laughed. The sound was so strange, coming from Declan. It was rarely heard, but he seemed lighter this evening. He was obviously still on full alert, but he seemed more relaxed now that they were out of San Diego.

"Yes, we're so used to eating every few hours that when we go a day without food our bodies think we're torturing them. We're a bit spoiled," he said, taking his second piece of bread.

"Yeah, I have friends who fast every once in a while. I think they're insane. I wouldn't mind dropping ten pounds, but I can't seem to stick with a diet longer than six hours," she admitted.

"Please don't ever diet. You're perfect."

She felt the heat of those words through her entire body. She enjoyed the sensation far more than she'd like to. The thought of him looking over her entire body was highly enticing.

"You're a wise man to say that, but believe me, we should all take better care of our bodies," she said.

He chuckled and she felt as if she'd won a gold medal.

"I don't like to brag, but when you have it, you have it," he told her as he leaned back and ran a hand down his flat abs. He was right, he really did have it.

"Mmm hmm, this is coming from a person with the right genetics," she told him with a roll of her eyes. There was no way she was going to tell him how much she appreciated that body he was so proud of.

"I work out," he insisted.

"Yeah, I'm sure you do. But enough of that. I want to enjoy my bread guilt free."

"Deal," he said.

The waitress returned with their drinks and took their order.

"This trip will be a good time for you to tell me what brought you to Edmonds in the first place," Declan said, taking her by surprise. Her smile fell away.

"I don't want to talk about that," she insisted.

"Why? I'd think you could trust me by now."

"I do trust you. But I don't think my past matters. I want a new future. If I quit walking where I shouldn't, maybe I can have that."

"Did you break the law?" he asked.

She shook her head. "No, I just, once again, was in the wrong place at the wrong time."

She couldn't help but feel her fingers flutter along her stomach. She didn't like thinking of the past. She didn't remember it all, but what she did recall wasn't good.

"I won't push you now, but it might help us," he told her.

"How would my past help?" she asked. If it would, she could understand why he'd need the info.

"Someone is targeting you. That might be more than a coincidence."

She thought about that for a moment. "Or maybe I just really need to think before I step out of my house."

"Everyone should think before they step out of their house. Have you seen some people's fashion choices?" he asked with a smile, but it didn't reach his eyes. He was trying to lighten the mood and she appreciated it.

"Yeah, but I can't say much about that right now. Look what I'm wearing," she pointed out.

"You look absolutely perfect," he insisted.

"I know your family now so it's easy to see how you know what to say. What I don't get is why you aren't like this more often."

Those words seemed to stop what he'd been about to say.

"What do you mean?"

"You come across so distant most of the time, but I can tell underneath it all you really do care about people," she said.

He shook his head and she waited. "Of course, I care about people, but that's dangerous in my job. I have to have a tough exterior or people can end up getting hurt . . . like you did today."

"Today wasn't at all on you. That was my fault. I wasn't careful," she told him.

Their food was delivered, and they went silent as they took their first bites. Declan had chosen a New York strip steak and she'd ordered salmon. It was delicious, and she was pretty sure she was going to finish it all.

"It will be better when we get home," he promised after a while. Normally silence in a date-like setting was awkward, but it wasn't that way with him. She knew Declan wasn't a man to talk just to talk, so she knew he was thinking when no words were spoken. She appreciated that about him.

"I don't know if it'll get better, but I do know I'll feel safer with friends around. It's not only me I have to think about, it's Timothy, and I'd die for him."

"No one will need to die. I'll take care of you both."

She sighed. "I know you'll do your best," she said. She hoped if they got their hands on her, his best would be enough. She prayed they'd leave her son alone. He had so much more life to live. She did too, but sometimes life wasn't fair.

It was late by the time they walked back to the hotel, and she was sufficiently full. She'd been tempted to stuff herself, but she hated feeling bloated. It was so much better to sate the hunger and stop.

As they entered the hotel room, sating other hungers was on her mind. Declan shut the door and she stood staring at him. She couldn't make herself stop.

He didn't move as his gaze locked with hers. She saw hunger ignite in his eyes. Her stomach clenched and she wasn't sure what to do or say. She knew it would be a mistake to sleep with this man, but a mistake she wouldn't regret.

"If you keep looking at me like that, I'm not going to be responsible for what happens," he told her.

Her core tightened as she pressed her thighs together. She opened her mouth to speak but couldn't find the right words. She was so dang lost right now. It was probably the adrenaline of the day . . . or the fact that it had been so long since she'd been with a man; she honestly couldn't remember the last time.

But if he made a move, she wasn't going to stop him. She wished she had the courage to make that move herself.

They both moved at the same time.

Chapter Thirteen

The first kiss she shared with Declan was unbelievable. His mouth connected with hers firmly, but with so much compassion and skill her knees grew weak. His hand wrapped behind her head and he held her while his tongue traced her lips before slipping inside and intoxicating her with his taste.

She was instant putty in his hands. Her arms wrapped around him and she held on tight while he took his time making her feel something she'd never before felt. She was his if he wanted her, and right now it felt very much like he did.

But he pulled back and she was confused. It felt as if there were weights on her eyelids as she opened them to look into his intense gaze.

"You've gone through a lot today, Angela. I don't want you doing something you'll regret in the morning," he told her, his voice rough but gentle. She might've fallen a bit in love with him in that moment. That should scare her enough to stop.

She didn't know what to say. The day had been hell. If she could change it, she would, but at the same time, would she have left town with him had it not happened? She wasn't sure she would've. And that would have been a mistake.

"At least you were there for me and my son. I don't know what we would've done without you," she said.

"You don't owe me anything," he said. "I'm going to take care of you until the end."

Her heart thundered as she gazed at this man who was so much more than he portrayed. He was kind even if he didn't want people to realize it. She wanted him more than she had before, and that was saying a lot.

"This isn't about owing anyone anything. I want to forget all the pain and fear. I want to feel what you make me feel by doing nothing more than looking at you. Please hold me, Declan. Please make me forget there's horror in the world," she pleaded.

His eyes darkened at her words as his fingers tightened behind her neck. She didn't think he'd walk away from her. She didn't want him to do what he thought would be the honorable thing. She wanted to be naked in his arms.

This time she was the one who reached up and kissed him. She started hesitantly, but as he responded, she deepened the kiss and became lost in his arms. When they broke away from each other, she could barely find her breath.

Her heart was beating fast, and all she wanted to do was find the nearest bed. That shouldn't be a problem. She'd wanted this man for a long time but had been too afraid to admit it even to herself.

With one final look that made her forget her name, Declan took charge and kissed her hot and heavy. The decision had been made and he wasn't wasting any more time. He pressed the full length of his body to hers and there was nothing on him that wasn't hard.

He pulled away long enough to lift her in his arms and his long strides ate up the distance to his room. He stood her in front of the bed and paused, allowing her to let the situation sink in.

"You can turn away," he said.

His words guaranteed she wouldn't. Feeling bolder than she'd ever been, Angela took a step back and watched panic invade his eyes. She felt wanted and powerful, and she loved it.

She reached out and ran her finger down the front of him, from his neck all the way to the bottom of his stomach. She stopped and gave him a flirty smile. He inhaled sharply and clenched his fists. He was allowing her to take the lead. She was sure that was a gift he didn't give many.

She reached for the hem of her shirt and slowly lifted it over her head, not allowing fear to take over. He'd saved her life today and had been kind and wonderful. Now she wanted to get lost in him. She wanted to make him feel good. Of course, that would make her feel pretty damn great herself—an added bonus.

The shirt flew away, and before she could change her mind she reached for the clasp on her bra. He reached for her and she stopped, pushing him down on the bed. He landed with a thump. She had no doubt he'd allowed it. He smiled as she continued stripping her clothes away.

He pulled his own shirt off and sat before her in just his jeans. "Holy hell, you are hot," she breathed. She was down to her panties and didn't want to slide those off yet. They were a whisper of lace that barely hid anything but keeping them on made her feel a little less self-conscious.

"Not nearly as sexy as you," he growled, reaching for her again. She pushed his hand away as she stepped up to him. Hoping she could figure this out along the way, she climbed on his lap, loving the heat of his arms as they circled her naked back.

She leaned down and ran her tongue along his lips, not connecting their mouths, but teasing him, before she pulled away. Her breasts rubbed against the peppering of hair on his chest and she felt wet heat flood her.

He reached up, cupped her head, and tugged, arching her back, making her breasts reach out hungrily. She nearly came when he leaned down and took a nipple into his mouth, sucking hard while his tongue circled the sensitive peak.

She held on tight while he lavished attention on one breast and then the other, making her stomach quiver and her thighs squeeze tight. She squirmed in his lap when he lifted his head again. He tried to kiss her, but she leaned back with a sultry smile.

"I want to suck on something," she said, her reward his sharp intake of breath.

She scooted back and ran her tongue down the side of his neck and over his hard chest, before kneeling on the floor and licking his abs. She undid his pants while tasting his musky skin.

He lifted up and she pulled his jeans and boxers away. Then it was her turn to gasp as his full erection sprang free, hard and smooth . . . absolutely perfect. She ran her fingers around the base of his thickness, then circled his tight balls before leaning forward and taking him in her mouth.

He was hot and salty and so beautifully hard. She moved up and down him while her fingers circled the throbbing flesh, and he groaned his pleasure, his fingers tangled in her hair.

"Baby don't make this end too quickly," he begged.

"Mmm," she said as she sank down on him again. The humming of her voice made him jump as another groan ripped from him. She wanted to keep bringing those sounds out of him. The more turned on he was, the more ignited she became.

She pulled back and stroked him several times, loving the gleaming tip of his arousal. She licked it up before running her tongue all the way down and across his base a few times before he was begging for more.

"Enough," he growled, as he reached beneath her arms and pulled her up. She wanted more but was so ready for him to be inside her she didn't fight him.

He laid her on the bed, and she held out her arms, wanting him desperately.

His eyes gleamed as he reached in his pants pocket and pulled out a couple condoms.

"I didn't think this would happen, wasn't expecting it to, but I was a Boy Scout," he said with a shrug.

She laughed, feeling more joy in this moment than she thought possible. "Thank goodness for being prepared. Thank you for taking care of me," she told him. She hadn't thought about condoms. There was no chance of anything bad happening, but that wasn't something she wanted to talk about. She just wanted to feel right now.

He set the condoms on the side table then climbed on the bed, taking his time to look down at her. She stirred beneath his gaze wanting his body on hers, not his eyes. He leaned down and kissed her, this time letting her know he was now in charge. She was perfectly okay with that.

He broke away from her mouth and lavished attention on her neck and chest, making her squirm beneath him. Each time his tongue swept over her nipples she arched her hips, begging him to enter her. But he was enjoying teasing her as much as she'd enjoyed doing it to him.

Then he moved down the curve of her stomach and laced his thumbs through her panties, at first tugging them up over the sensitive heat of her wet folds. She cried out at the friction. Then he ripped the panties away and she felt his hot breath replace the lace.

His hands moved beneath the curve of her butt as he lifted her at the same time his mouth connected with her core. He circled his tongue over her sensitive flesh and sucked, building the inferno.

A few sucks and swipes of his tongue sent her over the edge. She came with an explosion, her cry ripping from her as he continued licking until she begged him to stop. He ran his tongue over her wet heat a few more times before he leaned back, his lips red and wet, his eyes dark and on fire.

He climbed up her body and she spread her thighs, needing him inside her. He had a condom on in seconds. And then he was finally poised above her. She wrapped her arms around him while he looked down at her, his gaze so intense it was hard to look at.

"Please," she said when he didn't push forward. "I need you."

He didn't make her wait any longer. He pushed his hips forward and in a single hard thrust he was buried deep inside her. She was still trembling from the orgasm he'd just given her, and the fullness of him stretching her nearly sent her into a second one. He didn't pause, didn't let her adjust.

He pulled back and thrust back in, slow and steady, over and over again. Their bodies were covered in sweat as they moved as one, their pace slowly picking up speed. She let go of all thoughts as she came again, squeezing him tight. He kept moving. The orgasm drew on and on, and she didn't want it to end.

He picked up his speed, their moans synchronizing as they made love. He bent down and kissed her and she came again, this time more intense than ever before.

"Damn," he cried out as he buried himself to the root. She felt his release deep inside her, sending her over the edge with him. They shook together as the last of their orgasms faded away.

She was utterly spent. She couldn't move as he pulled from her and turned. He went still.

"Angela," he said with a groan.

"I don't know if I can again for a bit," she told him, thinking he was ready that fast.

"It isn't that," he told her. She barely had the energy to turn her head and look at him. She opened her eyes halfway.

"What is it?" she asked, her voice barely above a whisper.

"The condom broke," he said, apology all over his face.

She sighed. This really wasn't a talk she wanted to have, especially when she was feeling so dang good.

"It's okay, Declan," she assured him. "I haven't been with anyone in a very long time and I'm clean," she said.

"I have no doubt about that. I am too," he told her. She didn't think anything else. He wasn't the type of man who'd hurt a female in any way. "But there are other concerns with a broken condom."

This was what she absolutely didn't want to talk about. She wasn't ruining the moment. So, she'd assure him the best she could.

"It's okay on that too," she said. "There's no possibility of me getting pregnant . . ." She paused. She wasn't going to say forever. "Tonight."

"There's always a possibility," he told her. He'd turned on his back and pulled her into his arms. It was right where she wanted to be.

"It's okay. I won't get pregnant," she said again.

He stopped. Maybe it was her tone, or maybe he just trusted her. There was nothing they could do about it anyway. So, he'd have to let it go. She hoped he did.

"I don't want to ruin the night fretting over it anyway," he said. He held her tight. It had truly been a long day. Angela closed her eyes and was instantly asleep.

Chapter Fourteen

Tick tock. Tick tock. The clock was chiming each new second, minute, and hour. It struck midnight. It struck noon. Twelve chimes were heard in the old days. Now, you had to be somewhere in the city to hear that sound as everything had gone digital, but Declan still heard the chimes inside his own head.

He needed to break this case, and whether Angela liked it or not she was involved. And he believed it was more than just her witnessing the drug bust. He believed they'd been after her for some time, and whatever had happened to her before was a key element in all of this.

As much as Declan wanted to protect her and keep her out of it, he was left with little choice. He needed to shield her, and in order to do that he had to get to the bottom of what was happening.

He desperately wanted to serve the criminals up on a silver platter with no dessert, but when was it ever that easy? Maybe in the movies after some really great fight scenes. But in real life it didn't work that way. He wanted to be in the movies right about now. Hell, he wanted to be just about anywhere that didn't involve evil winning.

If one more person was killed on his watch, he might turn full-on Rambo or Terminator. He wasn't sure at this point.

They hadn't spoken about their night of lovemaking. And though the two of them had needed a lot more sleep than they'd gotten, he'd do it all over again to be in her arms. They'd made love three times, which had put them on the road far too late, but he'd had to let her get at least three solid hours of sleep before putting her in a miserable little car all day. He wasn't sure the thing could make it all the way back to Washington.

She'd smiled at him when he'd woken her with coffee and pastries and they had shared small talk, but that was it. He didn't think she regretted what they'd done. And he dang well hoped they'd do it again that night. How did a person bring that up? It was unchartered territory for him.

He didn't want to bring up sex, but he did want to bring up her past again. She'd had some sleep. Maybe not enough, but some. And she'd certainly had some other important needs met, so maybe she'd be in a more talkative mood.

"Can you tell me about your attack?" he asked.

She tensed next to him. But she quickly relaxed.

"Why do you want to know about that so badly?" she questioned.

"Because I think it's the same gang," he admitted. He didn't want her scared, but she was leaving him with no other choice. He hated it.

"But that happened in California," she said. "I was in the wrong place. I can't remember all of it. What are the chances the same people are in Washington?"

He hated that he was scaring her. He hated that she had to go through any of this.

"We've found a connection. Mario Vasquez is the leader in Washington. We've just found out his brother is Emilio Coronado, who's in California. It didn't take long for them to find you. The more we know about this gang, the easier it'll be to take them down."

She gave a humorless laugh. "It won't be easy at all," she said.

"Yeah, three years on this case makes me very aware of that," he said.

"Why would anyone want me? I'm nobody," she pointed out.

"But your dad wasn't. What gave you the idea to come to Washington?" he asked.

At those words, her face fell. He didn't say anything as he let the pieces click into place. She was calculating things and he could see she wasn't happy with the results. He gave her a little more time before he dropped the next bit of information he'd put together.

"Keera was led to Edmonds too. Your fathers knew each other." He'd recently figured that bit of information out. This gang was so much bigger than any of them had realized. They were good too. They weren't worried about making a statement as so many gangs were. They wanted to kill, maim, and rob their way through the US. That was their top priority, and anyone who got in the way was just another casualty that meant nothing to them.

"So, you know my dad was David Perez?" she questioned. She shuddered as she said the name. He understood why. The man was a monster.

"I should've known. You're FBI. There probably isn't much you don't know," she said with a sigh. "So why are you asking me if you have all the answers?" It was said with resignation, not resentment. He could feel her pain.

"I know what the reports say. I don't know what your account of it is," he told her.

"You realize this happened four years ago, right?"

"Yes, I know the dates, I know the story. What do you remember? What do you know?" That's what he wanted. She'd left once she'd healed, and no one had ever followed up with her again. He thought that had been a big mistake. But the division that had handled it had assumed it was a random attack like she'd thought. They hadn't made the connection to her father.

"The police weren't too worried," she said. That's when he heard the anger in her voice.

"I know you feel like a victim. You *are* a victim. But don't let them win. Sometimes it's hard for law enforcement to know when something is more than just a random attack. They are dealing with all sorts of cases. If something looks as if it can be wrapped up with a nice bow and closed, that's a win. I'm sorry I'm asking you to talk about this again. I'm sorry I'm forcing you to relive it. But when this is over you never have to think about it again," he assured her.

"I'll think about it for the rest of my life," she told him. He heard the tears in her voice, but she didn't allow them to fall. He was humbled by how strong this woman was. "How many times have women been attacked?"

"There have been multiple attacks. We have no way of knowing which ones were part of the gang violence. That's why we want your account. The more you can tell us, the more we will know what to look for."

She was silent for a few miles. "I don't remember much. I do remember the feel of the blade entering my stomach. But they smashed my head into the pavement and most of that entire week is gone," she said. A small sob escaped her. "I never forget the pain though."

"Do you have any recollection of who you were speaking to before the attack?" He was trying not to be emotional, trying to look at this like any other victim he was interviewing. He wasn't doing too well with that.

"No, not at all." She was quiet again for a few moments before she held up a hand. "But I've had dreams. The voice always changes, but the pain is the same, the fear grows worse. I can't tell you if there were ten people there or one. Part of me wants to know, but the rest of me wants it to just go away."

"Have you spoken to a professional about it?" he asked.

He didn't take his eyes off the road for long, but long enough to see the confusion in her eyes.

"Like a counselor?"

"Yes," he said.

"What will that help?"

"I'm not a big fan of them, but at this point I'd do anything to get you the help you need. I don't want anything else to happen to you," he said. And each moment he was with her the need to protect her increased. He was falling for the woman.

"I didn't do counseling. I had a son to take care of, and I just wanted to get away. My father's family told me Edmonds was a safe place. I should've known better than to listen to them. But that's where I ended up. Did my father want me dead?" she asked. This time a tear slipped down her cheek.

"I don't think so," Declan said. He meant it. "I think he wanted you protected. And someone sent you there to keep you safe. It was either the last act of a desperate man, or there's someone else involved. A possible secret guardian angel."

"But why send me into the territory of enemies?"

"I don't know. But whoever sent you might not have realized there were enemies. Criminals seem to think there's a code of loyalty among them. There's not. They will turn on each other every single time. There's always a price to pay."

"I fully agree with that," she said.

"Will you see a therapist when we get back? Let's get this case closed," he offered.

He let her think about it while they continued driving up I5.

After about five minutes she turned. "I'll help you close this because you've put yourself on the line for me, and I don't want you in danger. But when it's finished, I don't ever want to think about it again."

He smiled as he reached over, took her hand, and squeezed. "I promise you'll never have to think about it again once it's finished. No one will ever bring it up."

When he made a promise, he kept it. "Thank you, Declan."

He nodded, and then the car began making a noise. They didn't have time for this.

"What is that?" she asked.

"I don't know. Luckily there's an exit a mile up the road," he told her. "At least we can't say this trip is uneventful."

And just like that he was thinking about a few short hours before. He'd love to pull off and get another hotel room right now. Even though he'd made love to her three times the night before, he was more than ready to do it again.

This woman had stirred his body unlike any woman before her. He wasn't sure he'd be willing to let her go when this was all over. He was beginning to hope he wouldn't have to.

They limped the car to the exit. They were only to San Francisco and had a very long way to go, but they might get delayed once more. He wasn't far enough from San Diego for his liking, but he was doing what he could do.

He hoped it was enough.

Chapter Fifteen

Angela's stomach fell to the floor when the mechanic told her the news. The car was finished. There was no fixing it, no matter how much duct tape and bungee cords she could get her hands on. She'd had it for five years and it had been a good car, but it had taken its last ride.

"I don't know what to do," she said, pleading with the man to give her a different diagnosis. Declan hadn't wanted to go to the mechanic. He'd wanted to go straight to the junkyard.

"We've wasted four hours of our day on this," Declan said. He'd been impatient the entire time.

"I know you're frustrated, but there isn't a lot that can be done about it," she said.

"We should've gone with Owen like I wanted."

She threw up her hands. "I told you I couldn't leave my car," she said way too loudly. She hated raising her voice and forced herself to calm down. "But I guess it didn't matter."

She couldn't afford car payments, and she really couldn't afford to buy a car in California and pay all the extra taxes and licensing involved—not right now. She'd spent a lot of money, and her savings were quickly running out.

"Let's go," he said.

"Where?" she asked before calming herself. "I think we should take the bus." That was a logical next step. She didn't really need a car in Edmonds. It was a small town and she'd save money by not having one. That meant she'd be stuck there, but the idea of running again wasn't at all appealing.

"We're going to the car lot to get a vehicle," Declan said. His voice left no room for argument. He obviously didn't know her very well.

"For you? You have a car," she told him.

"I'm not riding on a damn bus, and you don't have a car anymore. We're going to get one."

He grabbed her hand, thanked the grateful looking mechanic, who obviously wanted them gone, and tugged her away. They could scrap the car.

"I can't afford to buy a car right now," she said. He was already calling the Toyota dealership. He ignored her as he spoke to someone. She heard him say cash and give his location. He hung up and looked at her.

"I'm buying it," he said, again with that no-nonsense voice.

"Over my dead body," she told him.

He raised a brow. "Not funny. And no dead bodies needed, just cash."

"You aren't buying me a car, Declan," she said, emphasizing it with a little foot stomp. He was turning her into an angry teenage girl, and she didn't like it.

"Do you want to get back to your son?" he asked, and she flinched.

"That was a low blow. Of course, I do." She wanted to punch the man . . . again. Damn, he inspired violence in her.

"Then stop fighting me." She crossed her arms. She might stop fighting with him, but he couldn't force a car on her. If she didn't sign the papers, there wasn't a thing he could do about it. But maybe they could rent a car to get home. She could afford that.

The dealership picked her up in a white Toyota Land Cruiser that was probably the nicest thing she'd ever ridden in. Her father always drove nice vehicles, but it had been a long time since she'd been in his home. And these seats were like sitting on butter.

"Is this available?" Declan asked, looking at the odometer, which only read one hundred twenty-three miles.

"Yes, sir," the salesman said, his eyes lighting up.

"We'll take it," Declan said. "If you get the paperwork done in less than an hour I'll throw in a five-thousand dollar bonus. We're in a hurry."

The guy was speechless for a minute, which Angela fully understood. The sticker on the window said the car was eighty-nine thousand dollars. Then the guy sighed as they pulled into the car lot. He seemed to be talking himself into saying something, and Declan laughed.

"There's nothing illegal about it," Declan assured him while he pulled out his FBI badge. "We really are just in a hurry and our car broke down."

The guy beamed again. "Okay then," he said. "I'll tell the manager, and we'll have you out of here in an hour."

The guy, who couldn't have been more than twenty-two or three, practically flew from the car into the dealership. This would, no doubt, be the best commission of his life.

"We just broke that kid's heart because we aren't buying this car," she said through clenched teeth from the backseat.

"We just made his quota for the month because we are," Declan said as he stepped out then opened her door and held out his hand.

"I refuse to fight with you in public," she said as the sales manager approached.

"Hello, Mr. Forbes. Kyle said you have a cash offer for this SUV," the man said as he held out his hand.

"Yes, with a 5K bonus if we have the keys in one hour. We're running very late," Declan said.

The man kept far calmer than Kyle, but there was no doubt he was happy about this sale.

"Well let's head inside and get the paperwork out of the way. Without involving banks or credit unions the process goes much quicker." He turned when they got inside and motioned another kid over. "Get this car to detailing and put it in front. It will be pulling off the lot in one hour and it had better be ready."

The kid nodded and rushed out to the vehicle. "Follow me," the manager told them.

Angela wasn't really sure what had happened. But an hour later she was standing next to the Land Cruiser with the key in her hand, not that it needed a key with a push button start. Several people shook her hand and thanked her, all with huge smiles on their faces, and then it was just her and Declan with their two bags.

Declan loaded them into the back of the sparkling clean car then looked at her. "Do you want to drive?"

"I don't like driving in the city if I don't have to," she said. She was so confused. He'd managed to get her to sign papers, and she was apparently the new owner of this car that was so far out of her price range she thought she might be dreaming.

"You'll be fine. It almost drives itself," he assured her.

She was practically shoved into the driver's seat. While all the paperwork was getting finished, she'd been given a lesson on how to operate the spacecraft. It was far more a rocket ship than a car. There were so many buttons, she was sure she'd never figure it all out. But she did know how to start it and use the blinkers.

The seat was already adjusted to her, and when Declan hopped into the passenger side, she didn't know what else to do but drive. She started it, the engine purring like a content kitten, and then they were on the road.

The map easily led them back to I5 and she tried desperately not to enjoy the ride. It was fantastic, the best thing she'd ever driven. Once they were out of traffic, she set it on cruise control, which also had a feature that slowed down and sped up if vehicles got in front of her. It *was* practically driving itself. She had a smile on her lips she didn't want to wear.

Declan let her enjoy the moment. "I'm not keeping this," she said. "It was so thoughtful of you, but there's no way I can accept it as a gift, and there's even less chance of me being able to pay for it," she told him.

"We'll argue about that after the trip," he said as he leaned back in his seat. "For now, I want to enjoy the ride. When you get tired of driving, let me know and I'll take over."

"I don't think anyone would ever tire of driving this," she mumbled, making him laugh.

"I've discovered I'm a bit of a vehicle snob. I like a smooth ride. I also love the safety features of Toyotas."

"I've always had cars and really don't like how low they are to the ground. But they've been affordable," she said. "And beggars can't be choosers."

He reached over and squeezed her thigh, making her insides stir. Their night together had been perfect. She desperately wanted more of that, and since they were so far behind, they'd surely stay at a hotel for at least one more night. She hoped they only had one room.

"You aren't exactly a beggar, Angela. You work damn hard for everything you have."

"I believe in hard work. I don't like handouts," she said as she pointedly looked at the car.

"There's a difference between a handout and a gift," he said as if a more than ninety-thousand-dollar gift was an everyday occurrence.

"I'm enjoying this ride far too much to argue about it. But believe me, we will have a face-down when we arrive in Edmonds," she warned.

"Do you mean a showdown?" he asked with another chuckle. She was more than happy to glare at him for correcting her. Sometimes things just felt good. And right now, she felt that way. The past forty-eight hours seemed a lifetime ago. She was sure it would all come back to her soon enough.

It ended up being much sooner than she was ready for.

Chapter Sixteen

Declan's phone rang and his first instinct was to not answer. He didn't want to speak to the director with Angela in hearing distance. He was sure whatever the man had to say late on a Saturday night wouldn't be good.

He'd have to tell her anyway, so he hit the answer button and waited.

"There's been another murder," Dorsey said, his voice frustrated and tired.

"Dammit!" Declan said as he slammed his fist into his thigh. He immediately felt bad when Angela jumped. "Hold on."

She glanced over at him with rounded eyes. "Pull over at this upcoming rest stop," he told her. Her face had gone a little pale and the smile she'd worn was wiped from her pretty lips. He hated this.

"Give us a few minutes and I'll call you back," Declan told his director before he hung up.

"Who was that?" she asked.

"The director. There's been an update. Let's pull over before we find out what it is."

She took the exit and smoothly parked the car in the back of the lot while he returned the call.

Dorsey picked up on the first ring. "Tell me what's happening," Declan said as a greeting.

"These guys stay a few steps ahead of us. I'm running out of options," Dorsey said.

"Who's the victim?"

Angela gasped next to him. He reached out and held her hand. He hated that she was hearing this and hated the fear in her eyes.

"Alice Smith, twenty years old. It was a gut stabbing and then her throat was sliced, left behind a bar."

"What's the connection?" Declan asked. It was tragic, but was it tied to their case?

"Witness statement says a female spoke to her before they exited the back door. The witness thought something looked off, so she peeked around the corner and saw a person approaching who looked a lot like who Angela saw. She called the cops. They got there too late."

"I'm glad she didn't go out there too," Declan said.

"Me too, or we would've had two victims," Dorsey said, completely certain of what he was saying.

"This sounds like Angela's case. Have the gangs officially merged?"

Angela's fingers went lax in his hand.

"We believe so. We think they're trying to shut down the Edmonds operation, and they're tying up loose ends. This victim might've been a girlfriend of one of the members, so they used another female to lure her out."

"Son of a bitch," Declan exclaimed. He'd had it with these senseless murders. Running drugs was bad enough but stepping up their game and brutally killing on top of it meant they were escalating fast. Previously they'd only taken out people who were in their way. Now they were seeking out victims.

"The media is all over this, Declan, so everyone's talking about it."

"Dammit. That's just going to wet their egos. They need to quit glorifying these guys' deeds."

"I agree, but it's a free press. There's nothing we can do to stop it," Dorsey said. The man sounded like he'd aged a hundred years in the past few days. Declan knew how he felt.

"The entire town is going to be in a panic now, making it even harder to flush these guys out. When people are scared, they look suspicious."

"Yeah, but maybe with public awareness there won't be as many victims available. Hopefully they batten down their hatches."

"The town has been put through hell the past few years and the cartel is just warming up. I'm worried we're going to get some vigilante groups," Declan said.

"I can't say I blame them. Their friends and family are being victimized."

"I don't want innocent people getting charged for taking the law into their own hands," Declan said.

"Like you wouldn't step up if it was your family getting attacked." That wasn't a question.

"Of course, I would," Declan told him. "But in case you didn't notice, I'm the law and won't get in trouble for it." Those words were spoken a little smugly, but he was done with this group of criminals.

Angela was shaking next to him, and he needed this call to end. "I'll call you back later. We're on our way home," Declan said. He hung up and turned to her.

"How many girls does this make?" she asked. Tears spilled from her eyes.

"One is too many," he told her. He pulled her over the console and into his lap, holding her.

Declan felt completely helpless, not a great feeling. He'd promised to protect her and that should include protecting her emotions. He was making it worse for her at the moment. But he couldn't hide this stuff. She needed to be aware of what was going on so she wouldn't make mistakes. Too many people died because they were careless. He wasn't going to let that happen to Angela or Timothy.

"Is Timothy okay?" she asked.

"Let me check on him." Declan continued holding her as he called his brother. Owen answered on the second ring.

"Hey, Declan," he said. Declan could hear Timothy giggling about something in the background.

"Where are you guys?" Declan asked.

"We just drove through Springfield, Oregon. We're going for a few more hours to Portland then we'll call it a night," Owen said.

"What's that noise?" Declan asked.

"I got the kid an iPad," Owen said with a chuckle. "I needed him distracted. Otherwise I was his main form of entertainment, and he asks a lot of questions."

Declan was shocked to feel a smile cover his face. "Yeah, eight-year-olds tend to talk a lot."

"Not when they have an iPad," Owen said proudly.

"That's lazy parenting," Declan pointed out.

"Good thing I'm not his dad then. I get to be the uncle who spoils the hell out of him."

Declan really liked the thought of that. If Owen was the uncle that meant he'd be Timothy's dad. He could handle that.

"I guess you have a point there," Declan said.

"Don't screw it up. I like having a nephew," Owen said.

"I wouldn't dream of it. We've had some delays so we're at least a full day behind you. Keep him safe," Declan said.

"You don't need to say that," Owen said, a bit offended.

"I know, brother. I'm just stressed."

"I know. Get her home safe too."

Declan disconnected. "Well, your son is being spoiled rotten. Owen bought him an iPad."

Angela gave a shaky smile. "That's an extravagant gift too, but a little more appropriate than a car."

He leaned down and gently kissed her. He couldn't stand not to any longer. "It will all be fine, Angela. I know it doesn't feel like it now, but I promise you we won't let them get to you or Timothy ever again."

"What if they do get to me again, Declan? What if they finish the job they started four years ago? I can't go through that pain again. I'd rather be shot," she said. She buried her head in the side of his neck and wept against him. "I hate crying over this. I hate worrying about myself, but I'm scared. I don't want them touching Timothy. I'd give myself up in a heartbeat for him. But I don't want them to have me either, and I feel selfish saying it out loud."

"It's far from selfish to want to live a healthy, normal life. You can say anything to me. You've been through more than anyone should go through. I can't believe you're still on your feet," he assured her.

"Sometimes I'm not," she said.

"Please don't be hard on yourself, Angela. I won't let them touch you again. They have to get through me." His voice was deathly. She hiccupped as she pulled away from his neck and looked up at him, so much trust shining in her eyes he wasn't sure what to think. He just knew he couldn't disappoint her.

"Someone interrupted the attacker the night I was hurt," she said. "I read the reports forward and backward. I never spoke to the witness, but this case sounds a lot like mine."

"I know." He wasn't going to lie to her.

"I would've ended up just like this girl if they wouldn't have been interrupted," she said. Her tears had stopped but she was still snuggled in close to him. She needed the comfort, and he didn't mind providing it—not one bit.

Declan had read that same report too many times to count. And she was probably correct. Someone had stopped what had been about to happen to Angela. She'd been knocked out after the first stab wound, and he was sure they would've gone in for the kill. It was so bloody, so vicious. He couldn't imagine the terror she'd felt, but she'd never feel it again because no one was going to get that close to her ever again.

Declan kept most of his thoughts to himself. He wanted her to be informed but she didn't need a tour of his mind. He had a lot of darkness from all he'd seen. She brought out the light buried deep inside. He wanted to do the same for her.

"I'll talk to whoever you need me to. I don't want any more victims. I don't want any more parents to lose their children . . . or any children to lose their parents. I don't want anyone else to live with the pain I've lived with. I want to remember so I can make it stop happening." The longer she spoke the stronger her words came out.

"You're the bravest woman I've ever met," Declan told her, meaning it. "And I've served with some exceptional women. Few who had suffered as you have would sign on for more. Thank you. Those words have so little value, but I mean them."

"There's a lot of value in a *thank you* when it's truly meant," she assured him.

"Trust me, it's absolutely meant," he told her.

"I can't promise I won't fall apart, but I'll do my best," she said.

"You can fall apart because I'm going to be there to help you pick up the pieces—every single time."

"Be careful, Declan. I might take you up on that," she said. He felt his heart thump, and it wasn't in a bad way.

"Good. Because I don't say what I don't mean," he told her. Then he pulled her to him and kissed her, this kiss a little firmer, this kiss letting her know she was his. He might not be giving her a ring or asking her to be his, but she was indeed his . . . and he realized he was hers.

Things that came easily never seemed to be worth it. This had been coming for a long time, and nothing in him wanted to change it.

"I'm going to drive now."

She smiled at him. "That sounds good to me. I'm a little shaky."

He kissed her again, then sat for a little while longer with her safely cradled in his arms. When they'd left San Diego, all he'd wanted to do was get her home. Now he wasn't in such a hurry. He wanted to drag this trip out. He didn't want her to pull away from him once they were back, and he was afraid that's exactly what she'd do.

He wanted to be a little selfish and keep her all to himself for as long as possible. Maybe then they'd have a real shot at making this a permanent thing. But rarely did people get what they really wanted.

Chapter Seventeen

"Timothy!"

Angela cried out in delight as she jumped from the SUV and rushed to hug her son, who was moving at Mach speed straight for her. It had only been three days but from the look on her face it might as well have been a year.

"Mom!" He launched himself into her arms. It was close to nine in the evening, but Angela had only wanted one more night away. They'd slept five hours and got a four-a.m. start to make it back to Edmonds.

On one hand he was glad to be home but disappointed on the other. He'd wanted more time with Angela before the rest of the world intruded.

"It's good to see you. Took you long enough," Owen said with a punch on the arm. "We were back yesterday."

"We had car trouble," Declan said.

"I noticed the new set of wheels. You didn't mention that," he said with a sly smile. "Are you trading in the Rover?"

Declan rolled his eyes. "I'm just giving you a hard time," Owen said. "I would've done the same." He laughed again. "And I'm sure she's giving you a hell of a time about it."

Declan grumbled. "I don't understand why she can't just accept it and move on."

"Because that would make your life too easy," Owen said.

"What would make his life easy?" Arden asked as he joined.

"She's having a hard time with the new car, but hers broke down and there wasn't much of a choice," Declan said.

"Yeah, that's a pretty piece of machinery. I'd take it," Arden said.

"Most people would."

"You guys are morons," Keera said. They gave her a blank look. She laughed. "You're very loving, amazing, beautiful morons, but still morons. Angela has a lot of pride and that's not a little gift. It's not exactly easy to accept."

"It's just a car," Declan said. "And I can obviously afford it."

"A very expensive one. She doesn't want to be judged. And the amount of money in your bank account doesn't matter to her."

"It obviously matters. It's reverse snobbery," he said. Then his eyes narrowed. "Who would judge her?" Keera laughed as she reached in and gave him a hug. She wasn't at all afraid of him anymore. He was going far too soft.

"None of us. She'll get used to it and love it," Keera promised. "You guys have been wealthy your entire lives and you're so used to it you don't think about it anymore, but the average person lives paycheck to paycheck. Their idea of a gift is a pair of discounted earrings. Give her some time to adjust to her new life as your woman. It took me some time."

"She isn't *exactly* my woman . . . yet," Declan muttered.

"I've seen the way the two of you have ogled each other for years. She's definitely *your* woman," Keera said, patting him as if he were a clueless child.

He didn't like how this conversation was going. It was making him shift on his feet like a teenager, and he didn't enjoy it one little bit.

"She *will* be mine . . . when I can convince her that's the only option," he said.

That made Owen and Arden laugh.

"What's so funny?" Kian asked.

"Declan trying to figure out his relationship status. Maybe he wants to change his Facebook button," Owen said, highly amused with himself.

"Ah, been there," Kian said.

"Never again," Roxie said as she placed her arm through her husband's.

"That's for dang sure," Kian said before leaning down and kissing his wife. The kiss grew uncomfortably deep in nanoseconds.

"Okay, okay, we *all* know how much you two are in love," Declan said. "We don't need a demonstration."

Roxie blushed as they broke apart and she snuggled close to Kian. "Sorry. The kids have been sleeping through the night and we're just . . . um . . . catching up," she said with a beaming smile.

"And we have lots of catching up to do," Kian agreed. "Want to go?"

She giggled again. "Not yet. We have to welcome Angela home," Roxie said.

Angela and Timothy stepped up to them right then. Thankfully she hadn't heard the rest of the crazy conversation. He wouldn't be sure how to explain that.

"Please don't change your schedules for me. I want to spend some time with Timothy and then sleep for about a week," she said. She wasn't looking any of them in the eye.

"Hey, we are mad at you for leaving, but not because you left," Roxie said.

"Nope, we understand that. We're mad that you didn't think we'd have your back no matter what. You're part of the family now, and that means we take care of you," Keera said.

"And we're so glad you're back," Eden told her. She was the first to give her a hug. "We all know what it's like to want to run. But this is your home, so no more taking off. It's safer for you and Timothy with a family who will do anything for you."

Angela's eyes filled with tears and she turned so she could brush them away. She took a moment before she responded.

"Thank you for understanding. I'm sorry. I was so scared I didn't see any other option," she said.

"I've been there," Roxie said. "And everyone opened their arms wide for me. We'll do the same for you because that's what family does."

"I love your family, but I'm not part of it," Angela reminded them. Declan wanted to correct her.

"That will be taken care of soon enough, I'm sure," Owen said before he winked at her.

Angela's cheeks went scarlet as she took a keen interest in her shoes. Declan wanted to wrap his arm around her, but he didn't want to embarrass her or scare her off. He still had to convince her she was coming home with him that night. That was going to be a fun conversation. He had no doubt he'd win, because she wouldn't put her son in jeopardy.

"Well, it really has been a long day, and I should get Timothy to bed," she said.

"I couldn't agree more," Declan said. "Do you have his bag, Owen?"

"Yep, I'll grab it."

Owen jogged to the house while everyone hugged both Angela and Timothy.

"We'll have a big dinner tomorrow night where you can tell us all about your trip," Eden said.

"Sure," Angela told her before she looked over at Arden. "Is there any chance I can get my old job back?"

Arden shocked her when he leaned down and gave her a hug. "I'm not saying this because I don't respect and care about you. I'm saying it because I do. You're family now and you won't be cleaning anymore. We'll talk about work after everything settles," he told her.

"I'm not too good to clean," she said with a narrowing of her eyes.

Damn, she was a sight to behold. Declan really might be falling in love with her.

"Hell, none of us are," Arden said as he held his arms up. "But we don't get paid to do it. It's the pleasure of owning a home. A pleasure I'd gladly give away."

"Good, then I want the job."

They glared at each other for a moment. Declan wasn't getting involved in that right now, but he truly appreciated his brother.

"We'll talk more tomorrow," Arden said. "You've had a long day of driving."

"That's for sure," she told him. "I'm ready to lie down instead of sitting on my sore butt any longer."

Declan had ways to make her a heck of a lot more sore without her complaining about any of them.

They said goodnight to everyone and climbed into her new car. She refused to drive, which he didn't mind because he could control where they were going. When he headed out of town, she turned toward him.

"Where are you going?" she asked. She was speaking quietly, very aware of Timothy in the back seat.

"To my house," he said.

"I have a place," she said before her eyes widened. "Or do I still have a place? I didn't think about that." She suddenly seemed lost.

"The apartment is gone," he said.

"Oh. I guess it's been almost two weeks. I really haven't had time to absorb that. We didn't have a lot of stuff, but it would've been nice to get it." She was trying to sound positive, but he wanted to ease her burdens right away.

"Your belongings are at my place. My siblings moved them a couple weeks ago," he told her.

"Thank you for saving my stuff," she said. There were still lines around her eyes as concern showed clearly. "But I can't stay at your house."

"We can argue about it tomorrow, but as you pointed out it's been a very long day and Timothy needs a bed. And my place is probably the most secure house in the state of Washington."

She smiled at him. "I have no doubt about that. I also don't have much of a choice tonight."

She seemed tired but not completely upset by the situation. Maybe she wasn't ready for their time to end either. He knew she wanted to be with her son as much as he wanted to keep her all to himself a while longer. He felt bad about that because he loved her son almost as much as he did her.

He pulled her car into the one empty space in his five-car garage. They didn't exit the vehicle until the garage was securely shut again.

"Are you hungry Timothy?" he asked as they walked inside the palatial house.

"No. Aunt Eden made Chinese food and chocolate brownies with lots of chips on them. I'm super full," he said before he yawned.

"You seem tired," Angela said.

"No, I'm not," he said before he yawned again. "Okay, maybe a little."

"How about we get you into the shower then snuggle up and read a couple books. I've missed reading to you the last few nights."

"Okay, Mom," he said.

"This way," Declan told them.

Angela gasped when she saw the room Timothy was sleeping in.

"When did you do this?" she asked.

"Wow, Mom, look at this," Timothy said as he ran over to the bed covered in camo with netting hanging from the ceiling. "It's the coolest room ever!" He jumped in the air.

"My brothers did it while we were driving," he said with a shrug. He owed them a huge thank you. "My brothers spent a day furnishing it, right down to the bookshelf loaded with every kid book they could think of."

"I'm never going to convince him to leave here," Angela said in exasperation.

Declan smiled. He didn't mind that one little bit. He was more than willing to give up his bachelor status. He was surprised that felt so easy to do.

There was a bathroom right next to his room, and when Timothy pulled out his new pajamas, he didn't complain at all about showering. As soon as he was gone, she turned to Declan.

"I truly appreciate all you're doing for me, Declan, but we can't make him think this is permanent. You can't make it so amazing here he won't leave with me."

"What makes you think I want you to leave?"

She let out a frustrated breath. "The situation sucks right now. I get that. And you want to protect us, and I can't thank you enough for that. But this *will* end eventually, hopefully sooner, rather than later."

"Then we'll cross that bridge when we come to it. Let's not stress about it right now," he said.

"It's hard for me not to. I've pulled Timothy all over the last few weeks and I want him to feel secure. At least school is out in one more week, so I don't have to worry about sending him back. I don't think I could right now. I'd be a mess the entire time he was gone."

"I agree. And I plan on having this wrapped up before school starts again. So, can we put living arrangements on hold for now?" He was practically holding his breath while he waited for her answer.

She gave him a tentative smile. "Okay, at least until tomorrow," she agreed.

Timothy came back out, and Declan was glad they didn't have to discuss her sleeping arrangements. He'd rather do that without any interruptions. He didn't want her to think she had to stay in his bedroom, but he was damn well going to make sure she knew he wanted her there.

He left her and Timothy to read together while he mixed himself a drink. After the last few days he wanted something strong. There was no doubt in his mind they were safe in his home. No one was sneaking up on them there. Maybe he'd keep her there under lock and key until he caught the bad guys.

He was starting to realize a part of him would die if something happened to her. He'd make sure that didn't occur. She was part of his life now, and that was all they needed to know at the moment. They'd figure the rest out day by day. Time really did seem to solve all problems.

Chapter Eighteen

In a bedroom the size of her last apartment, the last thing Angela should feel was trapped. But whether it made sense or not, that's exactly how she was feeling. Not trapped with Declan but trapped by her situation. She knew he'd brought her to his home to keep an eye on her, to make sure he could keep his promise.

He'd told her he wouldn't let anything happen to Timothy or her. She'd thanked him for that. If she fought him on where the two of them stayed, she wasn't allowing him to do what he'd vowed. She was going to have to stay at his place. She wasn't sure why she hadn't really processed that.

He was such a good man. She knew he wanted her in his bedroom—in his bed for sure. And that's exactly what she wanted too. But she was so confused. So many new things flew at her from all directions, and she hadn't been alone in days, weeks really. She was either at work with other people, or with her son, and she'd been with Declan twenty-four/seven for the past three days.

She'd needed time to think, to clear her head. So, she asked him to forgive her when she requested her own room the first night in his house. He didn't look disappointed, didn't guilt her, and didn't try to talk her out of it.

Two hours later Timothy was sound asleep, and she was in her monstrous room, unable to sleep. She tossed and turned on the ridiculously large and comfortable bed for over an hour before getting up and pacing the room.

It was beautiful and all of her clothes were in it. He wanted her in his bedroom, but he was honoring her decision. The more he did things like that, the more she was falling for him. She didn't want the case to drag on just to stay with him, yet she feared if she was there too long that's exactly what she'd hope for. Something definitely was wrong with her.

After five minutes of pacing she realized there was a balcony off her room. Though she was only on the second floor of the three-story house, she was hesitant to step out the doors. People were chasing her down. What if a sniper was out there?

Did she really want to live in fear and second-guess every decision she made? No. She refused to live her life that way. Declan hadn't told her to stay off the balcony. He hadn't locked the doors and he seemed confident in his home security. She wouldn't be surprised if he had sensors all the way around the edges of his property.

But still, she paced the room for an hour without opening those doors. Finally, she had enough of her fear and was feeling pretty warm, so she moved to the double French doors, ran her finger over the lock, hesitated for a few seconds, and clicked it.

It was frustrating how her heart thundered as she cracked one of the doors open. She wasn't going to turn back; she wouldn't live in constant fear. That wasn't okay.

The ocean breeze hit her, and she shivered as she stepped outside. The fresh air was exactly what she needed to clear her thoughts and ease her fears. She didn't look in the trees for someone aiming a red dot at her. Instead she looked up at the sky, grateful it was a clear night and she could see the stars.

Moving to the railing to enjoy the view, she couldn't imagine living in a house big enough to get lost in. She shuddered to think of keeping it clean. How did Declan handle that? She couldn't imagine he let strangers in to clean, but his place was immaculate.

Calmness washed over her. Watching the stars was as soothing as water. Maybe all of nature did that. Was that why people went camping? Sometimes it was nice to get back to the basics, but she couldn't live off the grid. She liked modern conveniences too much for that.

A power outage once in a while gave her an excuse for candlelight and scary stories. She loved a good fire and could stare at it for hours on end. But when the storms hit, she liked to be bundled, warm, and safe while she watched.

"I see you can't sleep any more than I can."

Though spoken in a normal tone, Declan's words caused Angela to jump so high she was pretty sure she could have qualified for the WNBA. Her heart thundered as she landed and turned in the direction of his voice.

He was leaning on the balcony about ten feet from where she stood, a slight smile on his lips. Her hand pressed to her thundering heart as she tried to get her breath back. She hadn't felt his presence there. She really *was* the first to die in a horror film.

She didn't reply right away because as soon as she saw him her heart began pounding all over again. The man was shirtless with chest and abs that made her wonder why he ever put on clothes. A low-slung pair of dark sweats with YALE written down one leg drew her eyes to that sexy patch of hair leading to her favorite place on his body. It took concerted effort to look away and meet his sparkling eyes.

"No, I couldn't sleep," she finally said. Her voice was husky and breathy at the same time. He didn't move, and she wondered if it was because he knew as well as she did that if they moved, they weren't going to stop until they were pressed together.

He broke eye contact this time, letting his gaze slowly travel down her shivering body. She was in no way cold, far from it, but she couldn't stop shaking. She knew she wasn't hiding much in the full moonlight, but she didn't try to cover herself. She'd needed some space that evening, had needed him to allow it.

Now she just needed him.

As his gaze roamed over her breasts, she felt as if he was caressing them. Her nipples hardened, easily poking the thin material of her nightie. Her breathing deepened, making her chest rise and fall. There was no hiding the affect this man had on her—and he hadn't even touched her. She had no doubt he was going to. She wasn't sure if he was waiting for permission. But she was unsure if she'd be capable of speaking right now.

The more he looked at her, the more she wanted him. She was in love with how it felt, with how much he turned her on. If she'd known years ago, she could feel like this she would've been seeking it out long ago.

"You're too far away," she said, her voice barely loud enough to carry over to him. But he heard her loud and clear. He didn't hesitate as he moved toward her. She took a step to meet him, letting him know he was exactly what she needed and wanted.

His unwavering gaze said so much without having to utter a single word. She'd never had a man desire her the way he did. It made her feel beautiful and invincible. Nothing bad could happen when she had a man like Declan Forbes looking at her with that intense gaze.

He stopped with only inches separating them and reached up, brushing his fingers down her cheek. She leaned closer, wanting him to kiss her, but he merely cupped her face and gazed into her eyes.

"You're so stunning," he said, his voice awed. "I can't seem to think of anything other than you and what I want to do with that luscious body."

"Kiss me, Declan. I don't want any more space."

She didn't have to ask him twice. Her body was on fire, and she knew he was just as aroused.

His arms wrapped around her, closing the space between them. His thickness pressed into her core as he lifted her leg, letting her feel how much he wanted her.

His other hand wrapped behind her neck and pulled her eager lips to his. She was his to take. There'd be no power plays and no games on that night. She wanted him to take her to heaven and never let her come back.

Finally, after what seemed like forever, his lips brushed hers. She was on fire and wanted hot and fast, but he was gentle and sweet, caressing and nibbling her lips. She brushed her tongue over his, tasting him, and he shivered in her arms.

He finally slipped his tongue inside, tracing her mouth, and she moaned as she pushed her hips against him. She wanted the few clothes they had on to be gone. She wanted him buried deep inside her. Nothing else would curb her hunger.

As their kiss grew deeper, his control weakened, and he pulled her tighter to him. She opened her mouth wider so he could touch every part of her. They were swaying against the railing as he pushed harder and kissed hotter. The heat between them intensified. If they weren't careful, they'd go up in flames.

His hand left her neck and traced the silk of her gown as he reached her butt and tugged her tighter to him. She ground against him, making him groan into her mouth, giving her more access. His fingers continued moving downward until he snagged the hem of her nightie and pulled it up, his short nails scraping her hot skin.

When he didn't find panties in the way, he let out a louder moan and his fingers clenched tightly into the softness of her butt. Only the sweats barely holding on to his hips were separating the two of them. She could take care of that if he'd give her one inch of space to remove them.

He ripped his lips from hers, and she whimpered as she reached for him. "I need a bed," he said and kissed her again.

She was floating. She loved how easily he picked her up in his arms, never breaking stride as he carried her across the balcony into his bedroom.

Had she known their rooms were side by side, she wouldn't have lasted as long as she had before stepping outside. She'd known a minute after she'd shut the door, she'd made a mistake. She'd wanted to be with him, not only because of the situation they were in, but because she was drawn to him and didn't know if that feeling was ever going away. She also didn't know what that meant. But right now, she wasn't going to think about it.

He set her on his bed and had his sweats and her nightie off in seconds. As they lay on top of the comforter, his hands traced every inch of her. She held on, scraping her nails along his back and butt, his arms and chest. She couldn't touch him enough.

After he'd caressed every sensitive place on her, he traded his hands for his mouth and tongue. He circled her nipples, sucking and nibbling, while his hands kneaded and massaged. He pressed his arousal against her leg, and she moaned and begged.

"I want you so hot you explode the second I enter you," he told her.

"I *am* that hot," she promised.

"Not yet, but soon," he assured her before his mouth clamped over her nipple and he nipped before running his tongue over it. She cried out his name feeling her orgasm coming closer and closer.

He nibbled, licked, and sucked until she was putty beneath him. If he asked her to turn, she couldn't. Her muscles were shot; her body was his. And he was playing it to perfection.

He ran his tongue along the inside of her thighs, but he skirted around the place throbbing most for his touch. He chuckled at her frustrated growl.

"I like you needy," he said against her stomach as he made his way back up her body. She couldn't muster the energy to reply, but she vowed to get payback the next time they made love—most likely a few hours after this finished. She was hungry for this man and was sure that would never go away.

Finally, he reached her lips, and as his mouth met hers, she felt her desire nearly peak. He was about to prove it was possible for her to come without touching her lower body. She was in awe of this man.

Suspended above her, she felt his tip at her entrance and spread her legs wider as she reached for his hips and tugged. Enough. She wanted him buried inside her for the rest of the night if possible.

"Open your eyes, Angela."

She shook her head. She knew she'd be a goner if she looked at him.

"Now, Angela. Open your eyes *now*."

It took so much effort, but she did as he said and cracked her lids open. He was looking down at her as if she was the most precious thing on earth. Tears stung her eyes. Looking at him was everything she knew it would be, and so much more. She had no doubt she was in love with him.

She had known this man for three years and the chemistry had always been there. She'd just thought it could never work. He was a Forbes and she was a nobody. He was hard and she was a pushover. They were oil and water. But even knowing this, it didn't seem to matter. She'd fought it, but he'd come for her. She was his for now—maybe for as long as he wanted. In this position she had no desire to fight what she was feeling.

There was no turning back. The more time she spent with him the more in love she'd fall. And there was no way for her to stop it, to get away from it. All she could do was hold on tight for the ride and hope when it ended, she'd still be able to walk away.

He pushed forward. Unlike the first few times, he went slow and steady. He let her feel every single inch of him touch her tight heat. She quivered beneath him as he filled her slowly, deeply, perfectly. And the second he buried himself she shook around him.

Her body let go and she came, squeezing him tight as she cried out. It was unlike any orgasm she'd felt before. It tugged on her from the inside out and went on and on. By the time she stopped shaking, she was a mess.

She realized she'd never taken her eyes from his. He looked barely on the edge of control, but he didn't move. He leaned down the slightest bit and ran his lips across hers, but he stayed in control even though she lost hers.

"Ohhh," she breathed, in awe of this man and how he commanded her body.

"I want to do that again and again," he said.

"Yes, please," she sighed. He smiled before kissing her.

She wrapped her legs tightly around him and held on tight, content to stay like this forever. That was until he began to move. He pulled back a couple of inches before pushing forward again. He did this several times, and she felt heat building again, steady and strong.

She cried out as her body released once more, gripping him. She couldn't keep her eyes open as he continued thrusting inside her, fast then slow, deep then shallow. He played her body like a fine instrument and gave her more pleasure than she'd known possible. And he held back his own.

Then he grabbed her hips and tilted her as he took long, deep, hard strokes. She screamed as another orgasm washed through her, this time pulsing so hard he had a difficult time thrusting inside her.

He finally let go, taking his own pleasure with hers. They shook together as both of them floated high in the sky, taking their time coming back to earth again. She held on tight, not wanting him to pull from her.

She needed to tell him he didn't need condoms. She didn't want that much material between them. She wanted flesh on flesh. Nothing else would do anymore.

They lay pressed together for minutes before he shifted. She whimpered as he pulled his still hard body from hers. But he never let her go. He removed the condom and pulled her tightly to him.

"We don't need those. I can't get pregnant," she sleepily told him.

"Are you sure?" he asked.

"I'm sure," she said.

"Good, because I want you without one."

She felt her heat clench at those words. She was so worn she could barely move, but if he pressed back against her she'd gladly fall into his arms. When it came to Declan she couldn't get enough. She never would.

She didn't even try to pretend she wanted to leave his bed. She was exactly where she wanted to be, and she wasn't going anywhere—at least not yet.

Chapter Nineteen

When Angela next opened her eyes, the sun was shining brightly through the massive bedroom window. For one moment she was confused and slightly scared. She stretched, feeling how achy her body was, and then the night before came back with a vengeance. And she smiled.

She was alone in Declan's huge bed, and she turned to see it was nearly ten in the morning. She couldn't remember the last time she'd slept so late. Her son was up at the crack of dawn, so she'd trained herself to rise early. She didn't like wasting her day anyway. Getting up late made her wonder what she needed to do.

Instead of jumping from the bed, she took a moment to relive her night. They'd only made love the one time, but he'd completely sated her. Maybe he'd thought she needed a night of uninterrupted sleep.

In all reality she had. She couldn't remember the last time she'd slept a solid eight hours. She hadn't so much as stirred all night long.

Taking her time, she sat up in the unbelievably soft bed. It would be pure heaven to spend an entire day in it—with Declan of course. Without him, nothing was quite as comfortable. It was odd how attracted she was to that man. Yes, he was gorgeous, but he wasn't the usual type of guy she looked at.

He was so tall, so wide, so foreboding, yet she wasn't frightened of him. All she wanted was more. Right now, though, it was good to have a moment alone without worrying about her son. Timothy knew all of the Forbes's well. He wouldn't be scared without her there for a few extra minutes. That didn't mean she was going to take too long.

It did mean she could gather her thoughts before finding her way through Declan's house to wherever Timothy and Declan were. She stretched and winced. She'd never been this sore in her life, and she had always worked hard jobs. Declan had managed to work muscles she hadn't known could get sore.

Climbing from the bed, she limped. She hoped that cleared up before the whole world knew she'd been loved thoroughly. They were having dinner with his family, and it would be mortifying if they saw her in this condition. They'd know instantly what the two of them had been up to.

She wasn't sure she could hide it anyway. The wives of Declan's brothers were master interrogators. Maybe they'd learned it from him.

She found her nightgown in a chair by the door and slipped it on. The balcony was clear for the walk of shame back to her own room. She was a consenting adult and there was nothing wrong with what she'd done, but she was a mother and didn't want to tell her son it was okay to go around sleeping with people—especially people you weren't even in a relationship with.

A shower would help before finding her son. The hot water might ease some of her achiness. She stayed under the massaging showerhead for a very long time and wasn't back to normal when she stepped out, but her limp was barely there. She couldn't believe how much her thighs ached.

Though she hurt more than if she'd run a dang marathon, she was smiling. It was a beautiful soreness, one that meant she'd had several days of intense pleasure over and over again. She'd take the achiness for nights like that anytime. She had no doubt it would happen again. Hopefully again and again and again and again.

She found herself humming as she got dressed. There were a few additions to her closet that she knew for certain hadn't been there when she'd left. She had no doubt Roxie, Keera, and Eden had helped with that. She was going to have to do something special for them. They'd become friends; she couldn't imagine losing them; she didn't want to give them up. She'd run, but they'd brought her back. This truly was home.

She needed to see her son, yet she was taking so long to get ready because she was hiding. What was this new day going to bring? They were back in Edmonds, and there was a lot to be done. She wanted to pretend life was normal, and she was just like anyone else, getting ready for an ordinary, possibly even boring, day. She'd never thought she'd wish for that.

She'd stalled long enough and finally left her room and found her way down the staircase. Declan had built his home exactly how he'd wanted it—a little bigger than average. The staircase was two times the size of a normal house's, and the ceilings were at least twelve feet high. There was no chance of feeling locked in this home. She really liked it.

She finally heard Declan and Timothy and followed their voices to the kitchen where they were sitting at the breakfast bar, laughing and eating.

Their smiles when she entered the room were like rays of sunshine bursting through the clouds on a stormy day, filling her with joy. She'd never spent time away from her son, and three days had felt like an eternity. She didn't want to be a clingy mom, but it was difficult not to be with all that had been going on.

"Are you hungry, Mom?" Timothy asked, though the words were hard to make out with his mouth full of what appeared to be a chocolate chip waffle. She eyeballed the whipped cream, strawberry jam, chocolate syrup, and sprinkles sitting on the counter then raised her brows at Declan.

"Is there anything but sugar for breakfast?" she asked.

"This isn't a daily thing. We're celebrating the two of you being back home where you belong," Declan said. "Among other things." He wiggled his brows as his eyes traced her body, which instantly flushed. She turned away so her son wouldn't see her blush.

She found the coffee pot and busied herself making a warm cup of heaven. That also gave her a second to compose herself before she faced her son and Declan again. If he made those same comments to her when they were around people she might have to hit him.

"I'm glad to hear you know it won't be daily," she said. "A healthy breakfast is important for growing boys."

"You say that every day, Mom. I just want sugar sometimes," Timothy said, batting his long eyelashes at her.

She moved over to him and leaned down, kissing him on the forehead. "And you get it *sometimes*. I just love you so big I want you to be strong and turn into a fine young man."

"I will. I eat my vegetables, even though I don't like them at all."

"I have to agree with you on that. Vegetables for breakfast aren't my idea of fun," Declan said.

Timothy laughed. "We don't have to eat them for breakfast," he said before he paused. "I don't think we do. But I always have carrots in my lunch and Mom makes all sorts of green things for dinner." He stuck out his tongue like he was gagging.

"It's soooo terrible," Angela said. "My poor, *poor* boy."

Timothy giggled before stuffing his mouth with more waffle. She cringed the tiniest bit, but they really did look amazing.

"Well, I guess I can't let you eat alone," she said. Declan chuckled and she glared at him. "You know I have a sweet tooth."

"I'm very aware of that. That must be why you're so dang sweet," he said.

She wanted to stay slightly aloof but there was no chance of that happening. She enjoyed being with him entirely too much.

She put a waffle on her plate and smothered it in butter before dousing it in syrup, a gooey mess of deliciousness she rarely allowed herself. There had to be over a thousand calories in this one small breakfast. She didn't feel guilty, though. She'd burned a lot more than that the night before. And she was sort of hoping to burn some more later that night.

"Mom, can I go to Mr. Kian's today? He said he's going fishing and I can go with him," Timothy asked. She was going to respond when he held up his hand. "But he said to make sure I ask, and if the answer is no, that's okay, too, cause it's up to my mom," he repeated.

She couldn't help but laugh. "Is that all he said?"

"If Kian is fishing, I don't see that as a problem," she told him. Her son had been through a lot this last month. To see him smiling and excited to be home made her heart full.

"We could go too, couldn't we?" she asked Declan.

"We could," he said. "Or we could go to the station and talk to some people."

Just that quickly she lost her appetite. She'd really wanted one day to forget about the horrors of the world. But that wasn't realistic. The sooner all of this was taken care of the sooner they'd get back to their lives. She wanted that even if it scared her that her time with Declan would end just as fast.

"Yes, that's a good idea," she said.

She disposed of the rest of her waffle before putting her plate in the dishwasher, took Timothy's plate, then reached for Declan's, but he grabbed her hand and stopped her.

"We can take a day off and do it tomorrow," he said.

"No, that was silly of me to suggest," she told him, but she couldn't manage to look him in the eyes. His finger came under her chin and he forced her to look at him. She found herself fighting not to cry.

"You know what, I'm making an executive decision. We're all taking the day off to go fishing. It's just what we need."

"Yea!" Timothy said as he jumped from his chair and began leaving the room.

"Where are you going?" she called. He skidded to a halt.

"To get ready. Mr. Kian said he'd be here in thirty minutes, and I don't know how long ago that was, but it seems like forever," Timothy said as he bounced on his feet.

"Do you need help?" she asked. He barely stopped himself from rolling his eyes, which he'd gotten in trouble for doing before. Then he smiled.

"I'm a big kid now, Mom. Remember? I can get ready by myself."

"Okay, yes, you are. You help me so much," she said.

He didn't say anything more and ran so fast from the room he slid when he turned the corner.

"He's growing up incredibly fast," she said, feeling the days flying by.

"That's because he has a mom who's taught him well," Declan assured her.

"I hope I haven't traumatized him too much. I try to keep all of this darkness from him." She stopped talking. "It's okay, Declan, we can get business taken care of." She didn't want to, but she was an adult and part of that meant she didn't get to run off whenever she wanted.

"Nope. I've decided we're going to play. It's well deserved. I want to play hooky from work. I'm already a few hours late so I might as well take the entire day off."

"Oh my gosh, I didn't realize this was a weekday. Are you going to get in trouble?" she asked. It was close to eleven in the morning. The day was half over. "You should have woken me. I'm sorry."

"You needed sleep. I did give you quite the workout last night," he said before pulling her against him and kissing her hard. "And I plan on doing it again, so take it easy today and stretch."

"Declan, shh, I don't want Timothy to overhear you," she said as she looked over her shoulder.

"We have at least ten minutes," he assured her before pulling her tightly against him, kissing her hard enough to take her breath away and send her pulse skyrocketing. Then there was a knock on the door.

"My brother couldn't have waited just a little longer," Declan grumbled.

Angela felt lightheaded as he released her. He gave her one more quick kiss then walked away. She took the few seconds she had to grab a towel and wipe the counter before Kian walked in. She tried pushing the kiss from her mind, but it was far easier said than done.

"How did you sleep last night, Angela?" Kian asked.

She felt her cheeks instantly heat as if he knew what she'd done. She couldn't look him in the eyes. He was probably making polite conversation because he knew she'd been stressed and traveling, but Angela wasn't good at hiding anything.

"Um, great, thanks," she said, not looking away from the counter.

"Oh, I know *that* look," Roxie said with a giggle.

"What look?" Kian asked.

"Oh nothing, darling. You and Declan go gather things while I chat with Angela," she said, dismissing the boys.

"I'm so confused," Kian said as the two brothers walked away.

"I want details and I want them right now," Roxie demanded the second they were alone.

"I can't give you details because my son will be rushing back in the room at any minute," Angela said. She finally looked up at her friend and Roxie was beaming.

"Was last night the first time?" she asked.

"I can't believe you're asking me that," Angela said with a gasp.

"Of course, I am. Was it?"

"I don't think I'll answer," Angela said.

"Oh my gosh, it wasn't. When was the first time? I want so many details."

Before Angela could refuse again, Timothy came skidding to a halt before them.

"Did I do good, Mom?" he asked.

She wanted to kiss her son over and over again for saving her. "You look great. Let's find Kian and Declan and see if they're ready," she said.

"This isn't over, Angela Lincoln. Wait until I get the girls and we corner you," Roxie whispered in her ear as they left the room.

"But I'm safe for now," she said with a smile as Roxie rolled her eyes.

"I get in trouble for that," Timothy said. Kids looked at the damnedest times.

"Yeah, me too," Roxie said.

"Everyone is able to come," Kian said when they found them in the living room.

"Yeah, Eden wasn't sure if she could. I'm glad she changed her mind. We have some much-needed girl time ahead," Roxie said as she wrapped her arm in Angela's.

Angela looked at Declan to save her, but he smiled and shook his head. She looked at him like he was a traitor. His answering look seemed to tell her he'd save her from everything in this world . . . except his sisters-in-law.

She had a feeling she'd be in a CIA-worthy interrogation before the sun went down.

Chapter Twenty

Being with Declan's family had been amazingly fun and had felt like being part of a sitcom. There was so much activity, so much love, and so much interrogation, Angela didn't know what to think.

Before Declan had come to California to rescue her, it hadn't been so bad back at home. There had been comments about the looks Declan and she had exchanged over the years, and some quips about the chemistry between them. But the girls hadn't pushed her too hard.

But now that Roxie had caught the scent of something *actually* going on between her and Declan, they were pushing hard for information—and doing their best at matchmaking.

The men seemed to be clueless while the women were better interrogators than the CIA. She wasn't sure how much longer she could avoid it. So far, she'd spent the day with Timothy glued to her side so they couldn't ask her the difficult questions. That wasn't going to last. The fishing trip was over with a bucket full of future dinners.

They'd returned to Declan's home and now it was time for the family dinner that seemed to be growing by leaps and bounds. Declan's father, Lucian, had talked them all into going to his good friend, Joseph Anderson's, place. Angela hadn't met the man yet, but she knew a lot about Joseph. How could anyone not know about the man? He owned half of Seattle, half the state of Washington, for that matter. She was afraid to meet him.

But with so many people around she wouldn't be of much interest to someone like Joseph. However, with the size of his property, she wasn't sure she'd be able to keep enough people around her to avoid being carried away by her friends.

She'd insisted on bringing something to the dinner. They'd told her not to worry about is as it was a party welcoming her and Timothy back, but she'd insisted on it being called a family gathering. She didn't like to be in the spotlight. And they couldn't have a dinner honoring her at a house where she hadn't even met the owner. She wanted to be just another guest, and guests brought food.

She was a good cook and took a lot of pride in that fact. She was also intimidated to be cooking for this crowd. But it was better than showing up empty-handed. She already was leaning too heavily on the Forbes family. She wasn't going to be a total freeloader.

She stood in Declan's dream kitchen with cookies cooling on the counter while she put together a macaroni salad and stuffed mushrooms. She felt as if she'd forgotten how to use a mixing spoon. She was a hot mess and it didn't appear to be getting better anytime soon.

"Mom, we're ready to go," Timothy said as he came skidding into the kitchen. She hated how jumpy she was. It was her son for goodness sake, and she was jumping as if a snake had crawled out of the sink drain.

"I'm almost finished, sweetie. Is Declan done in the office?"

"He said it wasn't a workday. He shut it all down and we threw the ball for a while. I'm definitely going to play baseball next year," he said as he jumped up on the barstool and grabbed a cookie off the platter.

"Really?" she said, her tension fading. "I thought you didn't like it."

"That was until Declan said he'd make me the best player on the team," Timothy said proudly. "I was throwing really hard."

"Declan's a busy person, Timothy. He might not be able to teach you very often. But I used to play softball. I could play catch with you," she assured him. She didn't want him growing too attached to Declan. This was all so complicated.

Her son was such a great kid. He was friendly and polite and loved life. He was eager to learn, and he wanted a male figure to look up to so badly. She hoped she wasn't utterly messing up his life by not giving him a father. She tried to make up for it. But there were some things a boy just wanted to do with a dad. She understood.

"I'm never too busy to throw a ball," Declan said as he joined them, sitting in the chair next to Timothy and grabbing his own cookie. "Where's the milk?" he asked with a wink at her son.

"I'll get it," Timothy said with hero worship in his eyes as he jumped up and grabbed a couple of glasses and poured them milk. He didn't spill a drop.

"My brothers and I used to toss a ball daily, either a baseball, football, or basketball. If it wasn't raining, we were outside doing something. If the rain drove us in, we'd find a gym to work off energy," Declan said as he ruffled Timothy's head and thanked him for the milk. He finished a cookie in three bites.

"I loved being outdoors as a kid. I need to get out more now," she said.

"Boys tend to have more energy to burn," Declan told her.

"That sounds slightly sexist," she said.

"Not at all. It goes back to caveman days when men hunted all day to feed their families. We're supposed to be outside using our skill and muscles," he said.

"These aren't caveman days anymore," she said.

"No, but if some huge natural disaster happens how many people do you think could survive without modern electricity and all the luxuries of home?" he asked.

She looked around his kitchen and raised her brows. He chuckled.

"I'm not saying I don't love a convenient life. I'm just saying if we get too lazy, we won't know what to do without all those conveniences. Look at the uproar over plastic straws. I have to admit I was irritated with the ban at first. Then I realized we survived a long time without them, and we can survive without them now. Do I like them? Yes, I do. Are they essential to my happiness? Not at all. Will I use them if they're around? Yep, I will. But I can drink from a cup and be just fine. I might spill some ice on me now and then, but I'll adjust. Humans adjust. We adapt. But if we get too lazy, we won't. So that's why I like throwing the ball and burning excess energy. I want to use my energy and not lose it."

"Wow, that's a good way to shut down an argument," she said with a chuckle. "I agree it's easy to get lazy. There are days when I don't have anything pressing so I'll curl up in front of the fire with a blanket and book and not move for a solid ten hours unless I need a drink or a bathroom. Those are few and far between, but they are absolute heaven."

"I can't say that's my idea of heaven," he said. "But when I'm sick I move less."

"There's nothing wrong with rest days. Even God took a day of rest," she pointed out.

"Nah, I just think that's the day he went fishing," Declan said. "He *is* a great fisherman."

"That's a very good point. I don't remember one of the six days of creation mentioning fishing. But there is a lot of sitting while fishing."

"If you're doing it wrong. I like the big fish that fight me," he told her.

"Of course, you do. I've never caught one of those."

"What?" He jumped up, making both her and Timothy look at him with concern. "That's an absolute tragedy. We're going to have to fix that as soon as possible.

Once you catch an eighty-pound halibut you'll never be able to trout fish again."

"I guess we'll find out," she said.

"I want to catch an eighty-pound halibut," Timothy said.

"That weighs more than you," Angela told him. "The fish might be fishing you."

"That would be so cool," Timothy said with a grin.

"Boys," she said with an affectionate smile.

"Yep, boys, can't live with us or without us," Declan told her.

"How many cookies have you guys eaten?" she asked as she looked at her depleted platter.

"I don't know. I wasn't paying attention," Declan said with a shrug. "They are good though."

"I can't take this tray now. There's hardly anything on it."

"Good. Then we'll have them when we get back home."

She liked her food being appreciated so she couldn't be too upset they were eating all the cookies, but she wasn't letting them touch her salad or mushrooms. The oven timer went off and she moved over to pull the pan out.

"Oh, those smell good," Declan said, suddenly at her side.

"Nope. Hands off. These are making it to the dinner," she said as she swatted him away.

"I just need to make sure they won't poison anyone," he said with pleading eyes as he gazed at the appetizer. She was so pleased he looked enamored with her food that she caved and placed two of them on a plate for him.

He wolfed them down. "Damn. These are the best mushrooms I've ever had," he said. "Come on, let me have a few more."

"No way," she said. "I found these warming plate things in your kitchen that you place in a bag to keep the food heated. These puppies are getting packed right now."

"Fine, let me go change real quick and we'll hit the road."

"Smart man," she said.

She was still smiling when Timothy and Declan rushed from the kitchen. She realized when she was alone again that she could get very used to their little domestic scene. She might get more used to it than she should.

For now, though, this was her life, and she was determined to enjoy every moment of it.

Chapter Twenty-One

Angela was grateful that Timothy kept the conversation going on the way to the Anderson mansion. She was nervous about going to this huge family event, and even more nervous about how she'd been feeling in the kitchen.

She'd already spent the afternoon with Declan's siblings, and she couldn't help but love it. She had a great time with them, enjoying the music and laughter and conversation. There was never a dull moment when the four brothers were together. They had an extremely tight bond.

Her first impression of the Anderson driveway was awe. It stretched on for about a half-mile, lined on either side with giant evergreen trees. The driveway itself was impressive. She couldn't believe she was about to see the famous Anderson mansion—that she was being invited to spend the evening there.

When they turned the corner and the massive house appeared as if it was reaching for the sky, she actually gasped. Even Timothy went silent.

"Is that a castle, Mom?" he finally asked.

Declan chuckled. "It's pretty dang close to a castle," he told him. "Mr. Joseph doesn't do anything on a small scale."

"Wow, I've never seen anything like that," Timothy said.

"Yeah, a lot of us haven't."

Angela had to fight rolling her eyes as Declan said that. She'd seen his parents' home, and though it wasn't as huge as the Anderson mansion, because that was their choice. The Forbes's could certainly hold their own with the Andersons. They were used to money and didn't know life without it. She didn't know if that would be a good thing or not.

Declan parked the car and rushed to open her door before she could. "This way," he said. Timothy jumped out and turned his head in all directions.

Declan grabbed their food, making Angela feel really silly about it now. She was sure there were chefs preparing the best of the best. Her food would be nothing. Hopefully they could tuck it away and no one would know where it came from.

They followed the sound of laughter to the side of the house and she had to fight not to gasp again as they neared a giant pool and an outdoor kitchen near huge tents set up with lanterns and heat lamps for when the sun went down.

This wasn't a typical backyard barbeque. That was for dang sure. She felt utterly out of place. A huge part of her wanted to turn and run, but she wouldn't do that to her son who'd already spotted a gaggle of kids.

"Can I go play?" Timothy asked. Declan nodded at her.

"Yes, just check in with me every once in a while," she called to his back as he jetted off.

There were at least a hundred people all laughing, talking, and dancing to the band set up in the corner playing a mix of country and rock.

"Wasn't this a last-minute thing?" she asked. "This looks like it was planned."

"They decided to do it when I said we were on our way home. We do a lot of get-togethers. Family time is important," Declan said.

"This looks like a wedding reception. I can't believe they put it together in a couple of days."

"Joseph does a lot of events. He can be ready in minutes. It helps that he has a staff who are capable and move quickly."

"We should put this food back in the car," she said, wishing she wouldn't have insisted on bringing something.

"As much as I want to keep it to myself, that's not going to happen. You worked hard on it. There's the food table." He spotted a long, *long* table where dozens of dishes were sitting, and he took the food over there. A couple of staff members smiled and thanked them, then set it out with all the other items.

Angela felt slightly better about it when Owen and Eden stepped up beside them and handed over a dish. "That's my favorite, Texas caviar," Eden said. "There's no cooking involved, and it always wows the crowd."

"Looks like we got here about the same time," Angela said, wanting to cling to Eden's side.

"Yep, Owen took forever to get ready," she said.

"Mmm hmm, except it was the opposite. My wife decided she wanted to try on a dozen dresses, then tried to trap me into telling her which looked the best."

"Well you look beautiful," Angela told her. "But you always do."

"Ah, thank you, darling. See, Owen? That's all it takes," Eden said with a grin.

"You look beautiful in everything you wear, especially sweats and a sports bra," he said. "So, I really can't give fashion advice."

She leaned into and gave him a kiss. "And I love that you think so."

"I'm an expert," he said.

She laughed with delight. "You're an expert at putting out fires . . . in more ways than one," she told him with a wink.

"That's just wrong," Declan said with a roll of his eyes. "I need a beer."

"I'll join you."

Angela and Eden followed the two men to where a huge open bar was set up. Eden grabbed a glass of wine for Angela and something sparkling for herself while the guys each took an ice-cold beer.

"It's good to see you, Declan," a man said as he approached with a beautiful woman at his side. "Who's the lovely lady you talked into coming?"

"Lucas, this is Angela Lincoln. Her son, Timothy, is running around here somewhere in the mob of children causing as much chaos as possible. Angela, this is Joseph's oldest son, Lucas Anderson, and his wife, Amy."

"It's a pleasure to meet you," Amy said. "We were told we're having a homecoming dinner for you tonight. I love any excuse for all of us to gather. Not that we really need an excuse."

"I can't believe how much effort went into this. When Declan said we were having a family dinner, I was thinking hot dogs and beer," Angela said with a nervous laugh. "I definitely like this better."

"Yes, the Andersons don't do anything simple, and since Joseph and Lucian are such great friends when the two of them get together a dinner becomes a gala event," Amy said.

"Well I'm glad I get to experience it. I might not find my son for a while, but he'll have some stories to tell, I'm sure," Angela said.

"Oh, if you want stories, I've got plenty for you. This family has all sorts of secrets."

"Darling, I thought we didn't share the secrets," Lucas said with an adoring look at his wife.

"Now that wouldn't be any fun at all, would it?" she asked as she leaned up on tiptoe to kiss her husband. They were obviously infatuated with each other. It was refreshing to see.

"You can tell it all. I've nothing to hide," Lucas said.

The band switched into a lively version of Friends in Low Places, and several people started to sing. Angela was overwhelmed with it all.

"Don't be intimidated by any of this. I know it can be a bit much. When I first met Lucas, I wanted to go running and screaming in the opposite direction. But then I got pregnant and, well, the rest is history. But after I got over my initial fear, I realized that, yes, they have a lot of money, but their hearts are even bigger than their wallets. Enjoy yourself tonight. You're going to be meeting a lot of new faces. There will be a quiz later."

Angela smiled at Amy. She instantly liked the woman. She'd love to know her story and how she met Lucas. Maybe they'd have time to chat more as the night went on. Or maybe she'd just read about it.

"We'll talk with you soon. I see my father, and I have a bone to pick with him," Lucas said.

"Uh, oh, looks like Joseph's in trouble again," Owen said with a laugh.

"That's nothing new. Dad's at his side. I bet the two of them are up to something as we speak," Declan said.

"They sure do love to meddle. I don't know how you got out of it," Owen said.

"I don't think I did," Declan said with a laugh. Angela had no idea what they were talking about. Owen clapped Declan on the back.

"Yeah, I don't think you did, either," he said with a wink.

"I'm not upset about it, though. That's the strange thing."

"Ah, if I could get a tear in my eye, I just might. That's about the sweetest thing I've heard in a decade."

"Yeah, yeah," Declan said.

"Even the hardest of them fall."

"What in the world are you guys talking about?" Angela asked, unable to hide her curiosity.

"You'll find out," Owen told her before he took Eden's hand and pulled her away to the beautiful wooden dance floor.

"Want to dance?" Declan asked.

"No," she said a bit too loudly. "I can't dance, and there are so many people around."

"I could drag you," he said, leaning in close and making her heart skip a beat.

"But you won't," she said, only about seventy percent sure of that.

"No, I won't. I want you to have a good time. But my other two siblings are approaching so that might be impossible. Do you want to make a break for it?"

"Yes, but I'll be brave," she said. The glass of wine was half gone, and she was realizing she might need several more to get through this night.

Kian and Arden approached with Roxie and Keera. "You guys beat us here," Keera said. "But it looks like most of the Anderson clan did as well. I guess we were taking too long."

"It's always good to make an entrance," Arden said.

"Isn't that a girl's line?" Keera asked.

"Nah, men like to make an entrance too."

"That's for sure. When you guys walk into a room together it definitely is a showstopper," Roxie said as she gazed at her husband.

"That's because I'm so dang cute they don't have to look at my ugly brothers," Kian told them.

"Mmm hmm, we all bow to you, Kian," Declan said with a smirk.

"I know. I *am* a doctor," he said with a waggle of his brows.

"Yeah, we've been told that a time or two," Arden said.

Angela loved listening to them banter. It was one of her favorite things in the world. The love between them was more than obvious, and they knew each other so well there wasn't a dry moment when they were together.

"Yes, we all know how hot you boys are. But the secret that makes people turn their heads is the hearts of gold you try so hard to hide," Roxie said.

"Damn, I love you, babe," Kian said. He pulled Roxie to him and kissed her long enough to make Angela squirm. No one else seemed to even notice. When he let go of his wife, her lips were red, and her eyes were sparkling.

"I love you too," she said as she reached up and brushed a bit of lipstick off his bottom lip. For all the two of them knew, no one else was around.

"Do you guys need to get a room? I'm sure Joseph has one or two to spare in this place," Declan asked. But then his arm wrapped around her, and she didn't know what to do. They weren't there as a couple. But she liked having his arm around her. It felt good—it felt right.

A gleam popped into Kian's eyes. "From what I've heard it's not us who need to get a room," he said with a chuckle. Angela tensed as she shot a warning look at Roxie, who gave her an innocent smile.

"Kian, I think I hear your name being called," Declan said.

"Yes, I think all your names are being called," Eden said as she and Owen joined them.

"Huh?" Arden asked.

"That is girl talk for get lost," Declan said. "I thought you would've learned that by now. The ladies want to talk without us."

"Oh," Kian said with a fake pout. "I guess we could disappear for a little while. But not too long. I want to swing you around on that dance floor."

"That's a date, darling," Roxie said. Then she shooed the men away.

And Angela was left alone with the women, exactly what she'd managed to avoid all day. She wondered if she could claim she needed a bathroom break and run for it. She figured these women were a lot smarter than she was, and they'd simply follow her.

One part of Angela didn't want to share with these women and another part wanted to tell them everything. She needed other women to talk to, and she had no one else. In the past few years she'd grown close to each of them. They had a unique friendship, and it felt good to be a part of the group.

That made it all the scarier. What if things went seriously wrong with Declan and she lost all of this because of it. Was it worth taking that chance? She wasn't sure she had a choice anymore.

"All right, I've been waiting all day to talk to you. When did you and Declan get intimate?" Eden asked.

"Yeah, you have no idea the amount of restraint it's taken us not to quiz you all day," Roxie said.

"I knew there were fireworks between the two of you, but I didn't know it had reached the sheet-tangling stage yet," Keera added.

Angela could honestly say she'd never been asked these types of questions before. She was utterly out of her element and didn't know what to think or say. She finished off her wine, and as if by magic, a waiter was there refilling. She liked this barbecue more and more by the second.

"I . . . um . . . well . . ." She found herself stuttering without having any answers for them. Should she spill it all?

"Look, these Forbes men are a pain to deal with. Each of us understands that, and each of us has had our own moments and stories, so just know there will be no judgment from any of us. We only want the scoop. Maybe we can work through it with you. If I'd taken the time to talk instead of running away, I wouldn't have wasted years I could've been with Kian. It's my biggest regret in life," Roxie said.

"I didn't want to like Arden at all," Keera said. "But he was always there, and the more he was, the less I could control what I was feeling. The first time we made love, I realized that's what sex was supposed to be like. Oh, and it only gets better and better as time goes on. I hate leaving his bed."

The other two women giggled, and Angela felt herself blushing at those words.

"I grew up in this town and knew Owen most of my life. He broke my heart. But we had to grow up, and I'm grateful for our time apart, but even more grateful to get to be with him every day now. I know they all have faults. You won't get judgment from us," Eden assured her. "I promise."

"Declan feels he needs to protect me," Angela said. "This isn't a relationship. He's just helping me and Timothy. I admit he's going above and beyond, but this isn't a love story." They looked at her with unbelievable looks. "I'll admit I have feelings, but I haven't had time to process them. And I don't see how this could work out to becoming more than it is."

"That's what all of us thought," Roxie said. "Love isn't always a choice, as some people say. I believe we can choose to love someone, and we can choose to stop loving them, but sometimes, no matter how much we don't want to, we can't help it. I didn't want to love Kian, but he was the only one for me. When I quit fighting that, my life became a lot better."

"The way Declan follows you with his eyes has a lot more to do with attraction than protection," Eden assured her. "I've seen it for years now, and it's only grown more intense. I don't think he's going anywhere, even when this case is solved. I've never seen him like this with another woman."

"Really?" Angela asked. She didn't want to feel hope. She was scared that would be a bad, bad idea. "Even if that's true, it's not just me I have to think about. I can see Timothy falling in love with him as well, and I don't want him hurt if this doesn't work out. But we aren't in a relationship. We're just sort of thrown together right now."

"But you're also sleeping in his bed," Eden said.

The three women stared her down as if daring her to deny it. She let out a sigh.

"Okay, yes, we've slept together . . . twice."

"Ah, now we're getting to the good stuff. How was it?" Keera asked.

Angela's face turned scarlet as she looked around, glad no one seemed to be paying attention to them.

"It was amazing, unlike anything I've felt before. It was so much more than sex," Angela admitted.

"Yeah, once you have really, *really* great sex, there's no turning back. You can never settle for mediocre again," Keera said.

"Then I'm probably screwed," Angela said.

"You are if he's doing it right," Eden said with a giggle.

"And they say men are bad," Roxie said with a laugh. "If they heard the way we talk, they'd be in shock. I love it."

All four of them giggled at that. The conversation wasn't nearly as bad as Angela had thought it would be. Maybe she really could tell these ladies anything. Maybe they could help her work through it all. She felt as if she belonged in this group and it was a great feeling.

"Let's go raid the snack table. I'm starving," Eden said.

That's when Angela noticed Eden was only drinking non-alcoholic beverages. The light dawned.

"Are you pregnant?" she asked.

Eden beamed. "Yes, but only three months. We're about to announce it. So much can go wrong in the first trimester I didn't want to say anything. But I'm eating three times as much as I normally eat so people are going to start noticing me getting really fat."

"Congratulations," Angela exclaimed. The women all hugged. Angela was a little jealous because she'd never again feel what Eden was feeling now. That reminder told her she couldn't ever have anything serious with Declan. He'd want to have children, a legacy of his own. And she couldn't give it to him.

She kept the smile on her face, but part of her joy dimmed at that cold reality. Luckily no one seemed to notice. She had a long night to get through, and she hoped she could shake off the gloom she was now feeling. She'd done it before, and she was sure she could do it again.

Chapter Twenty-Two

"You're a goner."

Declan was trying to tune out his brothers as he watched Angela walk to the food table with his sisters-in-law. He was pretty sure he was an absolute goner, but he wasn't going to give them the pleasure of admitting it.

As her smooth legs flexed while she walked, he realized he'd only seen her in a dress once before at a dinner a couple of years ago, and that dress had reached the floor. She'd been stunning then as she was always.

But the dress she was wearing now rested a few inches above her knees showing the smooth curve of her thighs and the muscled contours of her calves. She was wearing two-inch heels and looked good enough to devour.

All he wanted to do was walk over to her, lift her in his arms, and run his hands up that skirt, over the firmness of her ass, and around to that sweet spot that was making him hard even thinking about it.

He was fantasizing about the color of her panties, desperately wanting to know if they were lace or silk. He wanted to slide his fingers over every inch of her body. He knew the feel and taste of her, and he hadn't gotten nearly enough.

There was a breeze blowing in off the ocean and he watched as the skirt fluttered, giving him more of a peek at her olive skin that wasn't covered by nylons. He hated nylons. He'd rather she was bare and ready. That train of thought wasn't helping his condition at all. It was a good thing his shirt was untucked. In her presence that was a much smarter route to take.

"He's so gone he isn't even listening to us. Do you think he'll get a stalking order for ogling the witness?" Arden asked.

"I know I don't look at my patients the way he's looking at his protectee," Kian said.

"Yeah, I've saved a few women from fires and never undressed them with my eyes like that," Owen added.

"None of the people you've been around have been as delicious as Angela," Declan finally muttered. "But stop talking about her."

"What's going on between the two of you?" Kian asked. He was always the one to get to the point the quickest.

"Nothing. I'm protecting her," Declan said. There was a lot going on but he didn't think it was any of his siblings' business. Thinking that made him regret how much crap he'd given his siblings when they'd been going through relationship troubles.

He had no doubt it was payback time, and he was going to get it in full force. For one, he was the oldest and it was their pleasure to flick him crap, and for two, he'd always thought he was more advanced than them in being smart about not getting sucked into anything messy.

It didn't get any messier than it was right now.

However, he was a grown adult who'd been around the block a time or two and could control himself. He could take this nice and slow. That didn't mean he wasn't going to burn up the sheets while they were doing just that.

Hell, he was confused. He didn't know what to think or say. And he didn't want to tell his siblings that.

"Well, if you don't make a claim soon, it might not be an issue. There are a few single guys hanging around tonight at this party, and they are definitely noticing Angela's smoking hot legs. She gets hit on regularly at the diner as well. I don't know how she's still single," Owen said. He loved poking his brother the most.

"Does your wife know how you like to check out other women?" Declan asked.

Owen laughed. "I have zero desire to check other women out when I'm married to the most amazing woman on the planet. She gave me a second chance when I'd been an utter fool and I won't ever blow it with her again."

"You sure notice a lot about Angela," Declan growled.

Owen couldn't seem to stop laughing. "I notice a lot around me, and I hear even more from my very beautiful wife."

"Yeah, in case you haven't noticed our wives *really* like to talk," Arden said. "But I'm glad they're all so close. I can't imagine what it would be like to be one of those families where no one gets along."

"That wouldn't happen because we'd never be attracted to women who were like that," Kian pointed out.

"Well, to be honest, I've been attracted to some pretty bitchy women before," Arden said. "But the romance died off really quick . . . as soon as they started speaking."

"I remember when I was younger, I was attracted to a woman whether I liked her personality or not. The older I've gotten; personality determines how a woman looks."

"Now you do sound like an old man," Owen said.

"Or a mature one, unlike you," Declan told him.

"Growing up too soon sucks," Owen replied. "That's why I fight fires. I want to stay young forever."

"You're doing a damn fine job of it," Kian said. "Some of us have professional careers."

"You play with knives all day. You're no more mature than the rest of us," Arden said.

"Maybe you became a teacher so you could pretend to be a teenager forever," Declan told him.

Arden laughed. "No, if anything, hanging around teenage girls and boys all day makes me more grateful than ever that I've evolved. I don't know how our parents survived our childhood."

That got a grin out of all of them. "Because we're the world's greatest kids. I think we should give them a plaque that says so," Owen said.

"You *would* give them something that cheesy. I can't imagine what this conversation sounds like to an outsider," Declan told them.

"They'd probably assume we've had too much to drink," Arden said with a shrug. "Which happens on occasion."

"We've gotten off track here," Owen said. "Back to Angela and her singlehood. Are you going to stake your claim?"

His three brothers stood there and waited while he thought about his reply. He could make another joke, or he could be honest with them. He wasn't sure which would be better.

"She's mine," he said simply.

His brothers didn't mock him after that. They understood it wasn't easy for him to utter those words.

"Okay then. I can't wait for the wedding," Kian said with a smile. He might be joking, but Declan wondered if his brother was right. You didn't play with a woman like Angela. You didn't carry on a casual affair with her.

She had a son and she'd been through too much tragedy already in her life. Did that mean he was ready to commit? He never had before. He'd dated, of course. He was far from a monk. But the longest relationship he'd ever had lasted about a month, and he'd only seen the woman a few times during that time. He didn't do well with relationships. He didn't do well with compromise.

Declan was used to getting his way. And he knew compromise was the biggest word in any relationship. So, he was now claiming Angela. What in the hell did it mean?

Chapter Twenty-Three

"My friend, you have always thrown a great party," Lucian Forbes said to Joseph as the two of them sat back, away from the rest of the partygoers so they were able to look out at the crowd and see all of their family members.

"You as well. We haven't talked much the last few months. I don't like that," Joseph said. Then he looked around and Lucian laughed. Joseph scowled at him.

"I saw Katherine go in the house about ten minutes ago with my wife and a few other women. You might have ten more minutes to sneak a few puffs in," Lucian said.

"It's not sneaking," Joseph thundered. Several heads turned their way and Joseph quieted his voice. "I can have a cigar anytime I like. I just prefer to cut back on them."

But even as he said this he pulled one out of his pocked and inhaled its sweet scent. Lucian pulled one out too. There was nothing like a nice glass of brandy and a sweet cigar on a beautiful night filled with family.

"My wife gets on me when I have too many, too, so I know exactly how it is," Lucian said.

"What are you two yammering on about?" George asked as he came up and sat down. Joseph pulled out another cigar and handed it over.

"We're just talking about how blessed we are," Joseph told his brother as he leaned back. George laughed.

"I'm sure you are. But who are we matchmaking? That's the heart of the matter," George said. "I've been restless lately. I need a new project."

"Declan has been taking his sweet time with Angela, but we think it's finally moving forward," Lucian said. "She's been in town for three years now and the looks these two send each other are enough to melt paint, but neither have made a move no matter how many times they get thrown together. Now, with all this criminal activity, she's moved in with him. She and that beautiful son of hers."

"Nothing like the added bonus of an instant grandkid," Joseph said. He truly meant that. Family didn't have to be blood.

"You're smoking without me?" Richard asked as he joined his brothers and Lucian.

"We knew you'd be along," Joseph said. Joseph, George, and Richard were triplets, and though Richard had been taken at birth, you'd never know they grew up without him. The three of them were so well matched in personality that when they got together the world had better watch out.

Not only were the brothers as close as could be, but they were loyal to their friends as well. Once a friend, it was for a lifetime.

"I heard that last bit," Richard said. "So, Declan and Angela are finally making sparks happen?"

"Finally!" Lucian said. "I was beginning to lose hope. I knew they were made for one another. I just wasn't sure my son was bright enough to realize it."

"Yeah, we've all been there," George said. "There were times I wasn't sure I even liked my kids. I always loved them, but I didn't always like them."

"My kids were always perfect," Joseph said, puffing out his chest and taking a big puff from his cigar. "I guess not everyone is as lucky as I am though."

Richard, George, and Lucian all laughed at him.

Joseph glared as he took another puff. Then he smiled. "Okay, I might've wanted to hit them over the head once or twice. But look at all of them now," he said as he held out his arm so they could see their ever-expanding family out on the lawn.

There was laughter and love and true joy. There wasn't anything this family wouldn't do for one another. He was a very blessed man.

"They just needed some help along the way. There's nothing wrong with parenting, even after they are technically adults," George said. "We all get lost at times and need some guidance from Dad."

"I couldn't agree more," Lucian said. "You've done very well, and I appreciate the help you've given me with my family."

There was nothing Joseph liked more than acknowledgment for a job well done. He might not be able to brag to his kids about all he'd done for them, but he could certainly tell some stories to his brothers and friends.

"Joseph Anderson, what do you think you're doing?"

It was comical how quickly grown men could toss away cigars and try to put innocent masks on their faces. They looked like teenage boys in grandfather bodies. It was a picture-perfect moment.

Katherine Anderson had her hands on her hips as she stared down at her husband with a stern . . . and very affectionate look.

"I was just having a few puffs with the boys," he said. The only person he was ever this subdued with was the love of life. His wife was his entire world, and she would be until the day he died.

"Mmm hmm, a few puffs huh?" she said, not at all fooled.

"It's a party, darling," he pleaded.

Joseph was one of the most powerful men in the world, but he was no more than a purring kitten in his wife's presence.

"Which is why I let you get away with it for about ten minutes. Now that's enough. I want you with me for the next fifty years," she said as she reached out and took his hand, squeezing his fingers.

He still felt chills when she touched him. His love and desire for her would never disappear. From the moment he'd met her he'd known she was the one, and not once had that love faltered.

"You are so beautiful my lovely bride. I want even more years than that," he said, meaning it.

"You're a smooth talker and know exactly how to get out of trouble," she said.

"It's only smooth talking if the words aren't meant," he said. "Every word I say to you is from the heart. You are beautiful, kind, and still take my breath away. Not a single day goes by that I'm not grateful to have you waking up beside me each morning."

Her eyes shimmered with tears. "I'm not as eloquent as you, but of course I feel the same. Come dance with me."

She didn't need to ask twice. He could dance with her the entire night and still not have enough of holding her. They reached the dance floor and she melted against him. He was always careful with her. Katherine was petite and he was large. He never wanted to forget how easily he could hurt her.

He cupped her cheek and looked into her vibrant eyes. "You truly are the most beautiful woman here, darling," he whispered. Only with this woman did he mute his booming voice.

"You make me feel like I am," she told him.

She leaned her head against his chest, and Joseph looked out at the crowd of loved ones before looking up at the sky.

"Thank you," he mouthed. He was blessed and he thanked God every day for all he'd been given.

Chapter Twenty-Four

A week went by with no more answers than Declan had in the beginning. The gang was lying low. He was worried because these guys weren't going to stop. His property was secure. He had zero doubts of that. But the town wasn't, and he couldn't keep Angela cooped up forever. She'd go crazy, and it wasn't her fault there were bad people in the world.

But what if they got to her? His town was about the safest place for a person. The officials were aware of what was going on and would have their eyes out, but that didn't mean someone wouldn't be able to snag her. It could happen in an instant.

After the party at Joseph Anderson's house, she'd pulled back from him. Not completely, but she wasn't sleeping in his bed. And he didn't want her to feel she had to. He wasn't sure what would be taking advantage of the situation and what would be him showing an interest in her.

If they weren't living in the same house, it would be an entirely different matter. But he was protecting her, so there was a line he didn't want to cross. He wanted her to want to be with him, not feel obligated.

If he could read her that would be an entirely different matter, but he couldn't seem to. The way she looked and responded to him told him she felt something. But the way she held back made him unsure. He'd never dealt with a situation like this before. He'd never questioned whether a woman wanted to be with him. It was all new territory.

He didn't like it one little bit.

"Sit," he said when his brother's dog Max stood looking at him as if he was restless. He was dog sitting and had to admit Max was the smartest animal he'd ever been around.

He was pretty dang fond of the animal. Max had saved his sister-in-law Keera's life. The dog was a true hero with a unique personality. His brother would argue with the mutt, and Declan wouldn't admit it out loud, but man, it seemed like the German Sheppard could answer back and actually win. He didn't mind dog sitting at all.

As soon as Declan told the dog to sit, he seemed to give a bit of an eye roll, but he obeyed. He liked surveying rooms, so Declan could see why he'd been a valuable asset to the police force he'd served most of his life.

"Retirement must be good," Declan said, and Max seemed to smile at him. "Weird dog," he muttered. Max let out a breath of air almost like a mocking sigh. He really was a strange animal.

Declan walked in the back door of the hospital where Kian worked, glad Max was a service animal. He could take him anywhere. Angela had an appointment at the hospital to speak with a counselor. Maybe it would give them more leads. He could only hope.

"Hey, Declan," a nurse called out. "And hello, Max. You look mighty fine today." Max practically purred as she ruffed him behind the ears.

"Yeah, he knows how good he looks," Declan told her. She laughed before moving down the hallway.

He moved into the lounge where Kian was pouring a fresh cup of coffee. His brother turned and smiled.

"How's my favorite dog?" he asked as he moved over to them and gave Max a scratch.

"He's fine. So am I by the way," Declan said.

Kian laughed. With as much darkness as his brother had to deal with, Declan had a lot of respect for how positive he remained. From the time Kian had been born he'd always chosen to look on the bright side. Like everyone else, he had his moments, but he was truly a good man.

"What brings you in today?" Kian asked.

"Angela has an appointment, and I like keeping her nearby," Declan said.

"Have you discovered any more information on the case?" Kian asked. He'd been working long shifts and they hadn't had a chance to talk for the past week.

"We're stone cold right now. But I'm not worried. I'm waiting for what's next. I'm sure there'll be a showdown."

"And how are things going with Angela?"

Declan could pretend he had no idea what his brother was talking about, but he didn't see a point in it.

"I honestly have no idea what's happening. She's friendly, thanks me for the help at least a dozen times a day and makes some amazing food. But she's keeping her distance. I don't want her to feel obligated to me."

"I don't think she does. I think she's simply afraid," Kian said.

"Afraid of the gang?" Declan questioned.

"Well, there's no doubt she's afraid of that. But that's not what I'm talking about. I think she's afraid of what she's feeling. I know Roxie went through that. And in your case with Angela, she'd dependent on you as well, so that has to throw the entire dynamic off."

"I hadn't really thought about it that way," he said, grateful for his brother's insight.

"Maybe try talking to her about it. We never get anywhere with innuendos and trying to guess what someone is thinking or feeling. She might have no idea what's happening inside her."

"I can understand that; I'm not really sure what I'm feeling either."

"Well, talk to her and maybe the two of you can figure it out," Kian said.

"Is that professional medical advice?" Declan asked.

"Yep. And I won't even charge you for it," Kian said. "But I do have to get back to work. 'Tis the season for boating accidents," he added as he stood.

They walked from the room together and parted ways at the end of the hall. Declan went to the mental health clinic and found Angela sitting in the waiting area.

"There you are," she said with a smile.

Declan's stomach tightened at her words. He wished she was saying them to him and not to the dog. But Max knew who she was talking about. He gracefully walked to her and sat. She immediately reached out and started petting him.

"I wish he was yours and lived at the house," she said. "He's such a good boy."

"My brother absolutely didn't want him when I took him to his house to help with the case. But the two of them bonded. When Max saved Keera, my brother worshiped him. He's not going anywhere now. My brother loves him and so does Keera. She's going to be a mess when his time comes."

"Don't even talk about that. It absolutely breaks my heart that animals have such short lives. I don't understand it."

"Yeah, it sucks. But as long as we give them as good a life as possible while they're with us, we don't need to have regrets. I think animal abusers should have the same consequences as people abusers. If the laws were harsher maybe animals wouldn't suffer so much."

"I couldn't agree with you more. People who are cruel to animals, or to the young or old, are the biggest monsters there are."

"Yeah, I've never understood it."

She continued petting Max, who seemed to be very aware she needed comforted right then.

"Are you ready for this?" he asked.

The look she gave him was full of apprehension. He wished he could take some of her fear away.

"Not really. But I'm not sleeping well, and I know if I can help in any way, it'll make it better. I can't be a good mother when I'm scared and worried all the time," she said.

"I'm sorry. You have to let me know if there's anything I can do to make it better," he said. "I'm not just saying the words. I really mean them." She gave him a grateful smile before looking back down at Max. "Take him in with you. I think it'll help you feel calm."

"Really? They'll let me do that?" she asked. Some of the anxiety in her eyes lifted, and he was glad he'd thought of it at the last minute.

"Of course, they will. Max is a working dog, even if he's retired. He can go anywhere he likes."

Max looked up at him, seeming to say: of course I can. Declan really wished dogs could talk. He was sure the conversation would be fascinating.

"I want this all over with, Declan. I want to go back to a normal, even boring, life."

He smiled at her. "I don't think life is ever boring if you live the life you love," he told her.

"That's a good way to look at things. But sometimes a little boredom is good for the soul."

"It certainly can help us slow down when we need to," he agreed.

"Angela, we're ready for you," a woman called.

"Will you come in too?" she asked.

Declan was surprised. "Are you sure?"

"You need to know anything I talk about, so it would be better to get it firsthand," she said.

"Okay. Let's do this."

He wanted to take her hand as they walked through the doors, but he knew she needed to do this alone. He was just there to watch and be there if she needed him. He felt helpless again. He was determined to do something to change that because it was a feeling he couldn't stand. He wasn't a sidelines kind of man. He liked to be at the front where he could help the most.

Change was coming. He just prayed it was the good kind.

Chapter Twenty-Five

Angela was nervous as she sat across from the counselor. The lights were dim and soothing instrumentals were playing low in the background. This office was meant to relax its patients. Declan chose a chair in the corner of the room, so he was out of the way. She appreciated that. She knew he needed to hear what she had to say, but she didn't want to feel like she was being interrogated. She was beginning to think that's why it had been so hard for her to recall things before.

"You're safe here," the counselor said. "My name is Ava, and I've worked with many people. If you can't recall everything, don't worry about it. Let's just talk and see what we come up with."

The woman had a smooth voice that was very effective for calming her nerves. Angela did relax a little. It also helped that she had Max at her side, curled up on the couch with his head in her lap. She continued petting him while Ava talked.

"Have you spoken with a counselor before?" Ava asked.

"No. I spoke with the police, but never a counselor."

"Okay, well we're not going to do anything to make you too uncomfortable. It might be difficult recalling a traumatic past event, but we're going to do it as gently as we possibly can. I want you to sit back and close your eyes. It's much easier if you're fully relaxed."

"Are you going to hypnotize me?" Angela asked.

"No, but we want you completely relaxed so you can think about the night you were attacked."

"I try to avoid it," Angela said.

"I know. I also know you had a head injury. But everything is still there. We just need to try to find it. If we can't, we can either try again or try something else entirely. There's absolutely no pressure," Ava assured her.

She closed her eyes as she continued rubbing Max's head. She felt a bit sleepy. Relaxing was easing her anxiety.

"Let's talk about a normal Saturday night for you a few years ago," Ava said. "Tell me about a typical evening."

Ava had avoided going into the past so much she hadn't thought of that in a long time. But she smiled a little as she did, not focusing on the bad, but the good instead.

"I loved the weekends. I still do. Normally if the weather was good, I'd take my son to a park or out fishing. We'd do something outdoors. If the weather was bad, we'd go to a movie and skating or an indoor gym."

"Did you ever go out with friends?"

"Not too often."

"How about four years ago, the night you were attacked?" Ava asked.

Everything in Angela wanted to block this from happening, but she continued petting Max and pushed that thought away.

"Timothy was having a sleepover, and I decided to have a couple drinks on my own. I hadn't been to a bar in forever, but the apartment we shared was beginning to feel like the walls were closing in on me, so I walked two blocks down the road to a local pub. I'd been there a couple of times and it had always felt safe. People usually left me alone."

"What did you have to drink?" she asked.

"I was sipping on a lemon drop. I didn't have a lot of extra money, so I gave myself a two-drink limit. I ordered some French fries and waited for them."

"Where were you sitting?"

"I was at the bar. I didn't want to take up a whole table when it was just me. And I liked talking with the bartender. She was a young gal in her twenties going to college. She loved the tips she made working weekends. I was thinking it might be a good job for me, but I didn't want Timothy to have babysitters all the time."

"So you were talking to the bartender. Were there many people in there?" Ava asked.

"No. It was still pretty early. There were a few guys at a table laughing about something and a couple sitting a few stools down from me. But the bartender had a lot of time to chat."

"Do you remember her name?"

Angela concentrated. "Wendy!" she said after a moment. When she told me her name, I'd thought a frosty sounded good." She smiled at the memory. "I didn't say that though, because I'm sure she'd heard it before, and it was a silly thought."

"So, Wendy was talking to you a lot?" Ava asked, getting her back on track.

"Yes. She had a daughter and lived with her parents. We were both single moms so that gave us an instant connection."

"That's nice. How long were you there?"

"I ended up staying longer. Wendy gave me a free drink and we kept chatting. Then the bar started getting more and more people and she got busier. I thought about leaving, but I didn't have anything else going on that night."

"Did anyone sit by you?" Ava asked.

Angela shifted in her seat and Max snuggled a bit closer. It really helped.

"Yes," she said after a few moments. A woman sat down beside me. She wasn't too nice. She was complaining about the slow service, and I remember thinking I didn't want Wendy to overhear. She was working hard. So, I started talking to the lady.

"My new drink came, and the woman started talking to me about her day, her job, and her boyfriend. I couldn't keep up with her. My head was hurting all of a sudden and my stomach started turning. I didn't often drink, but I'd only had two and a half drinks over a two-hour period, so it didn't make sense to me. I hadn't eaten anything all day except those French fries, but I still shouldn't have felt that bad," she said.

"What happened next?" Ava asked.

It was all coming back to Angela with a vengeance and she wanted to hide, but she couldn't do that. She had to get through this. She held on to Max and hoped she didn't get sick as she described the most horrific moment of her life.

"The woman told me I didn't look good and offered to help me to the bathroom," Angela told her.

"Did you take her help?"

"Yes. I was so confused, and it's still blurry now, but I remember holding on to her arm as we walked. I couldn't see clearly. I looked at the ground as we walked. The woman said something about there being a line, and then she took me outside to a dark alley behind the bar."

"Were you concerned at this point?" Ava asked.

"No, I just wanted to throw up. My stomach was really hurting. I bent over and threw up for what seemed like forever. My head was pounding, and my stomach was on fire."

"Was the woman still with you?" Ava asked.

"I can't remember her being there anymore," Angela said. "But then I remember voices, so many voices. I couldn't lock onto any of them. I slid down the wall I was leaning against and tried to look around. There were people, but they were blurry."

"What were they saying to you?" Ava asked.

Angela tried to recall their words. "I don't know. But I remember hearing my father's name. I don't know if that's real or not. My dad was a drug dealer. He was a bad man."

"You heard his name?" Ava asked.

"Yes, I think I did." She went quiet for several moments. "And then all I felt was pain."

Tears rolled down her cheeks as she remembered the searing pain. Her stomach had hurt before, but it was nothing compared to how much it had hurt in the next moments. She kept petting Max who seemed to sense how much she needed him. A small whimper escaped him, and she concentrated on soothing the animal. It helped her not feel so much anxiety for herself.

"What happened next?" Ava asked.

"There was shouting, so much shouting . . ." She could practically see that blurry alley right then in her mind. "And then there was shooting pain in my head and the world went dark."

Ava was quiet for a moment as Angela sat there and wept. It was her worst nightmare, and she didn't want to remember it. She wanted it to just go away.

"Do you want to add anything else?" Ava asked.

"I don't think I have anything else," she said as she opened her eyes and looked into the compassionate gaze of the counselor.

"You did very well today, Angela. Very well."

"But I can't describe the people who hurt me."

"No, but you described what they were doing and how they did it. It's the same as other victims. We think it's the same gang. That's very good to know because we know how long it's been happening."

"So, this helped?" Angela said.

"Yes, very much. I'm just sorry it caused you more pain."

"I actually feel better," she said. Max leaned back and looked at her as if to say he was glad. She really loved the dog.

Declan came to her side and reached out a hand.

"You did amazing," he told her.

She took his hand and let him help her stand. She didn't feel like talking anymore though, so she nodded and let him lead her from the room, his hand in hers, with Max on her other side.

This was the way she wanted it for the rest of her life.

Chapter Twenty-Six

Declan walked Angela from the hospital without saying anything. Sitting silently while she spoke had been incredibly difficult. He'd felt her pain, and everything in him wanted to walk over there and pull her into his arms and tell her she didn't have to keep talking. He hated that she had to relive that moment, hated that fear in her voice.

He admired her strength and bravery after all she'd been through. When a person joined the military, they knew what they were signing on for, knew they could be in dangerous situations. But a single mother trying to live her life doesn't.

None of it was right or okay, but what he hated most about criminals was how they victimized people. They not only took whatever it was they were after, but they also stole a person's innocence and their sense of safety. Sometimes the victim was never the same again.

There was no doubt Angela had changed after her attack. He hoped he could give her peace of mind for the future and take some of that fear away. She had so much life left to live, and he didn't want her to have to do it halfway.

Declan had never had a desire to be anyone's knight in shining armor. But he found he wanted to be exactly that for her. Sitting back and watching as she suffered was the exact opposite of what he needed to do.

"We will get this guy and anyone who is still helping him," Declan told her after he couldn't take the silence anymore.

"I know you will," she said. She squeezed his fingers. He hadn't meant to hold her hand as they walked, but he was unable to let her go. It felt right.

They reached the parking lot and she stopped before getting in the car door he was holding open. She still hadn't let go of his hand and was still holding onto the dog. Maybe he and the dog were a cocoon that was keeping her feeling safe. He'd give her whatever she wanted.

"I'm glad Max was with me. That really helped. Do you think your brother will notice if we don't give him back?" she asked with the semblance of a smile.

"He might notice," Declan said. He wished he could give her the dog. Max might not be available, but he could find her one. He wanted to tell her so, but he wasn't sure what was in the future, and a dog was a long-term commitment.

"I can't believe how much stuff I'd blocked out," she said.

Declan didn't like standing out in the open like they were. There were too many potential threats around them. But she felt safe for now, and he wasn't going to rush her.

"Our minds are a powerful thing. When we can't take anymore, a button seems to flip to keep us protected. It's the same with the body. When we have a life-threatening injury our pain receptors will stop working. If you've been shot or bombed and you stop feeling the pain, you should worry. Pain might not feel like it, but it is our friend. It lets us know we're still alive and that we need to do something to make it stop."

"I've never looked at it like that, but it makes a lot of sense," she said.

"Everything in life happens for a reason. Even if that reason is senseless. You shouldn't have been attacked and you shouldn't have been shot at a week ago, but everything that has happened has made you stronger and more capable. I'm very impressed with the woman you are."

Tears sprung in her eyes. "I don't feel strong. I feel like I should've been more aware. I knew my drink had been drugged. I read the report. But I should've known better than to take my eyes off my drink in a public place. And then to follow a stranger was foolish when I was so sick. I just didn't think."

"Hey, don't do that," he said as he reached up and cupped her cheek. "You were sitting at a bar where you felt comfortable, having a drink. The person who did that to you works for a gang and has been trained on exactly how to distract her victims and how to do it with no one paying attention. I'm sure there was a diversion somewhere else in the bar to make sure no one saw her put the powder in your glass. That plan has been done many times before and we will stop it."

"I was targeted because of my father. I don't understand if he was the one who sent me to this town. I would've thought he'd send me away from it all before he died if he cared."

"I think he cared as much as he was capable. And I think you were sent here because whoever they were knew the Forbes family would help you."

She smiled, this time a real smile. "Are you talking about yourself in the first person?" she asked with a raise of her brow.

He gave her a crooked grin. "I wasn't referring to myself. I was talking about my entire family. Anyone who paid attention would've been well aware that we like to help those who need it the most."

"You really do that, which is fantastic. I can't imagine what this would be like without you. I'd like to think my dad did a good thing before he left this world. Maybe that helped in his final judgment."

"I like to believe we don't make that final judgment. That's difficult for me to say when I see the kind of evil that's out there. But we don't have all the answers. If there is this higher being, then He will know. I can't always sit back and hope someone else is doing the judging, but I can try to be a better person when I'm not furious."

"That's more than most people can say, so you aren't doing too badly," she said.

"I want to do so much more."

"We need people like you in the world so the rest of us can sleep soundly at night. I wish I could be a hero, but I'm okay with being a normal person too."

"You are a hero to me," he told her. "And to your son. Being a hero to one or two people is so much more rewarding than pleasing the masses, in my humble opinion."

That made her laugh, and he felt as if he'd won a gold medal. "I don't think there's anything humble about you," she said. She finally allowed him to help her into the SUV. He put Max in the back and jogged around to his side.

"Humble might not have been the best word choice," he agreed.

And just like that he watched her mood lighten. He loved seeing her more carefree and smiling. Her pain was always on the edge of the darkness that tried creeping up on her. But time really did know how to heal all wounds. Each day that passed brought her a little more peace.

He'd have to work on getting rid of all her demons. He wanted to be her hero. He didn't think he'd make a very good one, but he'd do all he could to prove himself worthy.

Maybe they did need to have that heart to heart. He wanted and needed her back in his arms again . . . sooner rather than later.

Chapter Twenty-Seven

Declan gazed out into the still sky, every sense on high alert. Usually the blackness of night calmed him, but tonight was different. He felt the walls closing in and knew it was only a matter of time before things came to a head. Sighing, he closed his eyes.

Declan sensed, before he felt, the cool tip of the rifle against his head. Surprise registered, and his thoughts raced over the last few minutes as he examined each second to see what he'd missed. How in the hell had someone managed to sneak up on him out here on his land? Outwardly he remained cool and calm, thankful for his years of training.

Focusing on the pressure and pitch of the gun barrel, Declan calculated the height of the man holding the rifle and the distance between them. Slowing his breathing, he began to plan an attack.

"Slowly open your eyes. Do not move or make a sound," a low, menacing voice whispered.

Relief washed over Declan. He'd know that voice anywhere. It had been a few years, but you never forgot your childhood best friend. Opening his eyes, he looked up into the dark gaze of Harrison Laurent. At six-foot-four, the former SEAL brought terror to his enemies, but to his friends and family he was as gentle as a teddy bear and loved with a fierce passion.

Grown men had been known to shake with fear in Harrison's presence, which made dating hard for his little sister, Kate. Declan had held a brief crush on Kate in their younger years, but that had quickly changed to a sisterly love.

If Harrison was there, then the third member of their childhood gang, Kaleb Stone, wasn't too far behind. Or maybe not. Kaleb had disappeared a few years ago, immediately after his wife's funeral.

Declan winced inwardly as he remembered the last time he'd seen his two friends. Kaleb's wife, Amy, had been kidnapped by insurgents while Kaleb was away on a mission. Her torture and death had sent shockwaves around the world.

Kaleb and Harrison still bore the physical and emotional scars of the failed rescue.

Completely broken, Kaleb had walked out of Amy's wake and hadn't been seen since. Harrison had retreated to a cabin in the snowy mountains of Austria but still visited his family's island occasionally and would go to various charity events run by the same family.

After making billions founding Telco Company, the biggest telecommunication company in the world, and being hounded by the paparazzi, the Laurent family bought an island where they could escape the glaring public eye. Over the years The Isle of Laure had evolved into a private oasis, catering to the desires of the world's elite.

It was so exclusive it wasn't found on any public map. Rumors swirled that there was a secret wing of the hotel. Declan could only guess what happened behind those doors.

Forcing his mind back to the present, Declan stood and embraced his old friend. How in the world did they know where to find him? Not even his nosy brothers and their nosier wives, or the queen of nosy herself, his sister Dakota, knew where he was in this spot on his land. His brothers had probably reached out to their brother-in-law Ace, who tracked down Harrison and Kaleb through his military contacts. Harrison had always been able to find the unfindable.

"What are you doing here?" he asked.

"The Big K and I heard you might be in trouble and came to see if you needed backup," Harrison said. With that, Kaleb stepped forward and the three men looked at each other, their childhood bond unbreakable even as grown men who'd witnessed unspeakable horrors.

Declan felt his steely heart crack as he looked from Kaleb's ice blue eyes to his cheek with the scarred reminder of his past. With sun-bleached blond hair and permanently furrowed brows, Kaleb was the shortest of the three but made up for it with his startlingly broad shoulders and steely gaze that could make the toughest men cower.

"Suck it up, princess," whispered Kaleb gruffly, using the phrase he'd used a thousand times when Declan would fall and scrape his knees playing army in the forest behind the Forbes estate. "No time for tears, it's too dangerous to lose focus now. Bringing down a drug cartel? Are you crazy?"

"No crazier than you two," Declan chuckled. How strange it felt to smile. Declan focused on the two men, becoming serious again. They didn't have much time before the drug ring scouts did their regular sweep and found them. Then they'd all be dead and no closer to cracking the drug ring for good.

"I have to," he said, squaring his shoulders. Harrison and Kaleb gazed at him with understanding. They'd all faced dangerous situations where making it out alive seemed impossible. Declan saw Kaleb give Harrison an almost imperceptible nod.

"Do you remember the combination code to our tree house?" Harrison asked.

"Of course," replied Declan. "You two made sure those numbers were forever burned in my brain."

"Call that number anytime from *any* phone, pager, radio, computer, or anything with a signal, from anywhere in the world, and we'll trace the signal and come get you out. Only the three of us know of its existence, and we'd like to keep it that way."

Declan was dumfounded at the gift his friends had given him. Not even the FBI had access to technology like this. Owning Telco Company and having one of your brothers as the most sought-after tech whiz in the world certainly had its perks.

"We've got your back," Kaleb said, gripping Declan's shoulder tightly. Declan didn't trust anyone but his family. However, at that moment he felt his small circle of trust grow to include his old friends.

"We also hear there might be a wedding," Harrison said as he sat.

"How in the world are you getting that information? We haven't talked in forever."

"You should know we are never far away," Kaleb said. "Even when we aren't physically here. I went off the deep end for a while, but that wouldn't have been what my wife would want. They won't win by destroying me."

"You already destroyed them," Declan pointed out.

"There's thousands more where they came from. I want them all," Kaleb said with a deadly resolve in his voice.

"I have no doubt you'll get them."

"Are you ready to leave the FBI yet? We have a project in the works," Harrison told him.

"What project?" Declan asked.

"When you're ready to leave, tell us, and we'll let you know."

Declan smiled. "I'm intrigued."

"Then don't take too long," Harrison said.

"Let me finish this case, then we can talk."

They nodded. The three men sat for a couple more hours catching up on the past two years. Then his two friends disappeared as quietly as they'd come.

Chapter Twenty-Eight

Angela had finally talked Declan into letting her out of the house on her own. She was sure he'd find a way to have her followed, but she wasn't going to worry about that. Part of her liked his overprotectiveness because she didn't have to constantly look over her shoulder. It was a very good feeling.

All she wanted was a normal day. She'd been cooking a lot, which she loved to do, and wanted to go buy her own groceries. Timothy was safe with Kian and Roxie, having another play day with their kids, and she wanted to have a few hours of alone time. She was grateful to Declan's family for that summer. She was sure Timothy would've gone stir-crazy locked away by himself with only his mother. Boys needed to play and laugh with other kids.

She pulled up to the store and stepped out of her beautiful SUV. She knew she couldn't keep it, but she wasn't going to argue with Declan about driving it for now. This was the first time she'd driven anywhere since they'd gotten back, and man, was it going to be difficult to walk away from such an amazing car. Part of her wanted to go on a nice long drive and just enjoy herself.

She was sure she'd give Declan a royal heart attack if she did that. The thought was very appealing though.

Instead she grabbed a cart from outside and walked in the store, heading straight for the produce aisle. She liked to use as many fresh ingredients as she could.

She had her cart half full when she saw Dr. Evans mumbling to himself over by the avocados. She stared for a little while and couldn't help but laugh at how confused he looked.

He finally glanced up and saw her. He must've known exactly what she was thinking, because he gave her a sheepish smile and shrugged. She decided to have mercy on the man and walked over to him.

"Troubles?" she asked.

"How in the world do people pick out fresh produce?" he asked.

"It's not that hard. Each fresh fruit and vegetable have a different consistency. Some are hard and some are soft. Some you can tell by smell and some by texture."

"Again, how are people supposed to do it? I just want to make fajitas," he said.

"Are you watching the home cooking network?" she asked.

"Yes!" he exclaimed. "I was sick last week and it was on, so I got sucked in. Paula Dean made some impressive dishes. I decided it didn't look hard to do and sounded a lot tastier than a convenience store hot dog, so here I am."

"Yep, many chefs for a day have begun that way," she said. "Do you need a little help?"

"Oh, heck yes," he said. "I can cut and fry if I can just get the right stuff." He was practically bowing in appreciation. Angela laughed.

"I'm sure any of the single ladies in town would love to help you with that part too," she told him.

"Hmm, I didn't think of that." He got a mischievous look in his beautiful brown eyes. "Wanna come help me cook?"

Her cheeks instantly flamed. She couldn't believe she'd missed seeing that coming. She looked at the avocados like they would jump out and save her.

"I . . . uh . . . well, I'm busy tonight," she finally said. She was *technically* single, but she still felt as if she were doing something wrong.

Doc Evans laughed. She wasn't even sure if Evans was his last name or he was Evan and people added the s to it. She wasn't going to ask now. Everyone just called him Doc Evans.

"I'm giving you a hard time, Angela. Everyone in town knows you're taken. It's a tragedy. I waited too long," he said as she handed him the bag with avocados in it. She hadn't taught him how to pick the right ones. She was all flustered now.

"I'm not taken, but I'm not looking to date," she said.

"Hmm," he murmured with that big grin in place while they moved over to the peppers.

"What is that supposed to mean?" she asked, hands on hips as he picked up red, yellow, and orange peppers. He didn't seem to need help with those, but it was hard to get a bad pepper.

"I like colors in my fajitas," he told her.

"I'm waiting, and I'm not easily distracted," she said.

He laughed. "It's so much more fun shopping with you than all by myself." He bagged his peppers then faced her again. "Fine. If you aren't taken, you might want to talk to Declan, because I think he's pretty much staked his claim."

"I'm not property to be claimed," she said. But even though she was saying it she also felt a warm glow flow through her. She liked the idea of being Declan's woman.

"He hasn't said anything like that, but it's more than clear how he feels about you."

They moved out of the produce section, and he tagged along with her, grabbing what he needed while she did her own shopping. She'd never gone shopping with a man before. It was rather strange but fun too.

"What has he said about me?" she asked in the meat department.

Evans laughed. "Guys don't have to say a whole lot for us to know what they're talking about. We also don't tell on them when they do say something," he said.

"Well, I feel perfectly chastised," she said.

"You shouldn't. I'm having a great time shopping. I never thought that would happen. I *really* appreciate you helping me. Plus, I get the added bonus of Declan being mighty jealous just as soon as he hears about it."

"What in the world are you talking about? Who is going to care about us shopping together?"

"No one will care, but they all love to gossip in a small town. Do you want to give them something to gossip about by laying a nice big kiss on me in the dairy section?"

She couldn't help herself; she began laughing. It took a full minute for her to stop.

"I can't believe you aren't snatched up. You are quite the man, Doc," she said.

"You can't lasso a true cowboy," he said, tipping an imaginary hat. "But when the time is right, I might just lasso my own little filly."

"I'm going to pretend you didn't just say that. It was far too cheesy," she said.

They placed the last of their items in the cart and moved to the registers.

"You're breaking my heart here. I'm giving you all my best lines," he said.

"Hi Doc, hi Angela," the young clerk said as she eyed them both. "Do you want this bagged together?"

Angela nearly blushed again. Evans was right, the entire town might end up talking about their little shopping trip.

"No, you can bag mine for me, and his for him," she said with a smile. She wanted to add that they'd just run into each other in the store, but she wasn't going to resort to that. She shouldn't have to explain herself.

"Okay," the girl who wasn't even twenty said, as she chatted about school with Evans. He really was a people person. She figured he could get the Buckingham Palace guards to speak in a matter of seconds. You just couldn't resist talking to the man.

They moved out to her car and Evans insisted on helping her load her groceries. They finished up and she looked around. She didn't want to head back home yet.

She pushed her cart to the return station, then stopped at his car to help him. He was finished by the time she got there.

"What are you up to the rest of the day? Where's Timothy?" Evans asked.

"Timothy is having a sleepover at Kian's house. I think I'm going to get a coffee and sit in the park." A shudder ran through her at the thought. But she wasn't going to go down any trails. She was staying right up front in view of the entire town.

"That sounds like an excellent idea. We already have people talking, so let's make it look like we're now on a date," he said with a wink as he held out an arm.

Angela couldn't help herself. She was really having fun. "You're going to get me into trouble, aren't you?" she asked as she wrapped her hand through his arm.

"Nah, but I might get my own ass kicked. I'm expecting Declan to drop down from the sky at any minute now in full Marine gear."

"I think you're overestimating what Declan thinks of me," she said. "And he hasn't been a Marine in a long time."

"Nah, there's a code among guys. We don't hit on our friend's woman, even if it isn't quite official. You are definitely *his* woman. However, we can tease the crap out of them if we want. And since I'm one of the few holdouts among my friends, I get to give all of them a hell of a time, especially since I'm so damn suave and amazing."

"You really are amazing," she said.

"After you, my lady," he told her as he let go of her arm and opened the coffee shop door.

"Why thank you, kind sir," she said as she batted her eyelashes.

"What are you two kids doing here?" They both turned to find Joseph Anderson at the counter.

"We're just enjoying a beautiful day," Evans said. Joseph looked at each of them with a bit of suspicion.

"And where is Timothy . . . and Declan?" he asked.

"Timothy is at a Kian's house for a play day," Angela said, deciding to ignore the second part of his question.

Evans was in too playful of a mood to do the same though.

"Not sure where Declan is, but you know what they say?" He put his arm around her back and she had to fight back a giggle. "When the dog's away, the cat's got to play."

Joseph's gaze narrowed a bit. "I don't think you got the saying right," he said. "But I have to run. My good friend Sherman Armstrong is waiting for me. We have a new project in a town close to here."

"Yes, the Veterans Center. I'm very impressed," Evans said.

"I did hear about that. It's truly amazing," Angela added.

"Yes, I'm very proud of my nephews. They're doing a mighty fine job."

"I heard about the addition to your family. That's fantastic," Evans told him. "I'm very happy for you."

"Yeah, I can't get enough family."

They said goodbye and Evans laughed as they stepped to the front counter.

"What's so funny?" Angela asked.

"I guarantee he's on his phone right now. That man is such a meddler, and he's probably already planned your wedding with Declan with Declan's father."

"What?" Angela gasped.

"How can I help you guys?" the kid at the counter asked.

"I'll have a peppermint mocha, extra hot with whip cream, and a blueberry scone," Evans said.

Angela took a second longer to think. "Um, I'll have a caramel macchiato and lemon cake."

Before she could pull out money, Evans slapped a twenty on the counter and led her away.

"You're going to make people talk more and more," she said. "I was having fun with it a bit ago, but now I'm a little concerned. I don't want to be looked at like some town hussy."

His smile fell away. "I'm sorry, Angela. I'm just kidding around. But believe me, no one will think of you that way."

"I *am* a single mother already. They might," she said.

He took her hand. "Not a chance. You've been here for three years, and they know your character. You're a hundred percent good just as you are."

"Thank you," she said. The boy brought their coffees and pastries and they moved outside. There was no sign of

Joseph or his buddy. They found a bench at the park and sat there for thirty minutes chatting.

It was a very enjoyable day. She wondered how the night was going to go. She wondered if Declan really would hear about it. She wasn't sure if she wanted him to or not. Would he be jealous? Did she want him to be? She was so confused she honestly couldn't answer.

She was tense as she made her way home. She didn't know when she'd begun to think of it as home. But home sounded good to her.

Chapter Twenty-Nine

Declan wasn't a jealous man. At least he never had been before he'd met Angela Lincoln. But he could seriously see red as he received reports about the good vet and Angela in town that afternoon. Of course, he hadn't let her go off on her own without having someone keeping an eye on her.

His man hadn't wanted to report what he'd seen either. Declan logically told himself that the vet was doing it on purpose. He knew Evans well and knew that was exactly what it was, but he couldn't help but want to smash the man in his pretty little face.

The vet might be playing, but what if Angela developed feelings for him? Declan couldn't begin to imagine how that would make him feel. She was *his* woman and he was deciding it was about damn time he proved that to her.

She'd gotten home an hour earlier and gone straight up to her room. He'd seethed in his office trying to calm himself. He wanted her to rush to him, throw her arms around him, and for the two of them to stop playing games.

He hadn't wanted to put pressure on her. There was enough of that already. But if he didn't get her into his bed soon, he wasn't going to sleep again. And a tired agent was a dangerous agent. Sleep deprivation was worse than drugs. The body needed down time in order to function.

He decided it was time for the two of them to have a showdown. He marched up the steps to her bedroom door. He debated whether he should knock or not. Too many years of being taught manners gave him that answer.

He tapped on the door. It hadn't been that long since the two of them had made love, but it felt like a year. He was so hungry for her he couldn't think of anything else. Declan was beginning to realize this need might never get sated—not with this one woman. Maybe this was because he loved her. Maybe that's how a marriage lasted through the test of time.

There was no answer on her door, so he tested the knob. It opened. He slowly pushed and called her name. There wasn't an answer. He immediately wanted to panic, but he assured himself there was no possible way someone had come into the house and taken her. There also was no way for her to sneak out. It was too dang secure.

He pushed the door farther open and noticed her bathroom door was shut. He stepped inside and shut the main door then moved to the bathroom.

"Angela?" he called.

"I'll be out in a minute," she said. He couldn't tell by her voice how she was feeling or what she was thinking. He didn't know if she wanted him to wait for her or not. But he wasn't going anywhere. He needed to lay eyes on her.

The door finally opened, and Angela came out. Everything Declan had planned to say flew out the window as his heart thundered in his chest and his breath left him. He stood dumbstruck by her sheer beauty and the intoxicating scent drifting toward him.

She was the most beautiful creature he'd ever seen, hands down. Her face, her body, the total package added up to a woman you didn't let go of. He wasn't a fool, and he knew when the game was over. It was over now, no chance of a rematch. He was hers for the taking.

Her eyes were gleaming though he could see she was nervous. She began moving toward him wearing nothing but a sleek black nightie that left little to the imagination. Her breasts were heaving, and the hem was brushing the very top of her luscious thighs. She was every man's darkest desire and his dream come true.

His every instinct wanted to grab this woman and plunge deep inside her hot, wet body. But he wasn't sure what she was doing, so he waited. It wasn't easy. She'd never done anything like this before, and if seduction was on her mind, he didn't want to stand in her way.

"You take my breath away," he whispered, his voice scratchy and full of need.

"I missed you today so I . . . made a quick stop before heading back. It was sort of last minute, but I . . . I . . . wanted . . . to, well, you know," she said, her cheeks heating up at the end of her stuttered sentence.

"You wanted to what?" he asked. He didn't recognize the sound of his own voice. The moment she walked out the door he'd grown hard. His arousal was throbbing in his suddenly too-tight jeans, and he wanted to strip them away. But this was *her* night and he'd try like hell to let her have it.

"Do you like my nightie?" she asked. She looked at his throat, obviously embarrassed to meet his gaze. He had to clench his fists to keep from pulling her to him.

"Oh, I very much *love* your nightie," he said. "I can't wait to take it off you, but I'm going to enjoy the way it molds perfectly to your body for as long as I can handle it."

"I have very little clothes on, and you're covered. That doesn't seem fair," she said with a flirty tone. She was enjoying herself. He loved that she was.

"I agree. These pants are killing me," he told her, enjoying this seductress she was becoming. He quickly took off his clothes, not leaving a single thing on.

Her eyes widened with pleasure at the sight of his arousal, and when she licked her lips he nearly came like a college freshman. He was done for and barely holding on to his last bit of control.

She ran her pink fingernail down the center of his chest and up again, circling one nipple then the other. He was squeezing his fists so tightly he knew his hands would ache tomorrow. She flattened her palm and pushed him back to the bed. He obeyed and sat. There was only one woman in this world he'd let do this, and she was intoxicating at this moment.

She pushed his legs apart and stepped between them, his arousal standing at attention, reaching for her. But she didn't touch him there. Instead she reached for his face before leaning down and kissing him. He couldn't take it anymore. He wrapped his arms behind her and pulled her tightly to him.

"You're a dream," he said before kissing her with all the hunger he was feeling. She groaned against his mouth. But too soon she pulled back and nibbled on his bottom lip before kissing her way across his clenched jaw. She ran her tongue down the column of his throat, then up to his ear where she circled his lobe.

She kissed her way back to his lips with a kiss so hot they were both panting when she pulled away. She squirmed against him, and he felt her wet heat brush his arousal. He could come right there without ever entering her. She was *that* hot, *that* beautiful, and *that* sexy. She was everything.

"Lie down," she demanded after breaking away from his lips again. He didn't want an inch of space between them, but he listened and pulled himself up on the bed, lying back. She stood over him for a moment, and the view was spectacular.

She climbed on the bed and leaned down, kissing him again before trailing her lips across his chest, sucking on his nipples then running her tongue over his abs. She moved lower but didn't touch his pulsing arousal. He groaned his displeasure.

She crawled back up, a wicked gleam in her eyes, and he wanted to spank her sweet little ass. She began moving down him again and he had enough. He wanted her to be a seductress, but it was his turn to play.

She let out a gasp when he grabbed her and flipped her onto her back, his hands pinning her arms down.

"What are you doing?" she asked in a husky breath.

"It's my turn to play with you for a while."

"That's not how this game goes," she said, but there wasn't much fight in her.

"I changed the rules," he said. "I can't help it when you look the way you do."

Talking stopped when he leaned down and sucked her nipple through the thin layer of silk she was wearing. She moaned her approval and he didn't have to hold her hands any longer.

He kissed and licked and massaged her breasts through the fabric for a while longer, loving how she felt. But soon he didn't want anything between them. He lifted her and carefully stripped the teddy, definitely wanting to see her in it again, and then she was lain out before him, a perfect piece of art.

He lavished attention on both breasts, making her wiggle and cry out as he sucked and nibbled. She begged for more. He'd give her the world. He was so hard he could cut glass at this point, but he wanted this night to last forever.

He danced his tongue across her flat abs and sucked on the inside of her thighs. He spread her legs open and took a moment to gaze at her wet heat. "So beautiful," he muttered, and she sighed in pleasure.

He had to taste her. He could do this forever and it wouldn't be enough. Her taste and smell were heaven. She arched her back as he sucked and licked her swollen flesh.

He wanted to plunge deep inside her, but not before he made her scream.

He swirled his tongue and hummed against her, and after a few more swipes, she cried out his name as her body stiffened and her thighs squeezed his shoulders. She pulsed against his mouth over and over, and he swept his tongue up and down her hot slit until the shaking stopped.

She melted into the bed, her body damp, a sweet smile on her lips. He leaned over her, enjoying how utterly beautiful she was. He didn't move until she opened her eyes, their dark depths glowing with pleasure.

No words were spoken as he slipped inside her, finally coming home. He moved slowly in and out as his head descended and he took her lips again. But no matter how many times he made this woman come, he wanted more. He stroked her, built her pleasure, and felt her release again and again while holding back his own.

Eventually he couldn't hold back any longer. Her name ripped from his lips as he let go, filling her with his heat. She shook around him as they came together in a perfect moment of bliss.

He collapsed on top of her where he lay for a minute before turning and pulling her into the cradle of his arms. They were both sweaty and hot, and he knew he could lie like that for the rest of his life.

"I really, *really* like that nightie," he said with a light chuckle.

She giggled against him.

"I should've bought one sooner."

"No, I think that was perfect timing."

They didn't speak any further, and soon he heard her slow, steady breaths, telling him she was sleeping. He lay there a while longer before getting up and shutting off the lights, then he carefully pulled the covers out and climbed in.

She reached for him in her sleep and he wrapped her close. This would be how they slept from here on out. She was supposed to be at his side. He had no doubt about that, and he wasn't going to argue about it anymore.

She was his. He was hers. That's just the way it needed to be.

Chapter Thirty

Angela's stomach stirred as she slowly woke. She was on fire, and didn't understand why, until she felt Declan's hands on her thighs. The morning sun was glowing in her room. She thought she'd been sated the night before, but at his touch, her body came instantly alive. She was ready for him that quickly.

"Good, you're awake," he said as he leaned down and nibbled on her chest, taking her nipple into his mouth and sucking. She couldn't stop her groan of approval.

"We should chat," she said, but the word ended on another moan.

"Unless it's about the weather, nope," he said before taking her other nipple into his mouth and biting down before sucking.

"But Declan . . ." she tried again. And he smiled as he raised his head. He leaned over her while continuing to run his hands along the curve of her body.

"My turn," he said. He then kissed her so hot she couldn't have spoken if she wanted to. His finger dipped into her heat and she moaned. She wouldn't mind always waking up like this. Who needed coffee when she had Declan?

"We're going to quit pretending there isn't something going on between the two of us. We're going to stop fighting it. You're going to sleep in my bed, and we're going to see what comes next." He said all of this while pumping his fingers in and out of her and circling his thumb around that most sensitive part.

She was coming undone and could barely hear his words. There was no chance she'd be able to argue, and maybe that was his strategy. But she was feeling too dang good to care about that right now.

He swept his thumb across her again and she came . . . hard. He let her catch her breath before making her look him in the eyes.

"Do you understand?" he asked.

"Yes, and no. I don't know what that means," she said, her voice breathy.

"It means you're my girlfriend, I guess." He stopped for a second and gave her a crooked smile. "Though I have never in my life used that term. With what the two of us have together, it just doesn't seem to fit, but we can think about that for a while."

"It's not just me, though, Declan. I don't want Timothy to get hurt in all of this," she said.

"I love Timothy, Angela. My entire family does. There is no chance we're going to hurt him," he told her. He spoke so easily of loving her son it brought tears to her eyes. She loved her son so much, and all she wanted was for the rest of the world to love him as much.

With those words she didn't have any fight left in her. She wanted this man, and she wanted to take what she wanted without thinking of all the what-ifs. She rarely did that, but she thought she could this one time. She needed this man.

"Make love to me," she told him.

She didn't have to ask twice. He climbed over her and slipped inside, and they didn't emerge from the bed for another hour. She didn't want to get up when they did, but Timothy was going to be home at any time, and she wouldn't put it past his brothers to come find them in the bedroom.

With reluctance they both rose and showered together. When they came downstairs, they found Kian sitting in the kitchen with Timothy, who was happy as could be munching on some sugary cereal.

"Good morning, sweetie," she said as she moved over to him and kissed him on the top of the head. "Did you have fun at Kian's?"

"Yes, we stayed up late watching scary movies then slept in past nine," he exclaimed. That was something they never did so she could see why he was excited.

"I figured neither of you would be up too early, not when you had the house to yourselves," Kian said with a wink that turned her cheeks pink.

Angela couldn't look at Declan's brother. She was too mortified, because she wasn't going to be able to deny what they'd been doing, but she certainly wasn't going to confirm it either.

"I'm glad you had fun, sweetie. I can't believe how quickly time is passing. You used to be too little to stay up half the night," she said.

"I'm almost a teenager, Mom," he said before stuffing another bite of cereal in his mouth.

"Well, you have a few more years until that dreaded time," she said. He was only eight. She didn't want him growing up too quickly.

"Did you know Kian and Roxie have a baby?" he asked.

"Yes, I do know that," she said. "A very sweet baby."

"Why don't you have a baby?" he asked with such innocence. But his words still stabbed her through the chest. She hoped it wasn't showing in her face.

"I have you. I don't need a baby," she said.

"But then I could grow up and it wouldn't make you sad," he reasoned.

She reached over and hugged him tight. "You are such a good boy. I promise to not be sad as you grow up just as long as you're still my son forever."

He laughed. "I *have* to be your son, Mom," he said, and she ruffled his hair.

"You *get* to be my son, just like I *get* to be your mom because it's the greatest thing that's ever happened to me."

"You always say that. I guess I'm pretty cool," he told her.

"Yes, you certainly are," she said.

"As much fun as it is listening to this conversation, I have to get home," Kian said. "Thank you for letting him stay the night. It was a lot of fun."

"Thank you for having him," Angela said. She walked over and gave him a hug. "You guys are amazing with my son and me."

He shifted on his feet but gave her a big smile.

"I'll walk you out," Declan said. Before he moved away, though, he leaned down and gave her a quick kiss. Her lips were tingling as he left the room.

"That's gross, Mom," Timothy said. "Kian and Roxie do that a lot too. Grownups are weird."

And with that he lost interest in the conversation. Angela guessed Declan wasn't going to hide their relationship in front of his family. She felt pretty good about that, even if it scared her a bit to be so open in front of her son.

On the other hand he didn't seem to mind at all. Maybe it was something that should be done just like ripping off a bandage. She wasn't really sure of anything. But she did know she was pretty happy for the first time in a long while. She hoped her bubble didn't burst.

Chapter Thirty-One

Declan had been at the office the entire day, and Angela had finally hit the point of no return. She was done being in the house. Because she felt guilty keeping Timothy locked up with her, she was letting him go to the other Forbes's houses too much to play with other kids, but that left her all alone.

She called Declan and told him they were eating dinner at her favorite Italian restaurant with outdoor seating. He didn't argue with her, but he insisted on picking her up. She wanted to fight him on it, but she had to give in sometimes. To win a war you had to lose some scrimmages.

They arrived just in time for the last outdoor seating of the night. The two of them had been inseparable for a week. She didn't fight being in his bed anymore. She also was well aware she was in love with him. Whether she'd wanted it to happen or not, it had, and there wasn't a whole lot she could do about—except keep it to herself. She didn't know what it meant, and she really didn't know if it would last when the danger was over.

"I'm starving," she told him.

"Nope. I've been told we never really starve," he said.

"Ah, yes, Eden preaches that. Didn't her dad used to tell her all the time that she's not starving, children around the world are the ones who feel real hunger."

"Yes, and it's enough that it's stuck with me," Declan told her.

"Well I'm really, *really* hungry," she said.

Their waitress, Cammy, brought their drinks and placed bread in front of them. Angela wasn't shy about picking up a piece and slathering it with butter. He followed suit.

"I don't know what's happening to me lately, but I can't seem to get enough food. It's insane. And my pants were tight today. You'd think that would scare me enough to get me to slow down."

Declan paused and looked at her. She couldn't read his expression. She smelled the wine and it turned her stomach. She set it down and focused on the bread instead.

"Maybe we need to do a pregnancy test," he said.

Her eyes widened as she looked at him, and then she was filled with sadness.

"I'm not pregnant," she told him.

"You could be, Angela," he said. She had no idea how he felt about that. He continued to eat his bread as he looked at her. "The condom broke the first time, and we haven't used any in a while."

She lost her appetite as she set the rest of her bread down and picked up her water glass. "I might be getting the flu or something, but there's no chance I'm pregnant."

"Why do you say that?" he asked.

She didn't want the romance to die so quickly, but she needed to tell him. It was only fair, especially if she was falling in love with him. She didn't want him to fall in love with a broken woman.

"When I was stabbed there was a lot of damage," she said. She refused to shed another tear about this. She'd stay strong.

"I know. I read the report," he said as he reached for her hand.

"I was told I won't have any more children," she whispered. It still broke her heart to say those words. It made her less of a woman. No man would want to marry a woman who couldn't have children.

He gazed at her for several long moments. "You do realize that even if you can't have children that doesn't mean there's anything wrong with you, right?" he asked as if he could read her mind.

"Of course, it makes me less of a woman," she said, voicing the thought she'd just had. His gaze narrowed.

"I don't ever want to hear you say something like that again. You are a man's dream come true, Angela. *You.* There's nothing more you need to give or add to the beautiful package you are." He was saying the right words, but they were coming through clenched teeth.

"Men want an heir," she said.

"There might be some men out there with that opinion, but would you want to date a man like that?"

She paused. "I've never really thought about it. I've just figured I'm too broken to marry."

"You're not even a little bit." He squeezed her hand. His jaw unclenched. "You're beautiful, kind, and loyal. I'm honored you're mine."

A tear slipped down her cheek before she wiped it away.

"I just wanted more kids. It was always something I dreamed of," she admitted. It was so painful to even talk about.

"Did you ever get a second opinion?" he finally asked.

She stared at him, not knowing what to say or think about those last words.

"What are you talking about?" she asked.

"It's been four years since the incident happened. There's a lot of trauma in a stabbing. Did you ever go back, and have it tested again?"

He didn't appear upset; he looked empathetic. But his words were scaring her a little, and sadly, giving her some hope.

"No. It hurt too badly the first time I was told. I wasn't going to put myself through that again," she told him.

She reached for the wine glass, and he slipped it out of her hands.

"I think we need to check again or take a test. I'm assuming you aren't on birth control. I should've asked you why there was no chance you'd get pregnant. I've never trusted a woman with that before."

She felt the color drain from her face.

"I wasn't trying to trick you, Declan. You can look at my medical records."

He squeezed her hand. "I don't think you're capable of lying, Angela. I know that. I'm just saying, we should check again."

She sat dumbfounded as the waitress brought their food. She couldn't even look at it. Her stomach was turning. What if he was right? What if there was a chance, she could have another baby? She'd given up hope that week in the hospital. She hadn't thought she'd ever have another child. She'd been so grateful to have Timothy. Some women could never have a child and they were okay with that, but she wouldn't have been.

"Hey," he said, getting her attention. "There's nothing we can do about it tonight. Let's enjoy our meal, alcohol free, and we'll look into it tomorrow."

"I don't want to get my hopes up," she said. "I won't be able to stand the letdown. I don't want to get pregnant now, but the thought that I could in the future would matter to me."

"If you are pregnant, we'll handle it."

"Handle it?" she questioned.

"I'd love my child, Angela. I hope you wouldn't think I could feel any other way."

"I know you would, but if I did get pregnant, it would've been under false pretenses. I swore to you there wasn't a chance."

"And that's exactly what you believed. But the body is an amazing thing. It can heal. And what's meant to be will happen."

She was speechless at his words. Timothy's biological father hadn't been nearly so kind. He'd thought she'd tried to trap him. He'd been a monster. It had been just her and Timothy for a long time. She wasn't sure what to think about what Declan was saying.

He leaned in and gave her a kiss, his lips lingering on hers for several moments. When he pulled away her heart was fluttering. She looked at this man she loved so much, and it killed her not to say the words.

"I'll take another of those," he said. She leaned forward and knocked her glass off the table.

"Oh," she exclaimed as she leaned over to grab it.

And that's when everything went very wrong.

There was a boom in the air. As she lifted back up, she watched Declan fly from his chair. Red splashed her as he grunted, falling to the ground.

"Get down," he ground out as another explosion ripped through the air.

Angela was frozen for a second, but then she slid to the ground next to him. He immediately grabbed her with his uninjured arm. His left one had a big bloodstain by his shoulder.

"Is that a gunshot?" she asked.

"No time. Crawl inside," he told her as he pulled out his gun. "Don't argue with me. Just do it, or lives will be lost." He'd never spoken so firmly to her before and Angela didn't even think of arguing. She moved quickly, not knowing what was happening.

"Come here," Cammy, who was the owner's daughter, said. She was behind the counter waiving her arm.

"I don't know what's happening," Angela said as she crawled across the floor.

"Someone is shooting at the restaurant. We've called the police."

Sirens were blaring in the distance. Angela huddled with Cammy and looked for Declan. Where was he? What was he doing? She wanted to go back to him, but she didn't want to put him in more danger. She had no choice but to wait. She and Cammy held each other as the clock slowed down.

Chapter Thirty-Two

Declan watched Angela go safely inside the restaurant. He didn't want to leave her, but he had to find the shooter. He'd been hit in the shoulder, but his adrenaline was running so high nothing was going to stop him.

He knew he was going to hurt like hell later, but right now he was pushing the pain aside. He'd been shot before. It wasn't critical if he dealt with it soon enough. He had time. He heard the sirens in the distance and knew help was on the way, but he wasn't going to wait for them. Someone had come after Angela and he wasn't standing for it.

He moved from the outdoor seating area, keeping himself low. He wasn't going to become an easy target. The streets were lit up, but there were also a lot of shadows to hide in. He didn't know if it was one person or multiple shooters. He didn't like this situation one little bit.

He moved ahead, no sign of the shooter anywhere. So he stopped and listened for the sound of steps, heavy breathing, or the click of a gun. His patience was rewarded. He finally heard steps as someone ran away.

"Like hell you will," he muttered as he jumped out from behind the car he'd been using for cover and went after the sound of the steps.

He was furious.

He didn't leave himself wide open, but he turned a corner and saw a short man fleeing the scene. He was fast, but Declan was faster. He was closing the gap between them. He wouldn't shoot the man in the back. He prayed he'd turn around. Declan wanted an excuse to put a bullet in this guy who had dared to come after his woman.

It was too late by the time the guy realized Declan was hot on his trail. He was only five feet away when the man turned, his eyes widening. He reached for his gun, but Declan closed the gap between them and threw the entire weight of his body at the guy, who had to be at least fifty pounds lighter than Declan. It was an easy tackle.

The man's gun went skidding away, and Declan started to feel the pain in his arm from the shot. "Not yet," he growled.

But the man got away from him as Declan felt darkness overtaking him. He couldn't let this man get up, get to his gun. He grabbed at his legs, but the guy laughed and kicked his hand away.

"Looks like you've lost a lot of blood," he said.

"Tell me your name," Declan demanded.

He laughed. "The cops are almost here. I can't give away all my secrets," he said.

"You don't need to," Angela said. Declan couldn't see her, didn't know where she was, and his panic increased ten-fold. She was supposed to be hiding in the restaurant. "I remember your face, Mario Vasquez. You *will* pay for what you've done."

Declan was fading, but he fought it as he turned his head. He watched in horror as the man in front of him pulled out another gun and took aim. Everything was starting to go black. He wasn't going to be able to keep his promise to her.

A shot rang out as sirens closed in. And Declan lost consciousness.

Chapter Thirty-Three

Angela waited in the hospital for the doctors to come out and tell her everything was fine. They'd assured her the bullet hadn't hit any major arteries, but they'd also said it was still a bullet wound and he'd lost a lot of blood. She was a total mess.

"Angela!" Roxie cried as she came skidding to a halt in the OR waiting room. Kian was right on her heels.

"I tried to get back there, but of course, it's my brother and they won't let me in," Kian said with frustration.

"They said he'll be fine," Angela said, but she still couldn't stop the tears. "Mario was aiming for me and he got Declan instead. I'm so sorry." She felt horrible. She was the one who'd insisted on going out. If they hadn't been there, Declan wouldn't be on the operating table right now.

"Don't you dare blame yourself for this," Roxie said. "This monster has been terrorizing the town for a long time, and Declan was closing in on him. He wanted you both, and Declan would gladly sacrifice himself for you, because he loves you."

"He's such a good man. He's done so much for me. I don't want to lose him. I'm so scared," Angela cried.

"We won't lose him. He's far too much of a badass," Owen said as he joined them.

"Those aren't words of encouragement," Eden told her husband as she sat on the other side of Angela. "But he is one heck of a tough man. I've known him my entire life, and I have no doubt we're going to be told he's okay any minute now."

"They have Mario in custody. You hurt him bad," Arden said with a glint of satisfaction in his eyes. "I just got off the phone with the police department. He's in surgery. They want to keep him alive to atone for his sins."

"They should just let him die after the terror he's put this town through," Keera said. She was such a gentle woman that those words seemed foreign on her lips.

"Oh, I have a feeling he won't last long in prison after all his abuse of women and children is known," Arden assured his wife.

"He needs to pay for what he's done," Angela said. "I was so scared. When Declan tackled him, his gun went flying. He told me to stay put, but I couldn't. I tried to stay back, but he was running after that man and I wanted to help. But when Mario pulled out his gun I had to make a decision fast, so I fired. Then the cop car arrived as he was falling down."

"You saved Declan. I have no doubt about it," Kian told her. "You did the right thing."

"I've never shot someone." She couldn't seem to stop crying.

"None of us ever want to do that," he told her. "But just remember you saved my brother's life. You're a hero."

Before they could say anything else a doctor stepped through the doors, and they all went silent. Kian was studying his face for signs of good or bad news.

"Your brother is ticked off, but he's just fine," Dr. Michaels said. "He's one tough man. He's coming off the anesthesia now and wasn't happy about being put under. I think he would've rather we used duct tape and fishing line." The man chuckled.

"That sounds like my brother," Kian said. "He's an idiot."

"Yeah, the tough guys always are. He'll be ready for visitors in about an hour. I normally like to wait a while, but I'm afraid he'll rip out his IVs and come hunting Angela down if she doesn't get in there right now. He's been very insistent."

"Can I see him?" she asked.

"Yes, follow me."

Eden squeezed her hand, then Angela was on her own with the doctor walking down the hallway. When she entered the recovery room Declan was in, she tried like crazy to keep the tears back. But she wasn't used to seeing her strong man look so weak.

He was shirtless on the table with two IVs in him, and he was so pale. There was a large bandage on his shoulder only a few inches from his chest. If that shot would've been a little lower, she would've lost him. She couldn't imagine that.

"Did he get you?" Declan asked. His voice was raspy, most likely from the oxygen tube they would've inserted during surgery.

"No. He didn't get me. I shot him," she said. She moved to his side and stood over him. He lifted his hand and she grabbed it. "He's in custody."

"Was it Mario?" he asked.

"Yes, it was Mario. We got him," she told Declan.

"Good. That's a start," he said.

"No. It's the end. You got the kingpin. Now you can put your case together," she said.

"I didn't get him. *You* did. You're the bravest woman I know," he told her.

"You've made me braver," she assured him. "And now he won't be chasing me anymore."

"I was so worried about you," he said.

"Declan Forbes, you scared me so much. You were shot and you went running after that lunatic. I will smack you when you're back to full strength," she said with a watery smile.

"Promise?" he said with a flirty wink.

"You drive me crazy," she said. And then she couldn't hold it back any longer. "And I love you."

He gazed at her like she was the most amazing person on the planet, and it made her heart swell with even more love than she thought possible.

"I don't ever want to live without you, Angela. Now crawl in this bed with me so I know you're okay. I need to sleep."

"I can't crawl in. It's against the rules," she said as she looked behind her.

"Screw the rules. I need you at my side."

She wasn't good at breaking rules, but she also couldn't deny him anything. She kicked off her shoes and carefully crawled into bed with him, making sure she didn't lie on his IVs.

"Don't scare me like that again—ever."

She laughed against his chest.

"You're the one who better not be scaring me," he said.

He closed his eyes and soon was breathing steadily. She tried to get up but he squeezed her hand and grumbled, so she just lay back. She didn't care if she got in trouble.

An hour later his family walked in and found them wrapped up together sound asleep. They all smiled.

Chapter Thirty-Four

It had been a week since they'd returned home from the hospital and Angela was still in Declan's house. They hadn't talked about it, and she was afraid to bring it up. But Mario Vasquez was behind bars and he'd been spilling it all.

There was no loyalty amongst thieves. His operation was shut down. Raids had been made, and over a dozen arrests had happened already. One of the biggest operations in the area had gone down in smoke.

Angela thought she'd feel joy at that. But she didn't. She was unsure of what the future would bring. She needed to get a job, move from Declan's house, and learn how to live again. But she wasn't sure how to do that.

Especially with the news she'd just discovered. She was in shock. That wasn't something even close to being on her radar.

She sat on the bathtub and gazed at the pregnancy stick, then at the other three next to it. She'd taken them over the course of eight hours. They all said the same thing; pregnant.

How in the world had it happened?

Well, of course she knew *how* it happened. She just hadn't thought it was possible for her. He'd already told her he trusted her. He's already said he'd love his child if she were to get pregnant. But *thinking* about a baby, and there actually *being* a baby, were two entirely different matters.

She was scared, but at the same time, filled with joy. She hadn't thought it possible to have a baby, and yet she was pregnant. And once again she wasn't married. But she'd done a great job with Timothy, or as good a job as possible being a single mom.

Unlike Timothy's biological father, she had no doubt Declan would want to be a part of their child's life. But what did it mean for the two of them? She didn't want to be in a relationship because of a child, and she wished they had more time to understand their feelings for one another before a child was brought into the mix.

Declan was so amazing with Timothy. It was special for her to watch the way the two of them had bonded. She'd been cautious, because she didn't want her son growing attached to someone who might step back out of his life. But she hadn't been able to stop it.

She came downstairs after sitting in her trance for too long. She was trying to figure out a way to tell Declan what was going on. She found him in the kitchen where he took one look at her and stopped what he was doing.

"What's wrong?" he asked.

"I wouldn't exactly say something is wrong," she told him. She began pacing the kitchen. "It's just that everything is up in the air and I'm confused."

She was growing agitated, but she didn't exactly know why. She was feeling claustrophobic in the giant house. That was insane.

"I understand," he told her. "We've been looking for Mario for a long time, and sometimes it's hard to settle after the bad guy has been caught."

"It has nothing to do with the case," she snapped. She was taking out her uncertainties on him when he'd done nothing wrong. "I'm just feeling trapped right now."

He flinched at her words. "Do you want to leave here?" he asked. There was hurt in his eyes.

"No . . . unless you want me to leave. It's just that I'm trying to tell you something and I don't know how to do it."

He remained calm, and she was grateful he wasn't trying to touch her. She didn't think she could handle that right then.

"Take your time and tell me," he said. She was even irritated that he was calm. She was so agitated, and he was just sitting there as if they were having a casual Sunday morning conversation.

"I'm pregnant," she blurted. She couldn't look at him. The room went utterly silent. She gazed at the kitchen counter as if it was the most amazing thing she'd ever seen. Still, there was nothing from Declan.

Finally, she couldn't take it anymore and had to look up. She was shocked to see him smiling. He wasn't speaking though, and she didn't know what that meant.

"Did you hear me?" she asked. "I said I'm pregnant. And there's zero doubt it's your baby. I just don't understand how because I was told I couldn't get pregnant, but I took three tests and they all turned blue."

"The body can heal," he said. "We'll get married right away."

Now it was her turn to go silent. She gaped at him as he sat back and sipped his coffee. He was talking about marriage as if it was simply the two of them going out to dinner.

"We aren't getting married because of a baby. I've seen people do that, and it's usually a disaster."

"We've already become a family. I've known you for three years and I respect you," he told her. "Timothy needs a father and I want to be that for him. And now we're having a baby. I don't want to miss out on a single moment of your pregnancy or our child's life. So, of course, we'll get married."

It wasn't exactly the proposal of her dreams, but he was making sense. They did get along, the sex was great, and she *did* love him. She just didn't want to say that right now. He hadn't told her he loved her. She knew he desired her and liked her. But that was a far cry from love. She wasn't sure Declan was the type of guy to be head over heels in love, and that's something she'd always wanted.

"We don't have to be married to have a family, Declan. I know you'll want to be part of the baby's life."

"I thought I'd be a bachelor my entire life. But then my siblings found the love of their lives and I found myself envying them. I've been intrigued by you from the moment our eyes first met, and those feelings have only grown in intensity over the years. I think we can have a beautiful marriage. And I think we'll make a fine family."

There were no words of love, but she didn't want him to tell her he loved her unless it truly was from his heart. Could she marry a man without love? She wasn't sure.

She loved him, and she had no doubt he cared about her and her son. Would that be enough? A lot of marriages were built on less and they lasted. But it scared her. She didn't want to end up divorced.

"We could just live together, Declan," she told him as she approached. "No one would judge us for that, not in today's world."

He cupped her cheek as he looked into her eyes. There was true respect in them. That was more than a lot of women got. She so wanted to tell him how much she loved him, but she held it in.

"I'd judge me. I *want* to marry you. My family will be thrilled. I think Timothy will be just as excited. Please marry me," he said. He leaned down and kissed her. It still wasn't the proposal of her dreams, but it was closer. There was no dropping to his knees, no heartfelt words of love. But there was respect and understanding. That was more than she'd ever had before.

"Maybe you should think about this," she told him. "Take a few days."

He laughed. "I won't change my mind. I'm one hundred percent sure of this."

He kissed her again, leaving her breathless. The nerves of the morning faded easily just by being in his arms. He calmed her. She hoped she could give him as much as he gave her.

"Okay, I guess we can get married," she said.

The smile he gave her was all the reward she'd ever need. He kissed her again, then pulled back.

"Can you be ready in a week?"

"For what?" she asked.

"The wedding," he told her as he stood. "We will want to do it quickly."

"We can't plan a wedding that fast, not even a small one," she said. "There isn't that big of a rush."

He laughed. "You haven't seen my family in action. If we tell them we want a fast wedding that's what will happen."

"Declan, you don't have to rush it. I won't show for a while," she said as she laid a hand on her stomach.

"I'm not worried about you showing. I can't wait for your stomach to round. I just want to make you my wife."

The words were spoken so simply and yet they were the most beautiful words ever said to her. This time she was the one to lean against him and give him a kiss. She truly did love this man.

"I'm going to leave it in your hands," she said.

He lifted her from the ground and spun her around, which was a mistake. She had to fight nausea.

"Sorry. I'm just really happy," he told her. "A week ago, with all the stress, I didn't think that was possible."

"I'm pretty happy too, Declan, and that's all because of you."

"Good. Now we need to talk to Timothy," he told her. She hadn't even thought of that. There was a poor mother moment.

"We'll do it together." If they were getting married, they'd be doing everything together for the rest of their lives. She could barely wrap her mind around it.

He kissed her again, this time slow and sweet. She sighed as she snuggled into his arms. It might not have been the proposal of her dreams, but it was heartfelt, and they had something to build upon. They were a family. She wasn't sure how it was all going to work out, but she was going to try to simply live in the moment. It wasn't such a bad place to be.

They walked hand in hand to find Timothy. She was sure her son would approve if that meant Declan would stay in their lives. And she felt like he truly was going to.

Chapter Thirty-Five

After their talk with Timothy, who was beyond thrilled, the day slipped away from Angela. There was still a nugget of fear that Declan was going to change his mind. She'd fought against this, so she was surprised by how much she wanted it. She needed to trust the man. He'd never given her a reason not to. But even if she did trust him, she needed a lot of faith in him to involve her son. She knew she could survive heartbreak, but she didn't want her eight-year-old to deal with it.

She lay in Declan's arms for hours that night unable to sleep. He seemed perfectly content as if there wasn't a worry in the world for him. By the time she fell asleep she was completely exhausted.

Sadly, Declan was already out of bed when she woke. Her favorite part of the day was waking in his arms, feeling his sweet kisses on her neck and lips. She knew once in a while she'd awake alone, but she didn't want to make a habit of it.

If they were going to have this wedding quickly, she needed to start her day. She had no idea how to plan a wedding. She wanted flowers and maybe a simple dress. She was sure Declan had already told his siblings, so she expected calls from her soon-to-be sisters-in-law. Maybe they'd help her. They'd had their weddings and probably had some connections.

She wasn't expecting the wedding of her dreams, but she wanted at least a few picture-perfect moments she could relish for the rest of her life.

Were they going to have a backyard wedding or a church wedding? How many people would he want there? Her friends were his family, so she didn't have anyone else to invite. That made it a little simpler.

After a long shower and some deep thinking, Angela made her way downstairs, hearing voices before she entered the kitchen. She hadn't had coffee yet and wasn't fully awake.

"Well, good morning, sunshine," Eden said with a bright smile as she entered the room. There were pastries and coffee all over the counter with the women looking at planners. The men were sitting at the table, laughing and talking.

"What's happening?" she asked. She moved to the coffee pot and someone tsked at her. "One cup a day won't hurt anything," she muttered.

Then she turned and looked at them. "Did Declan tell you already?"

"Yes! I think he would've had it written in the sky if he'd thought about it. He's so excited to be a daddy," Roxie said as she jumped up and hugged her. "Congratulations. We're beyond thrilled to have another baby in the family."

"Did he say anything else?" she asked.

"Oh, you mean about the wedding? Of course he did. Why do you think we're all here? We have to plan a beautiful one," Eden said.

"That *you* will love," Keera added with a sheepish smile. "And he told us we don't get much time because he wants you to be his wife immediately. It's so romantic."

The doorbell rang and Declan jumped up. "Good morning, beautiful," he said, giving her a quick kiss before he moved to the front of the house.

"I'm so confused," she said. She finished making her coffee and sat. She grabbed a cinnamon roll as her stomach growled. "But at least I know why I can't stop eating. It makes me feel a little better about getting fat."

"I loved being pregnant. I ate so many pastries the baker couldn't keep up," Roxie said.

"Yep, I'm there right now," Eden said. "We can keep him in business together. I love that we'll have our pregnancies together. Our children will grow up being best friends."

"I didn't think about that," Angela said, smiling for the first time that morning.

"First the wedding; we'll focus on baby stuff after," Keera said. "The wedding is only one week away, and there's *so* much to do."

"I was going to ask you guys if you could help me. I have no idea where to start."

"There's the blushing couple," a voice boomed, rattling the windows. That voice could only belong to one man. Angela turned to see Lucian Forbes walking in with Joseph Anderson.

"Welcome to the family, Angela. We're so grateful to have you and Timothy as a part of it," Lucian said as he leaned in and gave her a hug. "I called my good friend Joseph because he's a master at last minute planning, and we want this day to be special for you and my newest grandson."

"You really don't have to go out of your way," she told him. "A simple wedding is more than enough." She felt uncomfortable being the center of attention. This was all so overwhelming.

"Nonsense, my girl," Joseph said. "Every wedding is special and should be celebrated. I have an army of people coming to the house today, so be prepared to be swept off your feet."

The doorbell rang again. And it began.

When Joseph said he had an army of people coming, he hadn't been bluffing. Bakers, dressmakers, florists, decorators, a preacher, and beauticians all showed up at the house.

She had cake sample after cake sample, swatches of fabrics, tiaras, jewelry, and food thrust at her. Her hair was waxed and tweezed, her nails done, and her skin sprayed. As they played with her hair, the conversation never stopped.

She hadn't thought it possible. But between the Forbes family and the Anderson family, they'd managed to plan an over-the-top backyard wedding in ten hours. She wasn't sure what she'd said yes or no to. She didn't know which dress she'd be wearing. She was completely lost. And unbelievably, she was so happy she couldn't quit smiling. It was a tiring day but one of the absolute best of her life.

She didn't get to spend much time with Declan, but every time she found him across the room their eyes met, and she knew she'd made the right decision. She loved this man. The way he looked at her made her feel loved even if he didn't say the words.

Not much time passed before he'd walk by, touching her on the shoulder or hand, leaning in to give her a quick kiss. Yes, she'd made the right decision. It didn't look like there would be any mind changing. And she didn't mind that one little bit.

She and Timothy were going to have this amazing family to lean on for the rest of their lives, and she felt like she'd won the lottery. This new baby would be born into a family filled with love.

She was getting a happily ever after, even if it wasn't exactly the one she'd always dreamed about. Life wasn't about those perfect moments, though, it was about the journey you took to reach the happy ending.

Chapter Thirty-Six

Angela had never realized how much could be accomplished in a week. It was insane to think about. But she shouldn't have doubted the Forbes family. They'd even managed to give her a classy bachelorette party, making her truly feel like a bride.

But her week was over, and now it was time for the wedding. Gazing at herself in the mirror, she didn't recognize the woman staring back at her. Her dress was stunning, more than she could've ever hoped for. It hugged her tight on the top, then flowed out in layers all the way to the floor.

And the shoes. Oh, the shoes were the best things she'd ever placed on her feet. White and sparkly with her painted toes showing. Cushioned heels. She didn't think she'd ever take them off.

"You are the most beautiful bride I've ever seen," Roxie told her.

"I agree," Eden said.

"Stunning," Keera added as she put the last pin in place on Angela's veil.

"You've all been married recently so I find that hard to believe," Angela said.

"And each of us was the most beautiful bride ever on *our* day. Aren't you glad you're last, so you get the title of most stunning?" Keera asked with a laugh.

Angela couldn't quit smiling. She was apprehensive and couldn't believe this had happened so quickly, but she was also walking on clouds.

There were a couple hundred people outside the doors waiting for her to walk out, and she had to breathe deeply, in and out, telling herself the ceremony was just a small part of her wedding day. When it was all over she'd no longer be Angela Lincoln. She'd be Angela Forbes, Mrs. Declan Forbes, married to the most amazing man in the world.

She peeked out the window and heard music playing. Her son was with Declan, and he'd been beyond excited for their families to unite. He loved Declan so much, but not just Declan. He loved his aunts and uncles. It was so easy for him to settle into this family.

"I'm nervous," she said with a giggle. "I sure wish I could have a glass of champagne right about now."

"It's not champagne, but it's a close second," Eden said as she poured them both a glass of sparkling juice.

"We'll just have to drink double for the two of you," Keera said as she and Roxie had the real thing.

"To friendship and family. We came together because of circumstances and stayed together out of love. To the past, the present, and the future as it shapes us into the women we are meant to be. I love each of you, and I'm so glad to be here to celebrate your wedding day, Angela. Thank you for being a part of our lives," Eden said as she held up her glass.

"Here, here," Roxie, Keera, and Angela said. They clinked their glasses together and Angela had no more doubts or fears.

"Are you ready to do this?" Roxie asked.

"Yes, I'm ready," Angela told her. "Let's have a wedding."

Keera called out the door and Angela heard the music change. She'd requested her wedding song and a tear came to her eye as they began playing it. She hadn't wanted a traditional wedding march. She'd wanted something real.

So when *Something Just Like This* began to play, she smiled. She'd also requested a wider aisle because she didn't have a father to walk her down. She had her new sisters and she wanted them at her side.

They stepped out the doors and began walking down the rose petal lined path. Her eyes connected with Declan's and she knew beyond a doubt she was right where she belonged.

The look in Declan's eyes as she moved toward him made her feel beautiful and wanted. He was stunning in his tuxedo. And she had the naughty thought of wanting nothing more than to rip their clothes away. But not yet. She needed a few pictures first.

She reached him and he smiled as he took her hands while the women stood next to their husbands on either side of them. She hadn't wanted women on one side and men on the other. They were a team now, and she wanted to start her marriage the way she wanted to live their lives.

If asked later, she'd probably admit she didn't remember a lot from the ceremony itself. It was all a blur. He kissed her at the end when the preacher pronounced them man and wife, the most beautiful words she'd ever heard. And he took her breath away just as he did each and every single time.

They walked to their reception and she loved how Declan had insisted on all of the normal traditions: cake-cutting, toasts, and a first dance. He was far more romantic than he'd ever admit, but she wasn't fooled. This wedding had come together so beautifully all because of him.

They had music and dancing and stars above. It couldn't have been a more perfect day. As she melted against her husband, she still couldn't believe it was true. She laid her hand on his chest and watched the huge diamond glitter in the dim lighting.

"You went a little overboard here, didn't you?" she asked with a giggle.

"I just want men to know you're taken," he said.

She laughed. "I think men on Mars will know I'm taken since they can see it from there."

"All the better," he said.

She might be teasing him, but she absolutely loved her ring. He'd picked it out himself and it was spectacular.

"Have I thanked you today?" he asked as they swayed to the music.

"Thanked me?" she asked, purring like a kitten, so content to be right where she was.

"Yes, thanked you for taking a chance on me, giving me your trust, and becoming my wife. You've made my family complete."

She leaned back to look into his eyes and melted. This moment was something she'd remember from her wedding day even when she was ninety years old.

"That all came easy, Declan. I didn't know this much happiness was possible."

They paused on the dance floor as they gazed at each other. Then he cupped her cheek as he looked deep in her eyes. "It's not easy for me to use the word love," he said. Her heart was thundering. "But I do love you, Angela. I'll try to show you every single day how much."

She was speechless as she looked into the eyes of this man who'd given so much to her. There was no stopping her tears from slipping down her cheeks. It took several moments for her to be able to speak again.

"I love you, Declan. And I agree those are hard words to say. They make us vulnerable."

He smiled at her. "You're the first woman I've ever said that to that wasn't family. I will cherish you and never stop loving you. I didn't want to say that for the first time in front of everyone or I would've added it to my vows. But the more I do say it, the easier it will become."

"This was the right time. It couldn't be more perfect," she told him.

He leaned down to kiss her. It didn't take long to grow heated. The song switched to a fast number, and when he pulled back she was swaying in his arms.

"Are you ready to leave?"

"Oh yes, I want the honeymoon to start," she told him.

"We are *definitely* of one mind," he said with a laugh. Then he surprised her as he scooped her up in his arms and walked from the dance floor, their friends and family cheering and throwing confetti at them.

Not everything had been traditional at their wedding, and that made it the most perfect night of her life, because it was unique to the two of them, just like everything else had been.

Chapter Thirty-Seven

The actual honeymoon would come later. They'd both decided they wanted Mario convicted and their lives fully back to normal before they took off for a week or two. They also wanted to give Timothy time to adjust to this new family. He hadn't said much about the two of them getting married, and that worried Angela. Timothy seemed happy about the wedding. He'd stood proudly at Declan's side when she'd walked down the aisle.

She stepped out of the house and found Declan and Timothy playing catch in the yard. She loved the sound of her son's laughter. And Declan treated him like a son. Would that last forever? Would he still be so attentive after his biological child was born? It broke her heart to think he might not be. But his family was so good to Timothy. She couldn't imagine that changing.

"You boys seem to be having a lot of fun," she said as she approached. "May I join you?"

Timothy gave her a look and she had to keep herself from laughing. "Mom, I don't want to hurt your feelings, but you *really* can't throw a ball very good," Timothy told her.

"What? I'm great at throwing the ball," she said.

"No, you throw it underhanded," he said.

"That's because I don't want to hit you," she told him.

"Mom, getting hit is all part of the game. I can't be the best if I don't earn it," he told her.

His words filled her with pride. "You're growing up so dang fast," she said. "It scares me."

"Mom," he groaned. "You *always* say that. It's okay for me to grow up."

"When did you start comforting me instead of me comforting you?" she asked. "I think I need a hug."

He looked over at Declan for his approval and Declan nodded. Timothy ran up to her and gave her a big hug. She kissed his forehead. She wasn't having to bend down quite as far these days. It wouldn't be long until he was taller than she was, a terrifying thought.

"Mom, can I ask you a question?" he asked, suddenly serious.

She sat down on the deck. "Of course. What is it?"

He looked at Declan who came and sat next to her, then shifted back and forth on his feet. She was growing concerned. Declan squeezed her leg as if telling her to let him come to it on his own. That was hard for her, but she sat there waiting.

"Well, it's just that you and Declan had the wedding so that means he's your husband, right?" he said.

"Yes, he's my husband," she told her son. Declan took her hand and squeezed.

"Just like your mom is now my wife," he added.

Timothy chewed on his lip. She felt herself tense. She wasn't sure at all where this was going. She wanted to drag it out of him, but she knew she was like that too. Sometimes she didn't have the right words for what she wanted to say, and it took her a while to get them out.

"So, we will live here in Declan's house?" he asked. She didn't know how to answer that. She was glad when Declan stepped in.

"Yes, Timothy. We're all going to live in *our* house together. We might want a different one someday. I don't know what the future will bring, but no matter what we'll be in the same home together."

"I like that," Timothy said. Then he looked at his mom before looking back at Declan, a bit of anxiety in his eyes.

"You can ask me anything," Declan said. Angela's heart was breaking for her son because she could see how worried he was about something. She wanted to make it all better, but she needed to help him become a man too, and that meant letting him do things his way. She couldn't always step in. That wouldn't be helping him at all.

"So, are you my dad now?" he asked quietly looking down at his shoes. "Cause Grandpa told me he's my grandpa." The last words were barely above a whisper.

Angela held her breath as she waited to hear what Declan was going to say. Her son was being so vulnerable right now. But she trusted her husband. She never would've married him if she didn't.

Declan leaned forward as he looked at Timothy. "Do you want me to be your dad?" he asked.

Timothy looked up, a slight sheen in his eyes. "I've never had a dad. A lot of kids at school have dads and they love them. Some of the kids are like me and don't have one. A couple even don't have a mom. But I love playing with you and living here. I'd like you to be my dad," Timothy told him.

She was so proud of her son when he stared Declan in the eyes, being brave as he poured out his heart. She couldn't stop tears from filling her eyes and spilling over. She hadn't realized how much he wanted a father in his life. She'd tried to be enough, but there was a bond between fathers and sons she just couldn't fill.

"This is the happiest day of my life, Timothy, because nothing could be better than having you as my son. I already think of you that way. But knowing you want me to be your dad is the best gift anyone has ever given me. I love you, son."

He held out his arms and Timothy rushed into them, squeezing Declan tight. They stood that way for a long moment before Declan held out his arm and pulled her into their circle.

"We're a family," Timothy said with a big smile.

"Yes, we're definitely a family," Declan told him.

"I now have a great mom *and* a great dad," Timothy said. "That means on dad day at school I get to show you off, and you'll get donuts." Declan chuckled, but before he turned, she could've sworn she saw a sheen in his eyes.

Angela lost a few more tears with those words. She hadn't realized the impact not having a father around had on her son. She knew it had been out of her hands and she'd done the best she could, but Declan had given them so much by coming into their lives, and she wasn't sure she'd ever be able to thank him enough.

When she could speak again, she looked at Timothy. "How would you like to have a little sister or brother added to the family?"

Timothy's head tilted as he looked at her and then at Declan.

"It might be kind of fun to have someone to build forts with," he said. "But if I had a little sister, she couldn't be one of those boring ones that always looks in the mirror like Mandy. She'd have to be cool."

Angela laughed at his reference to *Last Man Standing*. She hadn't realized her son paid any attention to the sitcoms she watched.

"I can't promise anything. It will just be a roll of the dice," she said as she held her breath. She wasn't sure what she'd say if he told her an emphatic no.

"Well, I guess we could just train her," he said with a shrug.

That made Declan laugh. "She wouldn't be a dog," he said, laughing harder than she'd ever heard him laugh before.

"I could teach her to sit up and shake," Timothy said, giggling pretty hard himself.

"You are terrible," Angela said. "And I think that's how you're going to get out of babysitting."

He stopped laughing as he looked at her, the light dawning. "Are we *gonna* have a baby?" he asked.

She loved the word we. That meant this was *all* their baby. "Yes, Mama is pregnant," she told him.

His smile came back full force. "I guess I want a little brother or sister, because that makes me really happy," he said.

"Me too," Declan said. Then he grabbed Timothy's hand. "And the new baby won't mean I love you less. You will *both* be my kids."

Timothy's eyes filled again before he buried his head against Declan's neck.

"I love you, Dad," he said with a little sniffle. Angela held her breath.

"I love you so much, Timothy. Forever," he promised.

Angela's heart was so full she didn't know why it didn't burst. She had the perfectly imperfect family, and it was so much more than she could ever dream of.

Chapter Thirty-Eight

There were many people who said you needed to worry most when life was going too well. And for the past month, since her wedding, everything had gone amazingly well. There had been a time in Angela's life she believed those words. And then she'd met Declan and began to think there truly was a pot of gold at the end of a rainbow and luck in a four-leaf clover.

She began to believe the words, *happily-ever-after*, and she smiled at romantic comedies. She started thanking God again. Her fear began to diminish. But in the blink of an eye that could disappear so quickly.

This was her moment of waiting for the other shoe to drop.

She was walking through the forest she'd walked for years. Mario was behind bars so she was free again. She thought she was safe. Declan didn't know she was out walking. He thought she was simply running to the grocery store. But she was so happy she wanted a few minutes of quiet to reflect on how good her life was.

And then *he* was there.

It was impossible.

"You're . . . you're dead," she said, her voice barely above a whisper.

He smiled, making her recognize the evil in his expression. It must've been there all along, but somehow she'd missed it all those years ago.

"I've died several times," he told her. He was leaning against a tree, looking as if he had all the time in the world. She knew it wouldn't do her any good to run. She wasn't sure her legs would allow her to because they were shaking so badly.

"I don't understand," she said. Her face was tingling from confusion and fear. She'd felt fear before. She'd been shot at and chased down. Of course she'd felt fear. But this was different. This was a ghost from her past she'd never thought she'd see again.

He continued to smile. It was a look of victory. She'd discovered long ago he liked to get his way. He could put on a good mask, but once the veil came down, there was no hiding who he really was.

"I've had many names in life. When one name was no longer convenient, I came up with a new one and a new identity. A few plastic changes here and there and I'm a whole new man," he said.

She studied him. The fear lingered, but she felt herself calming. There was nothing she could do. She couldn't beat this man. He was too smart for her, had lived this life of deception for too long. He'd always win. With that knowledge, she felt a sort of peace fill her.

At the same time, her fingers circled her stomach, which was barely showing. This baby she was supposed to protect would never see the light of day. She was leaving one child behind and not giving the other a chance to take its first breath. That broke her heart. But nothing could be done about it. If she'd only listened to Declan, if she'd been more careful. But if-onlys didn't help her or her children right now.

He had changed. Part of that was aging, and part was cosmetic surgery. But there was no doubt it was *him*—the biological father of her child. She couldn't think of him and father in the same sentence without flinching. He'd never been Timothy's dad. He never would be. That role belonged to Declan, and she prayed he'd raise her son as his own when she was gone.

She now knew why Mario seemed so familiar to her. They shared features. She might've even seen him in passing when she'd been with Emilio. She wasn't sure. But all the pieces of the puzzle were beginning to slide into place. That didn't do her a heck of a lot of good at this moment.

"Who are you now?" she asked. "And why would you come back for me?"

His smile grew. There was no merriment in his expression, just pure evil. As she stood before him pregnant, she couldn't comprehend it. At some point in this man's life, he'd been an innocent newborn with no evil inside him. What had happened to make him who he was today? She'd never know.

"Haven't you figured it out?" he asked.

She shook her head. She didn't understand why knowing mattered. It wouldn't help her if she were dead. Maybe part of her hoped Declan would burst through the end of the trail and rescue her.

As she had that thought her phone vibrated in her pocket. She was glad she'd turned off the sound. But she was too afraid to reach in and hit the answer button. If it was Declan and she wasn't answering, maybe he'd grow worried and look for her. If she gave away that she had it on her, Emilio would snag it.

"Emilio Coronado," he said.

He let his words sink in. The light dawned as she gazed at him in horror. She had been a part of this gang all along.

"Why am I still alive? Why did you let me go for so long?" she asked.

"You weren't a threat then. And, believe it or not, I had a soft spot for you . . . so you lived. But I wanted to keep an eye on you," he told her.

"You did try to have me killed. I was stabbed. But someone interrupted. I don't understand why you didn't come back and finish the job back then."

His smile fell away. "That wasn't me. I wasn't happy about it. So I made a deal with your father and you were sent here. As long as you kept out of my business there was no need to take you out. But then you got in my brother's business, and you know how that goes," he said with a shrug as if they were discussing nothing more serious than the weather.

"I didn't know it was you. I was just in the wrong place at the wrong time," she told him. She didn't want to plead for her life, but if she didn't give it at least a little try then she wasn't worthy of being called a mother.

"It's just business, Angela. I'm wrapping up loose ends before I start over again. Your boyfriend has my brother. Now you have to go, but I find it's not so easy for me." He seemed surprised by his own words. She wasn't correcting him that Declan was now her husband.

"I have a son to take care of," she said. She wasn't pointing out her pregnancy.

"Yeah, I might need to take him, raise him the right way," he said with a shrug. The thought of this man getting his hands-on Timothy filled her with the worst fear she'd ever experienced.

"Please leave Timothy alone. He's a good boy and he knows nothing of this life. Let him grow up. Please," she said, unable to hold back tears as she begged this monster for her son's life.

"We need to go now, Angela. I don't want any last-minute rescues to happen. We'll talk more later," he assured her.

He took a step forward and Angela knew there wasn't much of a chance, but she wouldn't make it easy for him. She turned and ran, grateful her legs carried her. She thought for the briefest of moments she might actually get away. That was until a crack to her skull caused blinding pain . . . and the world went black.

Chapter Thirty-Nine

Declan felt all the color drain from his face. He'd been in the worst of worst situations, but never before had he felt the fear he was now experiencing.

He knelt down and picked up Angela's broken phone; a trickle of blood had splattered on its face. He stood and listened. She'd been gone at least thirty minutes. She could be anywhere.

As much as he wanted to let rage and panic take over, he couldn't allow that to happen. If she had even the remotest of chances, he had to act fast. He dialed a number and called in her abduction.

His gut had once again saved him time. She hadn't been gone long, but he'd had a feeling and tried calling her. She hadn't answered. He'd tried again. Still no answer. On the third try, her phone had been off. He'd pinged its last location and jumped in his truck.

"Angela's been taken," he said into his phone. He gave his location and hung up. He needed to get to the tree house. But he had to wait for the authorities. He knew the first hours after an abduction were critical in finding the person.

The next hour dragged on longer than any other in his lifetime. The cops, FBI, and Search and Rescue arrived. Declan filled them in on every detail he could, then he left before his brothers could arrive. He didn't have time for explanations. He needed the best of the best.

He went to his childhood hideout and was soon in the fort. It certainly wasn't a kid's playhouse now. He hadn't been inside in over fifteen years. A lot had changed. He didn't take time to look around at the monitors and technology. Lights were blinking, and before he had a chance to pick up the secret phone, Harrison's voice came over a speaker.

"What's wrong, Declan?" he asked.

Declan didn't need to ask how his friend knew he was there, and he didn't need to tell him something was wrong.

"Angela's been taken," Declan said, surprised with how raw his voice was.

"We're on our way," Kaleb said.

The line they were on disconnected. Declan dropped to his knees as he fought the urge to cry. He hadn't shed a tear since before he'd hit puberty. But the woman he loved had been captured after he'd promised her that wouldn't happen. He'd failed her. And he had no doubt it was Emilio and the gang.

He just prayed his friends got there in time.

It was less than thirty minutes later when he heard the click on the tree house door. Harrison and Kaleb stood before him, their expressions grim. Declan hadn't realized he'd never moved. He slowly stood, feeling hopeless for the first time in his life.

"She's pregnant . . . and the only woman I'll ever love," he said.

Harrison and Kaleb nodded. "We have no doubt about it," Harrison said.

"Let's get her back," Kaleb told him.

"I can't think. I can't stand back and be analytical about this," Declan said. "I've always been able to put my emotions on the backburner, but I can't with her."

Kaleb patted his shoulder. "Believe me, I know." Declan felt like a fool. This had to bring so much back for his friend. "But after losing my wife, I knew it would never happen again to someone I love. You're my brother and I won't let it happen to you. We put a tracker on Angela. We should've told you, but we didn't think it necessary unless a worst-case scenario played out. We're very familiar with the Coronado gang. And we have Intel you aren't aware of."

Declan shook his head. Harrison was already at a computer. "I don't understand."

"Emilio Coronado used to be Robert Crinoli. Before that he was Dean Withers. There have been other names," Kaleb said.

Light was dawning. Declan began having hope again. He hated that he'd lost it for a moment. "He's Timothy's biological father." It wasn't a question.

"Yes. He does mean to kill her, but it won't be easy for him or quick. He'll want to talk, want to get his closure. We'll get her, Declan. I promise you," Kaleb said.

"She's here," Harrison said. Declan and Kaleb turned to the monitor Harrison showed them. There was a binging light on it.

"Where is that?" Declan asked.

Kaleb moved over to a wall and pulled aside a picture where a keypad was hidden. He punched in numbers and a shelf filled with weapons popped out. He grabbed some.

"She's only thirty miles away in a remote cabin. I'll call a chopper to drop us a couple miles out. We don't want to get too close and alert him," Harrison said.

Declan nodded.

"Let's go get your wife," Kaleb said as he handed over a Kevlar vest. Declan took it.

"Yes."

They moved from the tree house; the chopper was there fast, and they boarded. Declan wasn't sure about all the connections his friends had, but he wasn't going to complain.

"Thank you," he told them.

"There's no need for that. We're brothers," Harrison said.

Declan nodded. He couldn't speak anymore.

Chapter Forty

How sad it was to wake for the second time in her life in pain, not understanding what had happened. Angela's head was pounding and fogginess blanketed her, but she'd learned over the years to not panic in this situation.

She'd had too many nightmares, had woken confused too many times. She calmed her breathing and tried to focus on what she remembered last. That's when her meeting with Emilio came back, front and center.

She tried to keep the panic at bay as she attempted to lift a hand. She couldn't. She opened her eyes and found she was tied down on a bed in a dark room. Both hands were cuffed to a metal post. There was no chance of getting away.

Still, she tugged on it.

"It won't do you any good."

That voice had brought her a thrill when she was a teenager. Now, it only filled her with terror and revulsion. She turned her head and saw him sitting in a chair in a darkened corner. There was enough light to see his beady gaze. She was completely at his mercy.

"Why are we here?" she asked.

"Because I haven't decided what to do next. I thought I'd kill you quick and leave. You're my final loose end. I'm finding I'm not ready," he said with a shrug. "It's very unusual for me. Normally, I make a decision and follow through without hesitation or remorse. That's how I've survived in this world."

He stood and came closer; everything in her wanted to move away, but she couldn't. She was his very unwilling captive.

"Time has been good to you, Angela, *very* good," he said.

Her stomach turned, and she had to fight to keep from puking when he sat on the edge of the bed and reached up, running his finger down her cheek and across her lip, resting his thumb on her bottom lip. She had to fight to keep from biting him. That would only lead to punishment, and she knew how cruel he could be when he was angry.

"We were so good together. I've never found another I've enjoyed as much as you. I thought many times of coming back for you, but that's against the rules. A new life calls for new whores. But you were different. I was younger then, but you were definitely special," he told her.

He reached behind her and cradled her neck. She had to bite her lip and hold her breath. She was so close to puking, and she wasn't sure what that would do to his temper. This situation seemed hopeless, but part of her was still optimistic she'd be found. She couldn't imagine what her death would do to her son . . . or to Declan. They hadn't had enough time together. She needed more.

"I loved you," she told him honestly. "But we ended. We moved on. Please let me go be a mother to my son," she said. She couldn't stop tears from falling.

He used his other hand to wipe her tears. The move was almost gentle, but she knew there was nothing kind about him. He was more fascinated by his own feelings. He didn't care at all about what he was putting her through.

He leaned down and kissed her hard while the hand that had been stroking her face moved down her throat and grabbed her breast. The tears came harder as she gagged into his mouth, her nausea too bad to keep at bay.

He jerked back and glared at her before the hand that had been groping reached up and flew through the air. She could hear the wind seconds before her face was jerked to the side from the power of his slap. She saw stars as pain radiated in her cheek, and she tasted copper in her mouth.

"Are you repulsed by me now, Angela? Because I remember a time I made you scream in pleasure," he said with a laugh that had no merriment. "I think I might have to prove again just how good I am."

She shuddered at what she knew was going to happen. She wouldn't be able to stop it. This man was going to torture her before he killed her. She forced her tears back. She wasn't going to give him the satisfaction of continuing to beg him. She wasn't going to scream.

"Just kill me. I'd rather that than have you touch me again," she said with as much courage as she could muster.

"I thought you wanted to go home to your son," he sneered. "Are you so selfish you'd sacrifice him for yourself?" The taunt hit her where it was meant to.

"You aren't going to let me go. I know that," she said.

"No, I'm not letting you go," he said. He reached up and ran his hand down her face and chest again, squeezing where he wanted. She gritted her teeth and looked at the ceiling, hoping if she didn't react, he'd lose interest.

A noise sounded outside, and his head turned as his eyes narrowed. It was probably nothing, but it made her heart speed up as she tried to push down the hope that filled her. She couldn't survive the disappointment of thinking someone was coming for her if no one was.

"I'll be back. Get in the mood really quick, darlin', or this won't be very fun for you," he said as he stood. He gave himself a moment to look at her from head to toe while licking his lips. "Yep, this will be a great night. It's exactly what I've needed for a while."

She fought it, but more tears fell as the door to the house closed. She tugged on her hands, but all she did was scrape them up. There was no way she was getting out of this.

"Goodbye, Timothy. I love you so much," she whispered. "Forgive me, Declan. You were the best thing that could happen for my son and me. I will love you with my dying breath."

She closed her eyes and waited . . .

Chapter Forty-One

It was amazing how quickly a rescue team could be formed with the right connections. The chopper landed and Declan was overwhelmed when six other men were there, fully armed, dressed in black, and looking *very* capable and *very* mean.

"I'm glad I called you guys," Declan said. "I thought I was the best, but I might have to give that up to you two."

Harrison clapped him on the shoulder. "We're not restricted by the government," he reminded him. "Come join us. We need more men like you."

"I'm in," Declan said. He loved the FBI, but it did restrict him. He wanted to do more, and he knew he could with his two best friends.

"Good. You start right now. This is the kind of stuff we do. People get to come home," Kaleb said. He didn't add, "unlike my wife," but they all knew he was thinking it.

They moved silently through the forest to the location where Angela was. Declan feared Emilio had somehow found the tracker and they were on a wild goose chase. But when they topped a ridge and found an old hunting cabin with a fire burning, he knew she was in there. He stepped forward to get her.

"Wait. We have one shot at this," Kaleb said.

Declan wasn't going to argue with his friend. The man had personal knowledge of just how true that was.

The nine of them stepped into a huddle. Harrison began speaking.

"You know what to do. Let's make a little noise to get this guy outside. We don't need him to be holed up inside with her where she could be hurt. Let him think it's an animal but get him outside. Then move fast."

The men all nodded. They moved forward in all directions, surrounding the cabin. Declan was about twenty feet from the cabin, behind an abandoned truck, when the front door opened. His gut clenched with the need to fight.

A man looked out, then widened the door before stepping onto the front porch, a shotgun in his hands at the ready. He didn't seem too concerned.

"A couple more steps is all we need," Kaleb whispered into the mic.

As if the man was a puppet, he moved to the edge of the porch and looked out. Declan wanted to rush him, but at this distance it gave the man plenty of time to pull the trigger. He had to count on the team.

And they moved quickly.

In a blur two men rushed Emilio from either side, taking him down before he had time to realize he was caught. He got out one scream before the night went silent again.

Declan jumped up and rushed to the cabin. He didn't need permission. He had to get to Angela. He burst through the door, his eyes already adjusted to the dim lighting.

She turned, defeat in her eyes as the door burst open. It killed him to see her like that. He slowed, not knowing how scared she was, and he moved forward.

"It's me, Angela," he said, his tone hushed.

She sobbed. "I was afraid to hope you'd find me, but I hoped anyway," she said. "I don't know how, but you're my superhero." Tears were streaming down her face as she twisted, trying to reach for him.

He held back his fury at seeing her tied down and handcuffed. But he wasn't going to show her. Luckily, he was law, so he reached into his pocket, pulled out a cuff key, undid the lock, then gently pulled her into his arms.

She curled up into him and clung on tight as her tears wet his shoulder.

"I love you," she said over and over again as she shook in his arms.

"I'm so sorry he got to you, love. I'm so sorry."

"It was my fault. I went for a walk. I know him, Declan," she said.

"I know, love, I know it all," he told her.

She leaned back, her eyes red. A bruise was forming on her cheek and he had to fight the rage waiting to erupt. He needed an outlet. He desperately wanted to step out those doors and beat the man to a bloody pulp. But holding her was more important right now.

"Did he hurt you?" he asked as he gently ran a finger across her cheek.

She shook her head. "Nothing bad. It would've been a lot worse if you hadn't gotten here when you did."

Nausea rose in his throat at her words. He could imagine what that monster had planned for her, but if he thought too long on that he'd react first and not be there for her like he needed to be.

"He shouldn't have had the opportunity to do what he did. I broke a promise," he said.

She gave him a watery smile. "You're my hero, Declan. Please don't say that, because it hurts me. I have faith in you. And we aren't going to give this guy any more power over you or me by thinking about him. I just want to go home. I want to hold my son while you hold us both."

He was so awed by this woman. "I've watched you for years now, and you humble me," he told her. "There are so many people who would justifiably fall apart right now, but your strength is what makes you who you are."

She leaned in and kissed him. "I get my strength from the people who have embraced me. I was scared and weak for a long time. Then I came to Edmonds and my life changed for the better. I'm so glad I was led here."

The sound of the chopper moving in sounded overhead, making it impossible to talk. Declan lifted her in his arms and left the cabin for good. It would be burned by the end of the week. He wanted no reminders of this night to exist.

They didn't speak as the chopper took them to the hospital even though she tried to insist she was fine. When he brought up the baby, she stopped arguing. They both held their breath until the sweet sound of their child's heartbeat filled the room.

"You're all clear," Kian said after about an hour, with suspiciously bright eyes. "I'm glad you came here now, but I should've been out there with you," he added with a glare at his brother.

"I know. I panicked," Declan said. "And I went to the tree house."

Kian nodded with understanding. "Well, that was a smart choice." Just then Harrison and Kaleb walked into the room.

"Hello, Kian," Harrison said as he shook his hand.

"It's good to see you both," Kian said.

"It's been too long," Kaleb told him.

"I'm going to get Angela home," Declan said as he helped her down from the table.

"That's a good idea," Kian affirmed.

Declan left with his wife at his side. She sat next to him in the truck that had been delivered to the hospital, his arm wrapped around her.

"I was afraid I'd never see you again. It was the worst part of all of this," she said as they pulled up to his house. "You and Timothy are my world."

"Timothy has no idea what's going on. He's at Owen's place right now. We can have him brought home."

"No. I want to hold him so badly, but I don't want him to see me shaken up like this. Let's get him in the morning," she said.

"Anything you want." They stepped inside the house, he lifted her into his arms again, and she snuggled against him as he moved up the stairs straight into the bathroom. "Do you want to be alone or do you want help?" he asked.

"I want help," she said, making his heart swell.

He gently stripped away her clothes and his, then stepped in the shower with her, washing away the grime of that man touching her. She clung to him the entire time. He'd never been so protective of another person. He was vigilant with his family, but it didn't compare to how he was with this woman he loved so much.

They didn't talk as they climbed from the shower, dried off, then walked to their bed. As soon as they lay down, she snuggled into his side and he rubbed her back, needing to touch her, needing to be assured she was okay.

"There's nothing I wouldn't do for you, Angela, nothing at all," he told her. He truly meant that.

"I feel the same," she said.

They lay awake a long while before he heard steady breathing telling him she was finally resting.

"I love you, Angela Forbes," he said.

She sighed as she snuggled closer. He was right where he needed to be with the woman he'd die for. Life could begin from this moment on. Every decision he'd ever made had led him to this.

And he was so grateful. Finally, he closed his eyes, and that night he dreamed of a beautiful future instead of the nightmares of the past.

Chapter Forty-Two
Four Months Later

"Can I have a few minutes alone?" Angela asked.

Declan leaned over and gave her a gentle kiss. Her stomach was so big it was hard to hold him from the front, but she could easily fit against his side. It was her favorite place to be. It was where she felt the most secure, the most loved.

"Of course. I'll be outside the doors."

She gave him a slight smile and then bowed her head while he walked away. She knew he'd give her five minutes or five hours—whatever she needed. The past month had been rough for her, but he'd been there every step of the way. She couldn't have asked for a more caring and wonderful husband.

Their love for one another grew each day. She no longer doubted it. It was easy to say I love you to someone, but when it was truly meant, those were the most powerful words in the world. Her favorite time he'd spoken them had been on top of the mountain when he went down on his knee and told her he was so grateful she'd become his wife. He'd given her a new ring with three stones in it to represent their past, present, and future.

They'd made love on that mountain and she'd known they'd last the test of time.

Then the trial had come.

They had an airtight case. It was over. It was truly, truly over. Angela hadn't realized she'd still lived in fear after Mario and Emilio were captured. But she had until the gang was officially dismantled.

She didn't have to be at the trial, but she'd wanted to be there. It had broken her heart to hear testimony from the family members of other victims like herself. There was so much corruption in the world, more than she'd been aware of.

The cartel trying to destroy Edmonds went much deeper than just their town. It was widespread throughout the States. But Declan and a huge team of dedicated FBI agents had cracked the case. It had taken three years and a lot of witnesses, but they'd done it.

It was over.

She wasn't sure what she was feeling as she sat in the empty courtroom. It really was over. No one else would be coming after her. No more cartels would sift drugs through the school her son attended. No more fires would be set, and no more people would be drugged and led out by that group.

She could sleep soundly every night knowing the members were either behind bars or dead.

She sat a while longer, letting it all sink in. Then she slowly stood. Movement was becoming more and more difficult. She was going to walk from that courtroom and say goodbye to it all. A nightmare might come once in a while, but they were already few and far between now. She was living a real life dream where evil wasn't welcome.

She passed through the courtroom doors and Declan was waiting.

"I love you," she told him.

He pulled her into his arms and smiled when her belly kept them slightly apart.

"I love you more," he replied, and she smacked his arm.

"I hate when you say that. You can't possibly love me more than I love you."

"I guess I'm good at the impossible then," he said.

He leaned down and kissed her like it was the first time. When he finally let her go, he took her hand so they could walk side by side. Each day with him was a brand new day in their lives together, and she was so happy for every single moment.

"Let's get on with the rest of our lives. This is all behind us now," Declan told her.

"Yes, to yesterday, today, and tomorrow," she said. "Now we get forever."

And they would. She had no doubt. She was in her happily-ever-after, and she would appreciate each and every moment of it.

Epilogue

Three glasses clinked together as Joseph Anderson, Sherman Armstrong, and Lucian Forbes sat back and smiled. The cigars were lit and the Scotch was of excellent vintage.

"There was a time in my life I didn't know so much happiness was possible, but that was long ago," Lucian said. "I can't believe all four of my boys have been so blessed with beautiful brides."

"Don't forget your daughter," Joseph said.

Lucian laughed. "No one will *ever* forget my spitfire of a daughter. With four big brothers, my little girl is one tough woman. I love all of their spouses and the babies they're giving me."

"I know. The time goes so fast," Joseph said. "I wish I could stop the clock."

"I'm so proud of all these young men and women," Sherman said. "There are definitely some sorrows in life, but the joys outweigh them every single time."

"What will we do now?" Lucian asked. "I feel a little lost."

Joseph's grin grew. He took a puff of his cigar as he sat back and looked at his friends.

"What?" Sherman asked.

Joseph looked at the securely shut door before looking at his friends again. "This is top secret," he told them.

"Well spit it out, old man. In case you haven't looked in a mirror lately, we aren't getting any younger," Lucian told him.

"You have to wait. The rest of the club is on their way," he said.

Of course, he was referring to his brothers and a couple more friends.

"I don't think I can wait," Sherman said. "You have piqued my curiosity for sure."

"Our families are taken care of. That's why I've thought of this," Joseph said.

"Thought of what?" Lucian and Sherman shouted.

"Okay, I'll give you a hint . . ." He leaned in and all their grins grew as he began speaking . . .

Preview for The Billionaire Wins the Game. See where Joseph Anderson comes to life and does his famous meddling for the very first time.

Prologue

"It's just not right, Katherine!" Joseph slammed his fist down on the table, making the dinnerware shake. "Those kids just don't listen to us — not one of them. Can't they see that we aren't getting any younger? I should've had grandchildren bouncing on my knees years ago."

Katherine smiled as she listened to her husband complain about his disobedient children. She knew what he said was nothing but empty words. He adored their kids as much as she did. She had to agree with Joseph, though, that a few beautiful women rocking babies would be an excellent addition to the house. She'd always dreamed of the day she'd be holding grandchildren while her table was surrounded by those she loved.

"Now, Joseph. You know if you go meddling again, the boys are going to disown you," Katherine warned.

"If they don't do something about this grandchildren situation, then I'm going to disown them," he growled, though with zero conviction in his voice.

"Since you retired last year, you've had too much time on your hands, Joseph Anderson. The boys have been tossed a lot of responsibility already. Are you sure you want to add more to their plates?" she asked, knowing the answer already.

"The boys are ready for love and marriage. They just need a helping push."

The decision had already been made. He'd have at least one grandchild in his empty mansion before Christmas.

Katherine suppressed her sigh, knowing nothing she could say would change her willful husband's mind. Where did he think their sons acquired that particular trait? Even with their flaws, she couldn't possibly love any of them, including her husband, more than she already did.

"Lucas will be first," Joseph said in his booming voice, startling Katherine out of her reverie. "I've already found him the perfect bride."

Joseph leaned back in his chair with a pleased expression on his face. Finally, he had a project to keep himself occupied — with the prize of grandchildren as his reward. Lucas was in for wild adventures come Monday morning.

Katherine watched the self-satisfied expression on Joseph's face and thought about warning her sons about what was coming. She decided against it because even though she didn't agree with Joseph's meddling, she really did want those grandbabies...

Chapter One

You can do this. Walk in there with confidence. Who cares if this family is worth more than Bill Gates and Donald Trump combined? You were hired for this position, and you need this job. They obviously see something in you, so keep your head held high.

Amy was giving herself a lecture on her long elevator ride up to the twenty-fifth floor of the Anderson Corporation. Her stomach was in knots as she began her journey into the corporate world.

She brushed a few strands of escaped golden hair from her face, more out of nervousness than necessity. She considered herself to be of average looks and tried to downplay the assets she'd been given. She wanted to be respected, not lusted after, like her mother. She had long hair she couldn't find the will to cut off, although when out, she always placed it in an unflattering bun.

She tended to hide her curves from the world. She was well endowed in what an ex-boyfriend had called "all the right places," and she was self-conscious of the fact. She also didn't like the fact that her green eyes gave away every emotion she was feeling, and that no matter how hard she tried, she couldn't manage to fix it.

She still couldn't believe she'd been hired as executive secretary for Lucas Anderson. Anyone who lived within a thousand miles of Seattle, Washington, knew who the Andersons were. Their corporation had a variety of divisions, which required a large staff. They dealt with everything from construction and farming to high-end corporate takeovers. Although their headquarters was in the U.S., they did business around the world, and she was excited to be a part of it.

Her job was in the corporate headquarters, working for the fairly new president, Lucas Anderson. All she really knew was that he'd taken over his father's position about a year ago.

Though she'd graduated with honors, she was still fresh out of college and felt a little bit overwhelmed at the prospect of working for such a powerful man. She hadn't actually met Lucas yet, just his father.

She'd first met Joseph at a college job fair toward the end of her senior year. He'd given her his card and told her to call after graduation, telling her he was impressed with her college transcript. She'd called the day after her commencement ceremony, and he'd gotten her in for an interview faster than she'd dared to even hope for.

As she continued the long ascent in the elevator, she let her thoughts drift back to the previous week when she'd interviewed for the job.

Amy took a fortifying breath as she stepped from the cab, looking up at the huge fortress of a home in front of her. Before she could blink, the yellow car pulled away, leaving her frozen at the bottom of the large cement staircase. There was no turning back now.

She slowly climbed the steps and approached the door, which was big enough to fit a large truck through. It seemed Mr. Anderson liked to do things on a much larger scale than the average person.

She rang the doorbell, though he must know she was already there as he'd opened the gates at the bottom of the driveway.

Within seconds, the door was opened by an older gentleman who, thankfully, was smiling.

"Hello, I'm Amy Harper. I have an appointment with Mr. Anderson."

"Good morning, Ms. Harper. It's a pleasure to meet you. Please follow me to the sitting room, where Mr. Anderson will join you shortly," the man said.

Amy nodded, then followed his quick steps as he led her through the overwhelming home. She couldn't help but look around as her steps echoed off the walls.

The home screamed luxury, from the gorgeous marble floors to the priceless pieces of artwork adorning the walls. The longer they walked, the more out of place she felt. She couldn't figure out what had ever made her think she could handle such a prestigious job as to work for the head of a multibillion-dollar corporation.

They walked through a set of oversized double doors and Amy looked around the warm room as her shoulders relaxed. A fireplace, so large she could literally walk inside of it, was burning what smelled like cedar, giving the room a comforting quality. Though the room was well lit, the light was soft, making the space incredibly inviting.

"Would you like something to drink while you wait?"

Amy shook her head and gave the man a small smile. She didn't want to appear rude.

"Go ahead and make yourself comfortable. I'll let Mr. Anderson know you've arrived."

Before Amy could respond, he exited, leaving her standing near the entrance. Eventually, she was able to make her feet respond to her brain and walked over to the comfortable-looking sofa. She sank onto the soft leather and leaned back. She wasn't kept waiting long before a rumbling voice startled her, causing her to sit straight up. She was thankful she hadn't accepted the drink or she would've spilled it all over herself.

"Good morning, Ms. Harper. I'm sorry to have kept you waiting. Sometimes it's difficult to get off the phone," Joseph said.

"I haven't been waiting long at all, Mr. Anderson. Thank you for getting me in for an interview so quickly. I really appreciate it." Amy jumped to her feet and moved forward to shake his hand.

"The pleasure's all mine. Now, let's get the formality out of the way. Call me Joseph, please," he said as he held out his hand.

Amy felt like she was caught before an oncoming train. She didn't know how to react. She couldn't be rude, but she was uncomfortable calling him by his first name. She took his hand as she shifted on her feet.

"Thank you. You can call me Amy," she finally replied, deciding to just not call him by any name.

"Now, let's sit down and chat. Have you been offered something to drink?"

"Yes, but I don't need anything." She didn't think she'd be able to swallow past the nervous lump in her throat.

Joseph indicated for her to sit back down on the sofa, which she quickly did, grateful to get off her shaky legs. He took the chair opposite her, then trained his light blue eyes on her face. The man was quite intimidating, standing well over six feet tall, with the broadest shoulders she could ever remember seeing.

He had snow white hair, just starting to thin a bit, and a neatly trimmed white mustache and beard. He was quite handsome for a man who must be in his early fifties at least.

"I was impressed with your résumé during the job fair at your school. If I remember correctly, you've held regular jobs since you were fourteen, then full-time work all throughout your schooling, correct? How did you manage to regulate your time to keep such impressive grades?"

"I've always believed in a strong work ethic. I made sure not to overschedule myself, and I took my classes a little later in the morning so I could work the swing shifts at my jobs. I didn't want to graduate with a lot of debt," Amy replied, happy in knowing she'd done exactly that and was pretty much debt free.

"Very impressive, Amy. Your résumé says you graduated with a degree in business finance with a minor in public relations. What are your future plans?"

"I haven't had a lot of time to think about where I want to go in ten years, but my goal has always been to get my foot in the door of a great corporation, such as yours, and work my way up. I know it's not an easy task, but I learn very quickly, and I'm not afraid of hard work or long hours. I'll do whatever it takes to learn all I need to in order to be a real asset to your company."

"What about marriage and babies?" he asked, never taking his gaze from her eyes.

Amy felt her cheeks heat at his question. She knew a lot of higher-up companies were afraid to hire young women because they'd sometimes get married, then need time off for having children and such. She didn't want to lie, but she knew her answer could lose her the job.

"I'm not involved with anyone right now, but I'd be lying to you if I said I don't want that to happen. I eventually want children, whether I do so in the traditional way or I adopt. I've always wanted to be a mother, but I can guarantee you I wouldn't let anything affect my job performance. I know the value of secure employment, and I can't be a great mother without first having a solid home for my child," she answered. She knew he didn't know her, but she could obtain letters of recommendation. She'd never once taken a sick day from work, and her school assignments had always been on time, if not early.

Joseph continued watching her for so long, it made her want to fidget in her seat. With sheer will, she remained still as she waited for his response.

"Do you have family or friends close by who'd be willing to help you?"

Amy was surprised by his questions. She'd never before had an interview with so many personal questions. It was throwing her off balance. She had all the answers to typical interview questions, but not the stuff he was asking her. She didn't want anyone to know the true circumstances of her personal life.

"I have a few friends, but no family here," she finally answered, feeling safe in her choice of wording. The reality was that she didn't have any family, period.

Joseph then switched back to asking a few more work-related questions and she relaxed, secure in her knowledge of the business world. She'd studied hard and spent the scarce free time she had researching large corporations, knowing she wanted a high salary job when she graduated.

Her real goals included working nonstop for several years while saving every extra dime she could so she'd be able to have a family. She'd been alone since she was a child, and she didn't want to die that way.

What Amy didn't know was that Joseph had already run a full background check on her, knew she was an orphan, and had much bigger ideas in mind than just an executive assistant position. He was looking for a potential daughter-in-law.

"Amy, it's been a true pleasure talking with you today. As you were my last interview, I can safely tell you that the position is yours if you'd like it."

Amy stared back at Joseph in shock. She hadn't expected to hear anything about the job for at least a week and found herself speechless as his words sank in. He smiled as he waited for her to compose herself.

"Um...thank you, Mr. Anderson. I...of course, I'll take the job," she finally stuttered, completely forgetting about his request to call him by his first name.

"That's wonderful. Welcome to the Anderson family corporation..."

The elevator sounding her arrival snapped Amy back to the present. *Do not blow this job, Amy. If it all works out, you could be completely secure within a couple of years.* With her final words of encouragement to herself, she took a deep breath and waited for the doors to open.

As she stepped onto the twenty-fifth floor, she was momentarily paralyzed with fear. It was the most beautiful office she'd ever seen. The doors opened up to a massive lobby, a round cherry wood desk strategically placed for easy guest access. Behind the desk was a stunning blonde who looked more efficient than Amy ever hoped to be. White marble columns flanked the entryway, leading to where Amy assumed the offices were located. Exquisite paintings hung on the walls, adding a depth of warm color. In the corner, a seating area offered soft leather furniture and an antique coffee table with a priceless chandelier overhead. She felt increasingly frumpy and inadequate as she stepped forward in her second-hand business suit and three-year-old heels.

"Can I help you?" the woman asked.

Amy snapped out of her temporary daze. "Yes, I'm Amy Harper, the new executive secretary for Mr. Anderson," she said with as much confidence as she could rally.

The woman looked at her blankly for a moment before slowly reaching for her phone. "Mr. Anderson, I have Amy Harper here who says she's your new executive secretary." She paused for a few moments. "Okay ... Yes, sir."

She hung up the phone and turned back to Amy. "Mr. Anderson says he already has an executive secretary and has hired no one new. He also said that if you're a reporter trying for another story about his family, all his answers are *no comment*." The woman looked dismissively at Amy before adding, "Have a nice day, Ms. Harper."

She didn't give Amy another glance as she turned back to her computer. As far as she was concerned, Amy was dismissed.

"Um, excuse me ... Shelly," Amy said, looking at the secretary's nameplate. " I was interviewed last week by Mr. Anderson. He told me to be in the office at eight A.M. sharp, so you may want to check again," she said a bit more forcefully. Shelly glanced up, as if shocked that the disturbing woman was still there.

Before Shelly had a chance to reply, the elevator chimed and in walked an older woman with smiling blue eyes. "You must be Amy Harper. I'm sorry I'm late but I got stuck behind a car accident," the woman said. "I'm Esther Lyon and I'll be working with you this week getting you trained for the new position. I was so happy when Joseph called to let me know he'd found my replacement," she said warmly.

Relief flooded through Amy, knowing the job was really hers, for better or worse. "It's so good to meet you, Esther. I was a bit nervous when Shelly said there wasn't a job," she said.

Esther looked over at the woman in question. "We haven't yet announced I'm retiring, though it's been in the works for some time. Shelly wasn't made aware of the situation. I'm sorry about any lack of communication.

"Walk with me, and I'll show you your new office as I talk a little about the history of this wonderful company. The original building was created a little over one hundred years ago, but in this growing city, many updates have been added since then. Joseph's grandfather,

Benjamin, started Anderson Corporation with little more than a prayer and a few dollars. As I'm sure you know, his hard work paid off. We're now global, with offices all across the United States and the world. Joseph was the next elected CEO after Benjamin's passing, but his son, Lucas, took over last year, and is certainly following in his relatives' footsteps. He's a brilliant man, and I'm sure you'll love working for him."

"I have to be honest," Amy said with awe. "This is all a little overwhelming. I mean, the history of this wealthy family, the amount of business to keep track of, even the building itself. I don't know how one man keeps track of it all."

"Oh, it takes a whole team, sweetie, believe me. Don't let yourself get worked up over nothing. The way to keep sane in this chaotic place is simply to do one task at a time. Look at the smaller picture, and before you know it, the day is done and you've accomplished far more than you ever imagined," Esther reassured her.

They walked down the hallway and through a large oak doorway into a huge office. Was everything in the building done on a much grander scale than your average place? In the middle of the room was a huge three-sided desk. On the surface sat a top-of-the-line computer and an overflowing in and out box. Two chairs were placed in front of the desk and one large chair behind it.

A bookshelf took up most of one wall, its shelves lined from top to bottom with many titles. Amy hoped she wasn't expected to read them all in a short time. Hopefully, they were only there for either decoration, or for when she needed a specific answer, though with the Internet, it was much faster to search online for whatever a person needed nowadays.

Natural light flooded the room from the floor-to-ceiling windows lined up on the back wall behind the desk. Amy was grateful for the uncovered windows, knowing if she got too stressed, she could take a minute to face the amazing city of Seattle while her stress had a chance to diminish. It really was an ideal office.

"Come in and have a seat. Make yourself comfortable while I show you what you need to get started. Before you know it, you'll be excellent on your own, no longer needing my help at all," Esther said kindly.

"I have my doubts about that, but I'm sure glad you're the one training me. You seem very nice."

"Thank you, Amy. Do you mind if I call you by your first name? I've never been huge on the formality thing. I feel that an office environment should be enjoyable, and *really* knowing who you're working with makes a big difference in making it so. Joseph became a dear friend of mine, and so did his beautiful wife, Katherine. I've watched their children grow into fine young men and have been treated like a part of their family. It's a good thing, too, because there are weeks you'll see far more of this office than your own place. You need to have a healthy working relationship with your boss."

"I'd love to keep it informal. Joseph said the same thing to me during the interview, and I didn't know how to respond, but I'm beginning to see this place isn't what I thought it would be. I was expecting a rigid staff and endless work," Amy replied. As she realized what she said, she quickly tried to correct herself.

"I wasn't trying to say hard work is bad, or being professional is a negative thing. I was just..."

"You don't need to explain, Amy," Esther said. "I understand exactly what you're saying. Before I was fortunate enough to get a job with Joseph, I worked for a large developer on the other side of the city. He was rude to me and his clients, never smiled at anyone, and didn't care about those who worked for him. He only cared about the bottom line. There are a lot of corporations like that, but this isn't one of them. They expect a great deal from you, but they're also willing to compensate you for your work. They treat their staff, from the lowest positions to the highest, with respect. The benefits are almost mind-boggling, but you'll soon learn why they can do this. They save a lot of money by having an incredibly low turnover rate, and they never hurt for more business, because they have repeat business in all their divisions. Even in bad economic times, they not only survive, but thrive."

Amy relaxed as she listened to Esther. The woman should be a recruiter for the corporation — not that it looked as though they needed to recruit. Before that moment, Amy hadn't realized quite how lucky she was to have gotten her job. It didn't matter, though. She'd work hard no matter what; she didn't know any other way.

Amy felt slightly overwhelmed as the two women worked together the rest of the morning. By the afternoon, she was starting to pick up on some of the tasks, though, and she really enjoyed Esther's company. They worked well together, and Amy wished she had more than one week of training with her. Amy had no mother and tended to enjoy the company of older women, especially when they were open and caring.

Esther put Amy on a project as she cleaned out her email. Amy was glad to find she was able to do the assigned task without asking for help. They sat in a comfortable silence as they worked for a few hours before they were interrupted.

"Esther, can you cancel my appointments for the rest of the day? I need to go to my father's. Before I leave, I also need the Niles reports if you've finished them."

Amy looked up as the most stunning man she'd ever glimpsed walked through a connecting door. He was looking at a piece of paper in his hand, which gave her a few moments to secretly observe him.

The first thing she noticed was his build. He had to be at least six foot four, with wide shoulders, a full chest, and a flat stomach. As his arm moved, stretching the obviously tailored dark business suit, she could easily guess he was solid muscle, not an ounce of fat daring to attach to his body. The white shirt clearly accentuated his golden tan. The outfit was complete with a loosened tie, making him look as if he'd just stepped out of a movie shoot rather than his office.

He ran his fingers through his dark brown hair, causing the short strands to stick out in a few places, making him even sexier, in her opinion. In the next moment he looked up, and his deep azure eyes met her startled green ones.

"I'm sorry, Esther. I didn't realize you had a client in here."

Amy was shocked by his words. Why was he calling her a client?

"Lucas Anderson," he said as he held his hand out to her. *I'm in trouble, big, big trouble,* was her only thought as she looked at his hand as if it were a snake. Skin-to-skin contact would feel far too intimate, even though it was simply shaking hands, but when had she ever touched a man of this stunning caliber? She also knew full well she couldn't refuse to shake her boss's hand.

As she hesitated an awkward amount of time, she saw him raise his eyebrows at her questioningly. Her face turned a nice shade of red as she finally broke eye contact.

She snapped out of her trance, realizing he was waiting for her to introduce herself. Finally, she stood and gave him her hand. "Hello, I'm Amy Harper."

Amy was rooted to the spot as his fingers closed around hers, her breath instantly held prisoner inside her lungs.

Chapter Two

As their hands touched, Lucas felt a surge of adrenaline rush through his body and straight to his groin, shocking him. He tightened his grip around her fingers, tugging a little, enough that she noticed. He didn't like the instant attraction — not one bit.

Amy was beautiful, sure, but so were thousands of other women he was in contact with. It seemed, though, that none of them had the power to electrify him with only a simple touch. The electric moment with Amy was a first for him.

As a myriad of emotions crossed Amy's face, Lucas found himself fascinated by her expressions. She didn't seem capable of hiding a thing from him, though he was sure she'd like to. Their gazes were locked together, her cheeks flushed and eyes wide as he watched a mixture of desire and fear play from deep within their depths. He found himself wanting to lean closer, shock her into gasping, opening those luscious pink lips, but somehow he managed to pull himself back.

He had work to do — important work. He certainly didn't have time to play with the obviously innocent woman.

Slowly, Lucas turned toward Esther, releasing Amy's hand at the same time. "When your guest leaves, step into my office and grab the paper on my desk. I have several letters that need to go out today and a few other tasks I want done before five."

"I think you and your father need to talk right away, Lucas," Esther said, stopping him.

"Talk about what?" He saw the hesitation on Esther's face and got a bad feeling.

"I sent you my notice last month and told you that your father would be hiring a new assistant."

"I told you then that I needed you to stay longer. I assumed the matter was settled," he answered a bit too harshly.

"Lucas, don't you dare use that tone of voice with me. Don't forget, I've seen you running around in nothing but a diaper. You knew when your father retired that I'd be leaving as soon as you got settled in. I stayed on to make sure you had a smooth transition, but now it's my turn to retire. I love this company but, like your father, I believe sometimes it's best to get on with things and bring in a new generation."

"I'm sorry about the misunderstanding. Can you work one more month so I can find an appropriate replacement to take your position? I'll double your salary, knowing it's an inconvenience," he asked, trying to forget Amy was in the room.

"Your father already conducted the interviews, and Amy's your new assistant. I've been training her all morning, and she's doing a remarkable job," Esther said and patted Amy on the hand.

His gaze turned immediately to the woman in question, the one who'd seared him with nothing more than the touch of her fingers. There was no possible way she could work for him — not even a chance.

◊◊◊◊◊◊

Suddenly, Amy found herself the object of Lucas's intense gaze. The minute he turned those cold blue eyes back on her, she felt her stomach drop. He had enough heat raging in his eyes to be a fire hazard. The intensity flowing between the two of them was enough to leave her shaking, though she really hoped her fear wasn't showing.

She tried to firm her shoulders and meet his look with an expression of indifference, but she was sure she wasn't pulling it off.

"I'll speak to my father about this, but I should've been informed of the interviews. Don't get too comfortable in your new position, Ms. Harper," he spoke with the utmost authority before storming through the doorway, shutting it a bit harder than necessary.

"I thought he knew I'd been hired. He didn't even know you were leaving," Amy said apprehensively. She could lose her dream job before it even started.

"Now, don't you worry about anything, Amy. It will all be just fine."

"I know you've worked here for a lot of years, Esther, but from the look on his face, he wasn't happy. I wouldn't get too set on retirement if I were you," Amy said, attempting to make a joke, though it fell flat.

"You'll find Lucas is far more bark than bite. He's riled up right now, but he'll settle down soon. Let's finish our work for the afternoon. By tomorrow this will be straightened out and you'll forget all about it," Esther promised.

Amy had her doubts, but there was no use in worrying about it. She figured she'd do the best job she could, and then *maybe* her position would be safe.

They got absorbed in their work, and the incident was placed on the back burner — still there, but put away for the moment.

◊◊◊◊◊◊

"Dad, how do you expect me to run this company when you're stepping in and doing things without letting me know?" Lucas was pacing back and forth across the parlor in front of his father.

"Now, Son, I told you when I left that Esther would be retiring once you got settled in. I also said I'd take care of her replacement. It's not my fault you forgot. And it's not Esther's fault you didn't take her resignation seriously."

"I take everything seriously. At the least, you could have let me know interviews were going on so I could be a part of it. I would've been just fine handling them on my own."

"I know you're more than capable of doing your job, but when you took over, I promised to tie up any loose ends left from my retirement. This was the final item I had to take care of," Joseph said, leaving Lucas with little argument.

"Dad, I know you're up to something. I just can't figure out what it is this time, but I'm capable of hiring my own staff. It doesn't look good for me when I don't know what's going on in my own offices."

"I interviewed about thirty people, and Ms. Harper was, by far, the most qualified candidate. Believe me, you won't have any problems with her. I checked her out extensively before sending her to you."

It was a good thing Lucas didn't know that Joseph was far more interested in her abilities as a possible wife than an executive assistant. Luckily, she really had done well in school and was more than capable of doing her job, and doing it well, for that matter. Lucas would've seen right through a woman who was only there looking for a husband.

Joseph felt Amy was a perfect candidate for Lucas. She was smart, strong, and had been through a lot in her short lifetime. She needed a family, and Joseph needed a daughter-in-law. It was a perfect match. Lucas would soon see that.

"You've left me with little choice. I don't think there's any way I can convince Esther to stay on at this point, now that she's made up her mind. I'll see how Ms. Harper works out, but if she doesn't work soundly with me, then I'll fire her and the next person will be someone I find, not you."

"I think that's a reasonable request," Joseph quickly agreed, wanting to change the subject. "Now, on to other business."

Joseph knew he couldn't give Lucas too much time to think about the matter. He was a smart boy, and Joseph didn't want him figuring out what he was up to. If Lucas had any idea how much Joseph wanted his sons married, Lucas would go running for the hills before he had a chance to fall in love with Amy. That just wouldn't do for Joseph. He wanted those grandchildren — the earlier, the better.

The two of them spent the rest of the afternoon going over the new benefits package Joseph had modified. Joseph might have retired, but he liked to stay involved. He'd go a little stir-crazy if he left the corporation completely. He'd promised his Katherine he wouldn't work seventy-hour weeks anymore, but he'd never agreed to forget about the corporation his grandfather had started. She understood that and was supportive of his remaining active with the human resources department. After all, she had a huge heart herself. It was why he loved her so much, even after thirty-five years of marriage.

◊◊◊◊◊◊

By the time Lucas left his father's house, his frustration had eased. When he returned to the building, everyone was gone for the day.

As he made his way into his office, he could smell a lingering scent of vanilla in the air, just a hint, but enough to remind him of his new employee. He had a feeling Amy was going to be nothing but trouble for him if he let her stay. The best thing for both of them would be for him to simply fire her. He knew his dad would be upset, but he'd support him.

As he stood in the connecting doorway to their two offices, he struggled with himself while remembering her innocent expression, so open and readable.

With a firm resolve, he stood straighter and turned his back to the room, silently shutting the door behind him. He was in control of his emotions, and there was no way he was going to let a stranger get under his skin. Women came and went from his life, serving an essential purpose, and then quietly exiting. His new employee wasn't going to get the upper hand and control any part of him — certainly not his emotions.

Lucas walked to his desk and picked up a file. He had a lot of work to finish that night, so he relaxed on his couch and started reading. It didn't take him long to feel his eyes start to grow heavy, then fall asleep before he knew what hit him.

Lucas often spent his nights in the office after burning the midnight oil. He'd always driven himself hard, putting work ahead of pleasure. He'd known from a young age that he was going to take over the family corporation. It was in his blood.

Lucas's last thought, before succumbing to sleep, was of vivid green eyes filled with hunger.

Made in the USA
Las Vegas, NV
29 December 2020